CW01637562

The Body Parts in the Library

A Library Ladies Mystery

Val Culley

East Wind Publishing

All the characters, locations and events portrayed in this work are fictitious.

The Body Parts in the Library

A Library Ladies Mystery

East Wind Publishing

ISBN: 978-0-9929443-3-9

For all the Library Ladies (and Gentlemen) everywhere who give wonderful service to their customers.

CHAPTER ONE

Two women were still out late in the evening in Upper Mickle, making their way home up the hill from the centre of the village. If anyone had been able to see them, they would have noticed they weaved about on the pavement rather than walking in a straight line. The small, slim one with dark hair had to hold on to the larger woman with long, blonde hair to keep herself upright. But although it was still quite light because it was nearly the end of May, it was such a hot, humid night that many of the residents of the small, south Yorkshire village had already retired to bed.

'I really enjoyed that meal,' Sallie Parker, the larger, blonde woman was saying to her friend. 'Marco was extremely generous giving us free Prosecco at the end, wasn't he?'

Jo Pudsey gave a hiccup and then giggled. 'It was good of them all to come to see us off,' she said, slurring her words.

'They felt sorry for us and they know it will happen to them eventually. We just happen to be the first library assistants in this area to be made redundant.'

'Still, they gave us a good send off,' Jo said, pronouncing the words with difficulty.

'Yes, they did, bless 'em. And I don't know when I'm going to be able to afford a lovely meal like that again, now I'm not working.'

‘Oh, but you’re a regular at Trattoria Marco. You’ll find a way. Something will turn up, I’m sure.’

‘Thank you, Mr Micawber. But I’m going to have to cut my spending drastically if I’m going to be able to manage on my small pension.’

‘You’ll get another job, no problem. You’ve a lot to offer an employer.’

‘But I shouldn’t have to try at my age. Once you’re in your mid-fifties, employers think you’re past it.’

Sallie stopped when they reached the village library. ‘Just look at it, our pride and joy for all those years and we’re going to have to go past it every day.’

They both stood still and gazed at the old, red brick cottage with its low hanging tiled roof. It had been converted many years before into the village library and they had both worked there happily until a week ago.

Inside, there was one large room lined with bookcases and a small kitchen and office at the back for the use of staff. Outside, the tidy front garden was abundant with flowers and fragrant rose bushes just like the gardens of all the other houses in the village.

‘Can you believe we’ll never go inside there again?’ Sallie asked.

‘Yes, I can. I’m determined never to set foot in there. Never, never, never!’

Sallie noticed the front bedroom windows of the houses on either side of the library were open, the inhabitants obviously trying to let in cooler air as they slept.

Afterwards she was to remember this and wish she had lowered her voice. But a few glasses of the house Trebbiano, followed by free Prosecco, had done their damage.

'A plague on all who enter there!' she declaimed.

'Don't be silly. Some of the volunteers and lots of the customers are our friends.'

'But they didn't mind taking our jobs, did they?'

'Yes, but most of them only volunteered because they didn't want it to close. They believe this village needs a library.'

'But it still makes me angry that so many of our customers have volunteered to work for nothing, even though they know we've been made redundant.'

'They had no choice if they didn't want the library to close,' Jo insisted.

'Some of them might have done it for that reason, but not all of them.'

'Yes, I suppose that's true. I do remember one of them telling me they'd always wanted a 'little' job in a library.' Jo mimed the quote marks round the word 'little' and giggled.

'Some of them, like that bitch Joyce Ferrier for example, have enjoyed seeing us lose our jobs.'

'You're right about her. She's made no secret of how pleased she is about it!'

'Some of them are definitely doing it because it makes them feel more important.'

'Yes, and they've not been exactly tactful while we've been working our notice, have they?'

‘So, what are we going to do about it?’

‘Nothing,’ Jo said wearily. ‘We can hardly lie down in the doorway to stop people going in.’

‘No, but there must be some way we can get our point across, so people understand what they’ve done to us. We have to get our revenge on the volunteers for taking our jobs somehow.’ Sallie was silent for a moment deep in thought.

‘Come on, let’s go home. Things will seem better in the morning!’

‘Will they? I’m not so sure. I’m going to think of something that will make them all realise what they’ve done to us. You just wait and see.’

‘That’s just the vino talking. We should both go home to bed. Tomorrow’s another day and all that.’ Jo giggled and hiccupped again.

They continued to toil up the road until they came to Sallie’s cottage, further up the hill on the same side as the library. Leaning against her gate, Sallie watched Jo cross the road and carry on walking along the pavement on the other side until she reached her own house. She watched her climb rather unsteadily up the steps to her front door. Jo turned and waved to her and Sallie waved back.

After Jo disappeared behind her front door, Sallie opened her own gate and walked down the path through her pretty front garden. She heard a noise behind her and turned round to see an upstairs window being closed in the house opposite. Thinking nothing of it, she turned back to her front door and put her key in the lock.

CHAPTER TWO

Library volunteer Verity Galling could feel her heart beating faster even before she put her key in the lock of the back door. She knew she would have only a short time to reach the alarm and stop it with her key fob and prayed it would work. Malcolm Bray had told them all it was vital to fob the alarm and stop it quickly. If the alarm company had to come out they would charge them for wasting their time.

Despite her trembling hands, Verity managed to get her key to turn in the lock and once inside quickly put her bag down on a desk and rushed back to the door to stop the alarm. But the tiled floor was wet and she skidded and nearly fell. She clutched on to the desk nearest the door to steady herself and took a couple of deep breaths before launching herself at the alarm. She held her key fob up to the panel and mercifully the ringing stopped.

She was breathing hard and was annoyed that the office floor was wet. It would be the fault of that useless cleaner the library employed, Tracy Dolby, who obviously hadn't mopped it dry after washing it, she thought.

Verity could already feel herself beginning to perspire. She had never been alone in the library before, but Malcolm, who was in charge of them, had said they all had to take it in turns to be the first one to arrive and set up. The other volunteers would arrive just before the library opened to customers.

She felt nervous about going into the tiny room at the back of the cottage, an old pantry where the keys to all the drawers and cupboards were kept in a locked cabinet, because she couldn't help thinking about the unpleasant stories she'd heard about the family who had owned the house years before it had been converted into a library. Clive Fenton, the library odd job man, was one of their descendants and everyone knew he wasn't completely right in the head.

Verity took all the keys from the cabinet through into the library and switched on the lights. She thought she heard someone, or something, move behind one of the book cases and stood listening for a few seconds, but everywhere was silent.

Hurry up, she told herself crossly. If Malcolm arrived before she'd done everything properly it would give him the opportunity to have a go at her.

She unlocked all the drawers behind the counter and then made her way across to the main door to open it.

She suddenly realised she hadn't switched on the computers and turned back quickly. She went round the desks switching on all the monitors and then bent down to switch on the towers underneath.

By now she could feel her cheeks were getting flushed. They'll all be here soon and they'll think her hopeless if she hadn't got everything done, she told herself. As it was, she had arrived a quarter of an hour before she was due to start her shift, to make sure she had enough time to do everything.

As soon as she had chance, she was planning to ask Rory Forster, the nice young man who had joined them, to help her find the relevant programme on the computer that enabled them to look at the library catalogue. She was supposed to have it open on both computers at the counter but couldn't remember how to do it and was worried about damaging them.

Verity made her way to the front of the library and turned the key in the lock of a large, wooden door that would once have been the front entrance to the old house before it became a library. Customers would now be able to walk in after ten o'clock, when the library opened.

She bent down in the small entrance area and unlocked the box that collected the books people posted through the slot on the outside when the library was closed. There weren't many today and could be carried in one pile to the desk. She planned to put them to one side until the nice young man came in and helped her find the correct programme to use to discharge them from people's accounts.

She thought Malcolm probably wouldn't notice a small pile of books on the counter. Oddly enough, the one thing about the library he wasn't at all interested in was the books, she realised.

Gathering them up in her arms to carry them to the counter, she noticed one that wouldn't close properly because something had been left inside.

She put the rest of the books to one side neatly and then opened the one that wouldn't close. Afterwards Verity would remember the book was a hardback by Jeffrey Archer. But right at that moment her only interest was in finding out what had been left inside it.

Verity found the object in the middle of the book and stared at it in disbelief. It looked like a thin, pink, uncooked sausage. She picked it up and held it closer to herself and peered at it through her glasses. Then she saw there was a fingernail at one end.

She realised with slowly dawning horror that she was holding part of a finger. It looked perfectly normal at one end but there was congealed blood at the other end with a piece of greyish bone sticking out. She dropped it, screamed and stumbled to the front door, opening it after a couple of tries because her hands were shaking so much she couldn't turn the handle. She ran through the front garden and out on to the pavement and screamed for help.

She was found a few seconds later, sobbing and holding on to the garden wall, by a woman accompanied by a large Dalmatian, who was on her way down the hill to the centre of the village.

*

Sallie woke with a dry mouth. A bright light was shining into the bedroom and she realised it was the sun, streaming in through a gap she had left in the curtains the night before. She took a sip of water from her glass on the bedside table, turned over and went to sleep again.

The next time she woke she looked at her watch, left next to her bed, and saw it was just after ten am.

After a few more sips from her glass of water she padded down the landing to the bathroom to have a shower. Then she put on a long, cotton skirt and a sleeveless, silky top and went down to the kitchen to make a pot of tea.

Her black cat suddenly appeared and rubbed against her legs.

'Sorry, Des, I know it's late, but we made a bit of a night of it last night.'

She put some food down in Desdemona's bowl and fresh milk and water in her saucers and the cat retired to her corner to have breakfast.

Sallie had arranged to meet Jo in the village for lunch later and after a couple of slices of buttered toast and two cups of tea, she felt ready to go out and face the world again.

Desdemona had gone out through her cat flap into the garden so Sallie locked the front door and set off in the direction of the village, enjoying the feeling of the sun on her face as she walked down the road.

Tracy Dolby, the library cleaner, was putting something into the boot of her car in the small parking area in front of the library as she went past. She was wearing what looked like a man's shirt over tight black leggings despite the heat.

'Morning Tracy,' Sallie called out to her cheerfully.

The cleaner turned and looked at her for a few seconds and then slammed the boot shut and with a toss of her dark brown ponytail walked away down the side of the library to the back garden.

What's got into her? Sallie wondered.

Further down the road she saw one of her former customers, Joyce Ferrier, coming towards her. She was small and thin with short dark hair, a sallow complexion and glasses with thick lenses. Sallie noticed she was dressed in her usual shapeless brown trousers and beige blouse, but because of the heat wasn't wearing her droopy cardigan with them. She had her Yorkshire terrier, Sebastian, on the lead.

Sallie had never been keen on Joyce but liked the little dog and had always kept up a civil relationship with her by taking an interest in Sebastian.

When Joyce got closer, Sallie called out cheerfully: 'Morning Joyce, how's the young man today?' Joyce never normally missed an opportunity to give Sallie an update on Sebastian, but on this occasion just stared at her grimly and pulled on Sebastian's lead when he tried to run up to Sallie for a pat.

Sallie stared in disbelief as Joyce stalked off without a backward glance, but then thought that perhaps Joyce was in a hurry to go and do her shift at the library.

She called at the deli on one side of the village green to buy a few things for the weekend and then crossed the road to go to the pub. She passed Dolly's Pantry on the way and saw Dolly Sweetman, the owner, arranging cakes on a stand in the window. Sallie had always been on the best of terms with Dolly and gave her a friendly wave but Dolly turned away abruptly to attend to something in the café.

Stranger and stranger, thought Sallie, as she carried on walking towards The Gentle Knight, Upper Mickle's only pub.

*

Jo woke, took a couple of painkillers, sipped some water and sank back into the pillows and closed her eyes.

The next time she woke up she glanced at the clock and couldn't believe it was half past ten.

She thrust her feet into her slippers and hurried down to the kitchen. Mutz, her large German Shepherd dog, was standing by the back door.

'I'm so sorry, Mutz. You must be desperate. Be a good boy and go down to the bottom of the garden. We'll go for a walk later.'

Jo opened the back door to let him out and refilled his bowls with food and water.

She put the kettle on for tea and filled a large cereal bowl with a sugary breakfast cereal and milk. She had nearly finished eating and was beginning to feel human again after the sugar injection when she heard scratching at the back door.

'Good boy, go and have your breakfast,' she said, letting Mutz back in.

She left him eating and took her tea upstairs with her while she looked for something to wear.

After her shower, Jo felt much better and took Mutz's lead down from its hook. The dog came running eagerly into the hall as soon as he heard the familiar sound.

She took him up the road away from the village in the direction of the open countryside to make up for neglecting him earlier. She saw Mr Johnson, an old gentleman, coming towards her. He had memory problems and kept forgetting to return his library books, but she had always gone to a lot of trouble to discharge them to a retrospective date so he wouldn't have to pay a fine and he used to thank her profusely every time.

'Good morning', she called out to him pleasantly, but he just glared at her and walked past without answering. He's obviously already forgotten who I am, she thought.

Once Jo had settled Mutz in his basket in the utility room, the part of the house that was the coolest at that time of the day, she set out to walk to the village.

As Jo passed the library she saw Clive Fenton, the odd job man, watering the garden at the front with a hose pipe.

'Good morning, Clive,' she said cheerfully. 'It's very warm isn't it? I bet those plants are glad to be having a drink.'

Clive looked puzzled, as though he hadn't understood anything she said. Then he seemed to panic, dropped the hose pipe on the ground and hurried away, leaving the water running out all over the path. He gets worse, Jo thought.

At the bottom of the hill, just before she got to the village green, she encountered Eileen Falls, one of the regulars at the library's Thursday afternoon Knit and Stitch group. Eileen was tall and thin and had long grey hair and large glasses.

'Good morning, Mrs Falls,' Jo said politely.

Eileen peered at her as though she couldn't make out who she was but then snorted disdainfully and walked past her.

I know she's got poor eyesight, but that's ridiculous behaviour even for her, Jo thought.

*

Sallie always ducked when she went into The Gentle Knight because the beam over the entrance was low, although she could just about pass under it without hitting her head. She knew that tall men, and particularly tall men who had enjoyed a few drinks, sometimes found out painfully that they couldn't.

The old flagstones in the entrance passage had been trodden on by customers for hundreds of years and the dark wooden doors to the bars on either side of the passage were very old, if not the originals. Sallie pushed open the door on the left and saw Frank, the landlord, with an empty bar in front of him, perched on a stool at the counter reading a newspaper and drinking a mug of coffee.

'Good morning, Mrs Parker, what can I get you?' he asked, folding up his newspaper and standing up ready to serve her.

'I think I'd better start with a black coffee. We made a bit of a night of it last night.'

Frank busied himself with the coffee machine behind the counter, while Sallie made herself comfortable on a bar stool.

'It's very quiet in the village this morning, isn't it? Everyone seems a bit subdued. I suppose it's because of the heat,' she said.

‘I think people are a bit upset about what happened to poor Mrs Galling,’ Frank said, putting Sallie’s cup of coffee in front of her.

‘Mrs Galling? Why, has something happened to her?’

‘Didn’t you hear the sirens earlier? A woman had to call the police out to the library, apparently.’

‘Why? What happened?’

‘Don’t you know?’

‘No, I don’t. This is the first I’ve heard about it.’

‘So it wasn’t you that gave her the fright of her life?’

‘Why would I want to give Mrs Galling a fright? Anyway, I don’t have anything to do with the library now. I was made redundant.’

‘Yes, but I’ve heard that after your night out with your friends in Trattoria Marco last night, you walked past the library and were overheard shouting about getting your revenge on the volunteers who’ve taken your job.’

‘Oh, that was just the wine talking. I didn’t really mean anything by it.’

‘Yes, but poor old Mrs Galling has a weak heart, so people are bound to be upset about it.’

‘What exactly happened to her?’ Sallie asked anxiously.

‘Somebody put a book into the library letter box with part of a severed finger inside it.’

‘A severed finger!’

‘Yes. That’s why Mrs Galling was so shocked that she ran outside. A woman going past came to her aid and phoned the police on her mobile.’

'Oh no! Poor Verity! But how could you think I had anything to do with it? Where would I get hold of a severed finger?'

'Well, it wasn't a real severed finger. It turned out to be the sort of thing you can order on the internet or buy from a joke shop. But Mrs Galling didn't realise and was horrified. It looked very realistic apparently.'

When the door to the bar opened a few minutes later Sallie was glad to see Louise Bainbridge come in. She didn't like people thinking she might have been responsible for scaring Verity. But she had known Louise for years and hoped she would believe she had nothing to do with it.

Louise looked pleased to see her. 'Hi, Sallie. I'm glad you're here because I'm meeting Emma, but I'm a bit early.'

Louise had been a housebound volunteer at the library for most of the years Sallie had worked there, choosing books and taking them to old people who couldn't go out and then visiting them again to collect the books to return them to the library.

Sallie looked at her and wondered how she could look so immaculate on such a hot day. She knew Louise was in her early sixties but she looked much younger. She had short, wavy blonde hair cut into a flattering style, lovely grey blue eyes and her face was perfectly made up as usual. She always dressed her petite figure in expensive clothes and today she was wearing cream linen trousers and a loose fitting white silk shirt. Two expensive-looking jewelled hair clips took her hair off her face and she looked cool despite the weather.

'Morning, Mrs Bainbridge,' Frank called out from the dark recess at one end of the bar before he had even seen her. 'What can I get you?'

Louise looked at Sallie's half empty coffee cup and said: 'I'll order us a bottle of wine and then we can go and sit in the garden.'

'Actually, I'm waiting for Jo to arrive.'

'I'll ask for an extra glass then.'

When Frank had given Louise a round tin tray with a bottle of wine and three glasses, she led the way down the dark passageway and out of the back door of the pub into the bright sunshine.

Louise put the tray down on a table with four chairs grouped round it well away from the door. 'I thought we should sit outside because I don't want Frank listening to every word we say,' she said, pouring them both a glass of wine.

After taking a sip, she put her glass down and leant back in her chair. 'I take it you heard about the drama at the library this morning.'

'Yes, Frank's just told me about it. He had the cheek to suggest I might have been responsible. And funnily enough, I had the feeling people were avoiding speaking to me when I was walking down into the village.'

'That's ridiculous! Anyway, it was a lot of fuss about nothing as it always is in Upper Mickle. Poor old Verity shouldn't be left to open up on her own. It was just a pathetic joke. But she had hysterics and ran out of the library and the silly woman who found her rang the police without bothering to find out whether the finger was real or not.'

'As if I would play a ridiculous joke on anyone like that!'

'Oh, of course I knew it wasn't you, or Jo. It must have been done by somebody very childish. Apparently you can get hold of these things easily. They're made from latex, but look very real, so I've been told.'

'I've lost my job and had to stand by and watch a bunch of volunteers take my place. If I wanted to spite them, I'd think of something a lot better.'

'Oh, I know. I would expect something really ingenious from you, Sallie.' Louise smiled at her. 'It was just a pity it had to be Verity who found it. Anyone else would have laughed about it. But you know what Verity's like. She's very highly strung and she gets terribly nervous about working at the library.'

'But I don't like to think people might really believe I was responsible.'

'Oh, don't worry about it. It will all blow over and be forgotten about in no time.'

'Anyway, considering there are so many volunteers, why was Verity left to open up on her own?'

Louise shook her head and put her glass down. 'The truth is they haven't got nearly as many volunteers as they expected to get. A lot of the people who put their names down at the beginning dropped out when Malcolm started to draw up a timetable and they realised they were going to have to make a regular commitment to work so many hours a month for nothing. Also, quite a few volunteers thought they were going to be working alongside you and Jo and when they found out you wouldn't still be there they decided they didn't want to offer their services after all. Technically there are only 13 of us left and one of them doesn't count really.'

'Why not?'

'Because they said people could do as little as an hour every three months and the person I'm talking about has taken it literally. He turned up to do the training and came in to help out for an hour right at the beginning and now he won't be on duty again for another three months.'

'That's ridiculous. How on earth will he be able to learn the job with a three-month gap between shifts?'

Louise just smiled again.

At that moment Emma Goodall, the vicar's wife, came out into the garden holding a pint of the pub's craft beer. Sallie thought, not for the first time, that she could have been a model in a magazine. Emma was tall and slim with long blonde hair taken back into a single plait and the sort of face you might see in a medieval painting, long with a straight nose and beautiful hazel eyes. She was wearing a sleeveless white cotton dress but her perfect figure made the garment look sensational.

'So, Sallie Parker, the talk in the village is that you're going to get revenge on the volunteers for taking your job. Was the finger in the library book this morning a warning shot, and, if so, what's going to happen next?' She smiled at Sallie mischievously.

CHAPTER THREE

When Jo reached the village green the first person she saw was Tom Cleaver, the sergeant from the neighbourhood policing team, who was on duty wearing a stab vest over his short sleeved, white shirt. He was talking to a little old lady she didn't recognise, who was wagging her finger at him and seemed to be giving him a hard time. He must be incredibly hot, she thought, as she watched him remove his helmet and wipe his forehead.

'Jo, how lovely to see you! I haven't had chance to talk to you since you finished at the library,' he said, his face lighting up as she came nearer to him.

'Hello Tom. I stayed at home for a few days, trying to get used to being a lady of leisure again.'

The little old lady snorted with disgust and stomped off, dragging her shopping trolley behind her.

'I've been wondering how you and Sallie were getting on after leaving the library,' he said, smiling down at her, oblivious to the old woman's reaction.

Tom was tall and slim, with grey hair cut short and a tanned face. Jo was pleased he was being friendly. He had been a regular visitor to the library over the years, enjoying the tea and biscuits and the chance to get warm on cold days, or cool down with the help of their electric fan on hot days.

'Everyone I've spoken to has cut me dead so far this morning. It's nice to see a friendly face,' she said smiling back up at him.

'Oh dear!'

'I'm starting to wonder whether I might have done something to upset people.'

He hesitated for a few seconds. 'Well, this morning there was an incident at the library.'

'What do you mean by an incident?'

'An old lady, who was working there as a volunteer, apparently found a severed finger in a library book being used as a bookmark.'

'Oh, my God!'

'She ran out into the street in hysterics and a passer-by called the police. Two response officers attended the scene quickly but found the finger was made of plastic. It was the sort of item people buy for Halloween parties, apparently. She was very upset about it, even though the finger turned out not to be real, so it seems a lot of people in the village are angry about it.'

'But I don't work there now so it has absolutely nothing to do with me.'

Tom looked uncomfortable. 'I'm afraid that people are saying you and Sallie were overheard talking outside the library last night about getting your revenge on the people who've taken your jobs.'

'Yes, but we didn't mean it! You surely don't think Sallie and I would play a silly joke like that? Anyway, it was only the wine talking last night. We would never actually do anything.'

'Yes, but people don't know that, do they?

'What was the title of the book?' Jo asked curiously

'I've no idea. Why do you ask?'

'The police should have asked for the title and got someone to look on the computer to see who had the book out last.'

'I don't suppose they thought of that,' Tom said gloomily.

'Anyway, I returned all my books over a week ago, before I finished working at the library. I've no intention of ever going in there again. From now on I'll use the big library at Mickleton.'

'Honestly, Jo, I don't think for one moment it has anything to do with you or Sallie. I just wanted to tip you off about what people are saying.'

*

When Jo joined Sallie and the others in the pub garden she wasn't surprised to find the conversation was all about the finger left in the library book.

'I haven't set foot in that place since my last working day,' Sallie kept emphasising.

While Sallie was visiting the ladies' loo, Jo spoke to Louise quietly. 'She was extremely angry last night when we passed the library on our way home from the restaurant. She was talking about getting her revenge on the volunteers. Maybe she went into her house to get the joke finger and a book to put it in, came out again and went to the library and posted it through the book drop-box.'

'I'm sure Sallie wouldn't do something so childish and pathetic,' Louise said at once.

Later while Jo was at the bar, Sallie said in a low voice to Emma: 'It's occurred to me Jo could have come out of her house and gone back down to the library after I'd gone inside. She'd been drinking heavily and isn't as used to it as me. In her inebriated state, she might have thought it was funny to play a joke on the volunteers.'

'Sallie, I am sure that it wasn't Jo…' Emma began, but stopped when she saw Jo coming back to the table.

Later, as they all left the pub, Emma whispered to Sallie: 'I do not believe Jo would have played that silly prank. You're going to have to trust her and she's going to have to trust you. All this will blow over soon and it would be a pity if either of you let it affect your relationship.'

Sallie was thinking about Emma's words while they were walking home back up the hill together. Emma's instincts were usually right.

Suddenly, Jo said: 'Why don't you come and have dinner with me tonight? It seems silly for us both to be eating alone this evening. We might as well keep each other company and have a nice meal together.'

'Thanks, Jo, that would be lovely,' Sallie said politely. She began to feel more cheerful again.

*

That night, while sitting in Jo's large, immaculate, black and white kitchen, the two women discussed the latest developments at the library

'It's so frustrating! If the finger was definitely in a library book, the first thing they should have done is look on the system to see who had the book out last. Then surely they would have realised we couldn't possibly have had access to the book?' Sallie said.

Jo put a plate of smoked salmon and prawns and a plate of brown bread and butter on the white table. She went to the fridge to get a bottle of wine to top their glasses up.

'I don't suppose any of the volunteers have had the brains to think of that,' Sallie added, helping herself to a prawn.

Jo came back to the table holding the bottle of wine and sat down opposite Sallie. She looked thoughtful for a moment. 'But the thing is, why should we be bothered about who played the practical joke on Verity? We don't work there now. It's up to Malcolm Bray and his team of volunteers to sort it out.'

'Yes, I agree. But they will have to find out who was responsible and let everyone know about it. I can't bear the thought of people in the village thinking we did it. You know what this village is like. By the time I went out this morning everyone knew about the excitement at the library and thought it was our fault. I ended up getting a very cool reception, even from people I thought were my friends.'

'So did I. Apart from Tom, no one acknowledged me on my way down to the village this morning.'

'So, we have to do something. It's really frustrating. If only we knew the title of the book, and who had it out last, we'd be able to prove we had nothing to do with it.'

'Yes, but it seems neither the police nor the volunteers have bothered to look into it.'

'I'm afraid that as far as the police are concerned no crime has been committed, so they're not bothered about finding out who did it. But it really annoys me that instead of having the sympathy of people in the village we're being treated like lepers. If we can find out who put the finger in the book, we could let Emma and Louise spread the word for us and then things would get back to normal.'

'Normal apart from the fact that neither of us has a job now.'

Sallie frowned. 'I'm afraid that's a much more difficult issue to sort out.'

After they had finished eating the salmon and prawns, Jo removed the empty dishes and put out new plates and cutlery. She went to one of the ovens in her range cooker and took out a large dish of lasagne.

'Wow, that looks good,' Sallie said appreciatively.

After Jo had served a generous portion for them both and put the dish back in the oven to keep warm, Sallie said: 'Of course, we could ask Emma or Louise to find out the title of the book. Then one of them could look up who had the book out last.'

'That's actually not a bad idea. I'll ring Emma after we've finished eating.'

Later, while Sallie was finishing off her second helping of lasagne, Jo looked round the kitchen for her mobile and then rang Emma.

'She's going to ring Verity and try to find out,' she said after ending the call.

Jo started to stack the dishwasher, but her phone rang only a few minutes later. She listened to what Emma was saying, laughing occasionally. When she had finished Sallie asked impatiently: 'What was so funny?'

'Emma said Verity couldn't remember anything about the book to begin with but then said it had a blue cover. Eventually she remembered it was by Jeffrey Archer.'

'Well, that doesn't help us much. There are probably loads of books by Jeffrey Archer with blue covers. It's bound to be his favourite colour being a Tory!'

'Emma says thankfully Verity suddenly remembered the title was Be Careful What You Wish For.'

'Good, that will give her something to go on. There will probably be only one, or perhaps two, copies in the library and she'll be able to see from the loan history which copy came back on Saturday.'

'Yes, but unfortunately Emma says she's not sure she'll be able to find out who had it last. She says she can issue books and discharge them and put them back into stock when they are returned, but that's about all she can do at the moment. She says she's not had chance to learn how the library's computer system works yet. Because there are only two counter computers and quite a few of the volunteers on each shift, she ends up shelving and tidying up while the men hog the computers.'

'How frustrating! If only we could somehow get in there for a few minutes.'

'I thought we were never going to set foot in there again on principle. I thought we'd agreed on that.'

'Yes, but this is different. We wouldn't actually be giving them any custom.'

'I wouldn't want to go in while all the volunteers were behind the counter.'

'No, neither would I,' Sallie agreed.

Jo thought about it for a few seconds. 'How about letting ourselves in while the library is closed? I still have a key to the back door.'

'I thought you'd handed your key in.'

'I did, but then afterwards I remembered I also had a spare key. It was given to me by a girl who used to do the odd casual shift for us. She gave it back to me after her last shift. No one ever asked for it and I thought it would be handy to have a spare in case I ever lost my own key, so I held on to it.

'I'd left the library before I remembered about it and then I thought, why should I be bothered about taking it back? No one remembered I still had it and no one would thank me for returning it, so I didn't bother. We could go and look now if you like.'

'We wouldn't be able to put any lights on because people would think it was odd at this time of night. They might ring Malcolm Bray.'

'I've got torches we could carry and anyway we could both find our way round blindfold if necessary after all the years we've worked there.'

'You make it sound so simple.'

'That's because it is.'

'Well, we wouldn't be able to go in at the front from the road because someone might see us.'

'No, but we could go down the little lane at the back and climb over the fence into the garden and then let ourselves into the back office. Then we could walk through into the library without switching the lights on and put on one of the counter computers. I bet they haven't changed the password. We could easily find out who was the last person to have the copy of the book that was returned on Saturday. What could possibly go wrong?'

*

A few minutes later they were on the footpath behind the library looking up at the high fence that ran along the end of the garden.

What had seemed like a good idea when they had been in the safety of Jo's kitchen didn't seem so clever, now they were standing outside in the dark and the only light they had was from two small torches. Sallie looked up at the fence apprehensively.

'Shine your torch on the fence and I'll see if there's any way I can climb up it. Then when I'm over the other side you can follow me and I'll help you get down safely,' Jo ordered.

Sallie shone her torch on the fence and Jo put her hands round the top of a concrete fence post and hauled herself up. Soon she was sitting astride the top of the fence looking down into the library garden.

'There seems to be a big pile of grass cuttings and weeds on this side of the fence,' she said, shining her torch down on them. 'Clive has helpfully provided me with a soft landing.' She flipped her other leg over the fence and jumped.

'Are you all right?' Sallie asked anxiously.

'Yes, I'm fine.' Jo sounded breathless as she got to her feet on the other side of the fence. 'Now you try to do the same.'

Sallie put her hands round the top of the concrete post as Jo had done and tried to haul herself up, but kept dropping to the ground again.

'Hurry up!' Jo said impatiently from the other side.

Sallie made a determined assault on the fence again and managed to heave herself up as Jo had done and scrambled up the fence till she was sitting on the top.

'Jump down!' Jo yelled, shining her torch on Sallie as she sat astride the fence breathing hard.

'I can't. It's too far, I'm scared,' Sallie said looking down into the darkness of the garden.

'Just jump. You'll be all right,' Jo shouted.

'I can't. It's too far to fall. I could hurt myself.'

'You won't hurt yourself, you'll land on leaves and weeds, I promise.'

Sallie, perched on top of the fence, shone her torch into what seemed a black hole below her.

'Jump down,' Jo urged her, shining her torch on Sallie from below, illuminating her as she sat there.

'I daren't. It's too far. I could break something,' Sallie wailed, looking down into the dark garden.

'No you won't, it's a soft landing. I landed on grass cuttings and weeds and I'm okay.'

Sallie clung to the top of the fence with both hands, scared of falling over into the garden.

'Oh for goodness sake, let go and jump down, before someone looks out of their window and sees you perched up there.'

'I'm sorry, I can't. I've never been good with heights. I thought you knew that. That's why I couldn't go up ladders at the library.'

'For pity's sake, let go and jump!'

Sallie reluctantly released her grip on the fence and then, losing her balance, lurched sideways and fell rather than jumped into the garden, leaving her long, white cardigan attached to the top of the fence.

'Ouch! I've landed on some thistles and been stung,' she shrieked.

'Never mind that. You've left evidence that you were here.' Jo shone her torch on Sallie's cardigan.

She helped Sallie up from the pile of weeds she was lying in.

'Why do you always have to dress in so many long, flowing garments all the time, as though you're about to go and tell people's fortunes at a fair?'

'Well, why do you always dress as though you're going out to do someone's plumbing?' Sallie retorted, looking pointedly at Jo's outfit of jeans and white polo shirt.

The two women stood facing each other in the garden angrily, both breathing hard.

Then a beam from a powerful torch illuminated them. 'What on earth are you two doing here?' Tom, the beat sergeant asked. 'We've had a call from a resident saying they'd seen people behaving suspiciously on the footpath behind the library.' Tom was accompanied by Wasim, a tall, handsome young constable the girls both knew and liked, who had also visited the library regularly.

'We weren't behaving suspiciously. We have a key to the library. We just chose to come in round the back,' Jo said calmly.

Lights started to go on in the upper rooms of houses nearby.

'Well, let's get you both out of here and then we'll talk about this properly,' Tom said firmly.

'But my cardigan's still on top of the fence!'

Wasim went over, lifted Sallie's cardigan down and handed it to her.

'We'll go back to my house,' Jo said. 'This time we might as well go out through the front garden.'

‘Oh, thank goodness I haven’t got to climb that fence again,’ Sallie said with relief.

CHAPTER FOUR

Back in Jo's kitchen, Tom and Wasim sipped mugs of coffee while Sallie and Jo explained themselves. After they had revealed why they were trying to get into the library using Jo's spare key, Tom thought about it carefully.

'They're always telling us to use our discretion more, aren't they, Wasim? So that's what I'm going to do. You didn't actually break into the library, you just climbed over the fence, but I believe you had no ill intent so there's no point in taking it further because it's in no one's interests. What I'm expected to do now is give you both a warning. So, stay away from the library from now on and don't give people any reason to complain about you to us again,' he said sternly, looking at Sallie.

He then turned to Jo and smiled. 'I would hate to see you get into any trouble so I suggest you give me your spare key and I will hand it over to Malcolm Bray when I get the chance. Then you can't be suspected of anything that happens in the library in future.

'You're lucky it was us who came along. I was giving Wasim a lift because his car is in the garage when we heard the library mentioned over the radio, so I said we'd take a look. But don't go getting any more bright ideas because if we get any other complaints we'll have to act next time.'

Jo glanced at the kitchen clock: ‘It’s less than an hour since we left here to walk round to the library. How did the police hear about it so quickly?’

Wasim said: ‘Someone living near the library was looking out of their back bedroom window and saw two people behaving suspiciously on the footpath flashing torches about.’

‘Does everyone in this village have nothing better to do than look out of their windows all the time?’ Sallie demanded.

‘In my experience a lot of them don’t and they seem to like looking out of their windows,’ Tom said. ‘So, Sallie, you must bear that in mind next time you decide to act suspiciously.’

‘I never consciously decide to act suspiciously. And, anyway, how did they know we hadn’t been playing tennis and hit our ball into the library garden? Jo has a tennis court in her back garden.’

‘Yes, but people will know she hasn’t got a floodlit tennis court, because they all know everything about everyone round here.’

They all laughed and the library was quickly forgotten as the conversation moved on to other things.

When the two officers had finished their coffee and got up to go, Jo gave Tom her spare library key and the girls promised again they would keep well away.

Tom said they would walk Sallie home and Sallie got the feeling it was an offer she was not expected to refuse. Mutz had been sleeping contentedly in his basket in the kitchen all the while they had been talking to the two officers. Tom gave Mutz a friendly pat before leaving and the dog just snuffled happily. It occurred to Sallie to think he wasn't much of a guard dog, despite the fact he often barked fiercely at her.

The two police officers walked with her to her front door, and watched while she unlocked it and saw her safely inside the cottage. She felt like a naughty schoolgirl being taken home by the police after being caught playing truant.

She poured herself a glass of wine and sat on the sofa next to Des and stroked the cat's thick black fur while she thought about things. She felt a few twinges because of her fall from the fence and knew her best white cardigan was now torn and no longer smart enough to go out in.

'The annoying thing is we're no further forward,' she said to the cat. Des purred contentedly in reply.

*

When Sallie woke up the next day she quickly remembered it was Sunday and turned over to go back to sleep again.

There was nothing to get up for. From now on every day was going to be the same. There was going to be no difference between the working week and the weekend. She had the whole week in front of her to do her chores and potter in the garden, things she used to do on Sundays.

Her left side ached and she remembered her fall from the fence. Then she remembered how distant people had been with her because they believed she had been responsible for the prank that had upset poor Verity. Different thoughts kept coming into her mind and she knew she wouldn't be able to get to sleep again so she got out of bed and went down to feed Des.

After a cup of tea and a refreshing shower she looked for a book to take out into the garden to read in the sunshine. It was so quiet as she browsed among her books that when her phone rang it made her jump.

Jo sounded very bright and purposeful. 'How about meeting me in the pub for lunch?'

'No, I don't think so. I really can't face people. It will probably be all over the village about us being caught by the police breaking into the library last night.'

'Nonsense! It will be a good thing for us both to be seen out and about, carrying on normally showing we've nothing to be ashamed of. Come on, Sallie. When have you ever let what other people think bother you?'

Put like that she found she couldn't refuse so she went upstairs to find something smart to wear to boost her confidence.

*

As she was on her way down to the village green, a short, stocky man in shorts and a sleeveless vest, with a fat bulldog on a lead, deliberately stepped in front of her to make her stop.

'About that book I ordered. When's it going to come in?' he asked belligerently.

Sallie looked at him. He seemed familiar but she couldn't put a name to him. 'I don't remember ordering a book for you. Could it have been my colleague, Jo?'

'I don't know, you all look the same to me.'

Sallie took a deep breath. 'My colleague, Jo, is small and slim, with short dark hair and pretty, elfin features. I, on the other hand, am taller, broader and have long blonde hair. So, of course, I can understand completely how it must be difficult for you to tell us apart.'

'Never mind all that. What about my book?'

'I have been made redundant by the library and replaced by a large group of volunteers. Ask one of them.'

'They said they didn't know anything about it and that you'd probably done it wrong. I paid a pound to reserve that book. When's it going to come in?'

'I don't know and I can't check for you because I no longer work there. I haven't set foot in the library for more than two weeks now.'

The man glanced down at his dog sitting comfortably on the pavement and jerked on his lead. 'That's not what I've heard,' he said with an unpleasant leer. 'Walk on, Bartholomew!'

*

The pub was quiet and Sallie and Jo had a peaceful lunch with no interruptions to their conversation.

Frank, the landlord, read his newspaper sitting on his stool behind the bar and didn't make any remarks about their adventures of the night before as they were ordering, so they didn't know whether he had heard about their exploits or not.

'I suppose I'm going to have to start looking for a job this week,' Sallie said with a sigh after they had finished eating. 'But it's difficult to know where to start.'

'The Job Centre should be able to give you some ideas and also tell you if you are entitled to any financial help, so I'd begin there if I were you.'

'Are you going to start looking?' Sallie asked.

'No, I think I'll stay at home for a few weeks and enjoy the summer and take stock. I'm not saying I never want to work again, but I don't want to rush into anything. There are a few jobs I want to get done on the house and then I'll see how I feel.'

'Well, I'm afraid I haven't got that luxury. I won't be able to use my savings to top up my pension indefinitely, so the sooner I start job hunting the better.'

Just then the door to the bar opened and Louise came in accompanied by a tall, dark-haired man, who Sallie realised must be her husband, Don. Sallie looked at him with interest. She hadn't seen him out and about with Louise much. She knew from chatting to Louise over the years that he worked long hours managing the string of shops he owned, leaving Louise to spend his money on their large, smart house and her extensive wardrobe. Louise had made no secret of the fact that this arrangement suited her. But she had recently told Sallie that Don was thinking of taking early retirement and had already started working as a housebound volunteer for the library, alongside her.

Don was powerfully built with a good head of curly hair and dark eyes. He wore a short sleeved shirt open at the neck displaying a lot of dark chest hair.

When Louise saw them she said: 'How lovely, the girls are here. Get a bottle of wine for us, Don.'

She came over and pulled a chair across from another table to join them.

While Don was still at the bar she said in a low voice: 'Are you both all right? I heard about what happened last night from Tracy Dolby.'

'How on earth did she find out?' Jo asked crossly. 'She doesn't live anywhere near the library.'

'Oh, you know what this village is like. Things get round in no time at all and Tracy always seems to know what's going on. That's why I keep her on as a cleaner. She's not exactly thorough, but she keeps me up to date with the village gossip.'

'It was a lot of fuss about nothing. I remembered I had a spare key to the library and thought it would sort things out once and for all if we could get into the library, switch on one of the computers and find out who was the last person to borrow Be Careful What You Wish For.'

'Be Careful What You Wish For? Why, what's that got to do with it?'

'It's the book the finger was found in, according to Emma,' Sallie explained. 'We thought if we could find out who had the book out last and who had put it in the drop-box, we could prove it was nothing to do with us.'

'Oh, I don't know why you're bothering. It will all be forgotten soon enough.'

'Well, I've given my spare key to Sergeant Cleaver and he's going to pass it on to Malcolm Bray. There's no way either of us will be able to get into the library in future, so we can't be accused of anything else.'

'If I were you I would forget the whole thing and concentrate on enjoying this fantastic summer. You are ladies of leisure now. Let Malcolm Bray have all the hassle of running the library from now on.'

Don came over to the table with a bottle of wine and fresh glasses for them and a pint of beer for himself.

'It's so hot here I won't notice any difference when I go to Spain on Tuesday,' he remarked as he sat down.

'He's going over there to shout at the Spanish builders again,' Louise explained as she poured the wine. 'Everything seems to take ages to get done out there and we're worried the villa we're having built won't be finished in time for when we go in October.'

Don grinned. 'Well, you know what they're like. They're constantly taking long breaks so they can go home for a siesta. And when you ask when something's going to be done, the answer's always – mañana.' He gave a loud laugh and took a swig of beer.

'Anyway, I want him to check everything's been done properly so far,' Louise put in. 'I'll be choosing the soft furnishings and small items at the end, you know, all the fun stuff, but there's no point in me going with him this time. I don't do building sites,' she said with a shudder.

'Of course you don't, dear, and anyway I'm quite capable of giving them a good kick up the backside. I don't need help from anyone.' He laughed again and drank his beer. Sallie was struck by his self-satisfied manner.

*

Later, as Sallie and Jo walked up the hill together, Sallie suddenly said: 'Whatever does Louise see in an obnoxious prat like that?'

'Sallie! You can't say that!'

'Well I just did!'

'It's not terribly fair.'

'I've never spoken to Don before so I had no idea what he was like. I didn't like all that criticism of the Spanish and their way of life. It must be very hard working on a building site in heat like this. I couldn't help thinking that if you look down on the Spanish and their customs, why on earth go and live there?'

'It's because he's preparing for his retirement. Louise said he's already had a heart scare and he needs to hand over his businesses to someone else to run for him if he wants to live to a ripe old age. That's why he's become a housebound volunteer with her. She wants him to get used to living a different kind of life when he's retired.'

'Oh, so he's not just another volunteer who couldn't wait to take our jobs?'

'No, not at all. He just wanted to do some voluntary work to see what it will be like when he's retired. Remember, Louise has been doing it for years. She didn't want us to lose our jobs, but she's had to agree to work alongside Malcolm Bray and his team to be able to carry on doing the housebound deliveries. Don offered to do it with her, to help her. They're not actually going in and doing shifts on the counter like the others. Once their villa in Spain is finished they'll be spending more time out there, so someone else will have to take over the housebound deliveries then.'

'I can see Emma getting lumbered if no one else comes forward.'

'Yes, I think you're probably right, so in a way it's good she's one of the new volunteers.'

'I agree. I don't resent her getting involved with the library at all. As the vicar's wife she felt she had to help because she didn't want the library to close. So I don't mind her volunteering. It's just the other self-important busy bodies I resent.'

'I must say I envy Louise for having a man willing to do things for her. That's what I miss now I'm divorced. For a long while I thought I didn't need another man, but sometimes I think it would be nice to have someone you could rely on, don't you agree?'

'It's so long since Chris went off with his young girlfriend, I can't remember what it was like to have a man to help me with anything,' Sallie said sadly.

CHAPTER FIVE

Eileen Falls peered through her glasses at the lock on the back door of the library and tried to push her key into it. She grew more and more irritated as the key failed to turn.

She scrutinised it again and then tried the key the other way round. Finally, the lock yielded and allowed her to open the door and enter the office. She plonked her handbag down on one of the desks and stomped back across the room to look at the alarm she had set off. She raised the fob attached to her key ring and held it up to the alarm to try to stop the noise as instructed, but it carried on bleeping. She examined it and realised she had been holding her fob up against the wrong place. When she tried again, the awful din stopped.

After fetching the keys from the small room at the back, she switched on all the lights and put on the staff computers. As she went to switch on the public computers she noticed a book lying on the returns trolley. She felt a surge of irritation. All those people on duty on Saturday and no one had bothered to shelve it! She would never leave the library while there were still books on the returns trolley.

It was a paperback biography about some television gardener. Just because you can plant a few flowers and scatter a few pebbles around, it doesn't make you a celebrity, she thought. She picked it up and held it closer to her so she could read the cover. It doesn't make you a good gardener, either, she thought, when she saw who the book was about. She marched over to the corner on the opposite side of the library where the biographies were kept. As she went round the end of one of the bookcases she saw something lying on one of the easy chairs. It was long and white and looked like a stick.

She couldn't tell what it was, even as she got nearer to the chair, so she picked it up to look at it. As she brought it closer to her face she realised it was a bone. She was so shocked she dropped it. Feeling suddenly hot and dizzy, she opened her mouth to scream but no sound came out. The room started to spin round and she found herself falling…

*

Geoffrey paused dramatically with his scissors in one hand and a lock of Sallie's long blonde hair in another. 'So, big Eileen came crashing down. Apparently she hit the ground hard. The other volunteers had to send for an ambulance. There's never a dull moment, is there?'

Sallie looked at his enthralled face in the mirror above her own. 'But what caused her to faint?'

Geoffrey went back to cutting her hair for a few seconds. 'She was in there on her own because she had arrived earlier than everyone else,' he said, relishing telling the story bit by bit.

'They will have asked her to go in early to set up.'

'Oh, right. Well apparently she went round a corner to shelve some books and found a human bone on one of the easy chairs.'

'No!'

'Yes, apparently it was a large leg bone and she didn't know what it was so she picked it up and held it right up to her eyes. She's got terrible eyesight, apparently.'

'Yes, I know, she has to wear very thick glasses.'

'Anyway, when it dawned on her what she was holding, she fainted. She's a big lady and she hit the floor hard. The other volunteers found her when they came on duty. They're worried she might have injured herself seriously.'

'Oh! Poor Eileen, I do hope she's okay.'

'Well they carted her off in an ambulance, so they won't know for a while. Is that enough off the back for you, Sallie love?' he asked, holding up a small mirror and showing her the back of her hair, which was much shorter and now curled neatly under.

Sallie looked at the reflection in the big mirror. Her hair was now short and neat, emphasising her blue eyes and flattering the shape of her face. 'Yes, that's great, thank you.'

Just then the shop door opened and someone came in, but Sallie didn't bother turning round to see who it was.

She said: 'Yes, it looks a lot tidier and a bit more businesslike, cut like that. Thanks, Geoff. Only, I wanted to smarten myself up a bit because I have to start job hunting this week, thanks to those lovely, kind people who have volunteered to do my job for nothing.'

She heard Geoffrey's partner, Roger, take a sharp intake of breath from somewhere in the background, but took no notice.

While continuing to snip away at Sallie's hair, Geoffrey said: 'The thing is, Sallie love, people didn't want the library to close. I'm sure no one wanted you to lose your job, but people were told by the council that if no one was prepared to volunteer to run the library for nothing it would close.'

'Oh, I know, I understand all that. Some people, such as Emma, the vicar's wife, thought it was their duty to volunteer to keep the library open, but she still feels sorry for me and Jo because of what's happened to us. I have absolutely no quarrel with her, or people like her.

'It's just the ones on a power trip, who think volunteering at the library makes them somehow important, that I resent. They're mostly pathetic little nonentities who have nothing else going on in their lives and taking over the library is the most exciting thing that's ever happened to them. It's people like that I resent.'

'Yes, I think we get that, duckie. After all, you were overheard saying only the other night that you were going to think of a way to get your revenge on them all.'

'Yes, but to be fair, I'd been drinking. I didn't really mean it. People say all sorts of things when they've had too much to drink.'

'Oh, I know what you mean! When I've had too many cocktails I can be really mean to Rog. Sometimes I don't know why he puts up with me.'

Sallie said: 'Everyone knows you and Rog think the world of each other. You can forgive the people you love if they aren't very nice to you sometimes and he will know deep down you didn't mean it. Just as I didn't mean any of the things I said about the volunteers on Friday night. I'd had too much to drink.'

'Yes, but someone put the finger in the book and now the bone on the chair.'

'Oh, don't tell me I'm getting the blame for that as well!'

Geoffrey paused while he skilfully cut a few layers into one side of Sallie's hair.

Then he stepped back and looked at her hair from a distance. 'Well, you were caught by the police trying to break into the library on Saturday night.'

'Yes, but we didn't get inside, so we had no opportunity to put the bone on the chair.'

'I know, but people are saying you could have tried again later when the police had gone.'

'But we didn't! Honestly, Geoff, it's so unfair. Jo and I had nothing to do with either of those incidents at the library but people are still treating us as though we were responsible. We're determined to find out who's behind it, so we can prove once and for all it's nothing to do with us.'

Roger suddenly appeared behind her with a cup of coffee. 'Here you are, Sallie love, strong and dark, just how you like your men,' he said, putting it down on the ledge in front of the mirror.

'Rog!' Geoffrey squealed, pretending to be scandalised.

'I've just had old droopy drawers in,' Roger continued, ignoring him. 'She was telling me she feels people aren't giving the volunteers enough credit for giving up their time to run the library for nothing.'

'Droopy drawers?' Sallie asked, puzzled.

'You know who I mean, little Joyce, with the stretch brown trousers that hang down because she's hardly got any bottom.'

'Oh yes, of course!' Sallie immediately turned round in her chair to see if she was in the salon but there was no one there.

'Oh, she's gone now,' Roger said immediately. 'It didn't take long. It was only a fortnight since I'd cut what little hair she's got and I did it really short last time because that's what she asked for.'

'Why did she want it cut again?' Geoffrey asked, adding to Sallie: 'Not that I'm one to ever turn away trade.'

'She said she just happened to be passing and suddenly decided she wanted more off her fringe. She's a bit strange, but then I don't think she's got much else going on in her life. I hardly took anything off her fringe, but she quickly said it was fine and got up to leave.'

'Well I hope you charged her.'

'Of course I did you big…'

Sallie cut in quickly: 'Do you think she heard what I was saying to Geoffrey?'

'Oh yes! Loud and clear. You could have probably heard it outside the shop in the street, the way you project yourself. That's why I think she was so keen to go, all of a sudden.'

'Do you think she saw me in the shop and that's why she decided to come in?'

'I'm sure it was. I could tell by the way she stopped at the window and then turned back to the door that she'd spotted you and she was definitely eavesdropping on your conversation with Geoffrey.'

'But why?'

'She was perhaps hoping you'd let it slip you were responsible for the practical jokes at the library.'

'But I've already told you both that Jo and I have had nothing to do with it.'

'Oh, yes, we know!' they chorused.

*

After leaving the hair salon, Sallie was planning to go to Dolly's Pantry for a cup of coffee to see what sort of reception she got there. She had taken only a few steps down the street when she encountered one of her regular customers from the library. Mrs Whittaker was a dignified old lady with grey, wavy hair, who despite the heat was wearing a cream linen jacket with her usual Scottie dog brooch on the lapel.

'Oh, hello Sallie! How nice to see you. How are you getting on?'

Sallie opened her mouth to answer, but Mrs Whittaker said: 'I'm glad I've met you because I'm a bit worried about something. Do you mind if I ask your advice?'

'No, of course not. I'd be happy to help.'

'Well, I've had a letter from the library saying my books are overdue and that I owe some money on them, but I know I took them back in good time, so I'm a bit shocked. What can I do about it?'

'When you took them back, did you hand them in at the counter, or did you put them back through the letterbox?'

'I handed them in at the counter, I always do.' Mrs Whittaker was decisive.

'Have you been into the library to ask about it?'

'Oh yes. I told them I'd returned them and pointed out who I gave them to. It was a young girl and she was behind the counter when I went back in but she said she didn't remember serving me. How can I prove I took the books back?'

'Did they offer to do a shelf check for you?'

'No, they didn't.'

'Well, if you can remember the titles, you could go in and try to find them on the shelves yourself and take them to the desk and ask them why they are still showing on your account.'

'I could do, I suppose. But how could I prove I hadn't put them there myself to get out of paying the fine. Also, they said even if I found them at home, I would still have to pay the fine. But I know they're not at home because I took them all back before they were due, as I always do.'

She looked at Sallie hopefully. 'I don't suppose you would come in with me and vouch for me.'

Sallie felt terrible. 'I can't, I'm afraid. Now I've been made redundant I can't interfere. In fact, I've now been warned to stay away from the library. But why don't you wait till either Emma Goodall or Louise Bainbridge are there. They'll be much more supportive and helpful than the others, I'm sure.'

'Oh all right. I'll keep going in until I see one of them behind the desk,' Mrs Whittaker said, looking dejected as she walked away.

*

Sallie hadn't walked more than a few more yards in the direction of Dolly's Pantry when she ran into Emma.

'Hi, Sallie. How are you getting on? Have you got time for a quick coffee?' the vicar's wife asked.

'Yes, in fact I was just on my way to Dolly's.'

They were soon sitting at a table for two by the window waiting for Dolly to notice them. Sallie saw that the café owner was resplendent in a pink and white flowery cotton dress with a full skirt over layers of net petticoats as she sashayed over to take their order.

She ignored Sallie but was effusive towards Emma.

'Hello, my darling, how lovely to see you in here.'

Sallie said: 'Hi Dolly. How are you?'

'All right, I suppose,' the café owner said brusquely.

'We'll have two cappuccinos and two pieces of chocolate shortbread, on me,' Emma said decisively, closing her menu.

When Dolly had gone, Sallie said: 'She obviously thinks I'm to blame for all this nonsense at the library.'

'Oh, you mustn't worry about it.'

For the first time Sallie noticed her friend didn't look very happy.

'Is everything OK?'

'Yes. Well no, I'm a bit upset, I suppose, although it's nothing to worry about really. I shouldn't let it bother me, but it does. I've had an argument with Malcolm Bray.'

Sallie was immediately interested. 'What was it about?'

'Well, not content with being chairman of the Library Committee in charge of all the library volunteers, he's chairman of the Battle Re-enactment Committee and the Village Show Committee. He's just so pompous and ridiculous. He wants everything done his way and isn't prepared to see anyone else's point of view.'

'Why, what's he done?'

'He says he wants Howard to travel miles out of the village to say a prayer before the battle re-enactment and then almost immediately to be on the platform for the opening of the summer show on the village green. Then he wants him to judge several competitions during the afternoon before being back at the site of the battle to say a few words at the end. Howard's got a wedding at the church in the morning and Saturday afternoon is usually his time for putting the finishing touches to his sermon for the next day. Poor Howard works seven days a week and hardly ever takes any time off and yet Malcolm didn't think he was asking too much of him.'

'What a prat!' Sallie said, before biting into her chocolate shortbread. 'Has he got nothing better to do in life than to sit on committees and boss people about?'

'It seems not.'

Emma took a sip of her cappuccino. 'Howard will feel it's his duty to run about in the heat doing everything that's asked of him. He may be the vicar, but he's a human being too. That's what people such as Malcolm never seem to realise. Howard's got a few health issues hanging over him at the moment, so I don't want him to have to work too hard.'

'He's going to have to learn to say no to people.'

'It's easier said than done,' Emma said with a wry smile. 'Anyway, that's enough of me moaning. How are things going with you? By the way, I love your hair. Is that Geoffrey's handiwork? It's a lovely cut, it enhances your bone structure and makes your lovely blue eyes seem even bigger.'

'Thank you. I'm trying to smarten myself up ready for job hunting.'

Sallie told her all about her adventures on Saturday night with Jo, and how Jo had eventually given her spare library key to the police to be handed over to Malcolm Bray.

'I'm glad Jo did that because now no one can say you could have let yourself into the library.'

'In the future, yes, but what about this bone that's suddenly appeared on a chair in the library? According to Geoffrey and Roger, people think Jo and I put it there. But where would we be able to get hold of a human leg bone?'

'It wasn't human,' Emma said. 'George Bloodworthy, the butcher, is one of the library volunteers and when he came on duty this morning and saw it, he said straight away that it was a cow's leg bone. Anyone with a dog would be able to get hold of one from a butcher, apparently. Most people wouldn't have thought it was from a human being, but unfortunately Eileen has very poor eyesight.'

'Why would anyone put a cow's leg bone on a chair in the library?'

'Someone is out to make mischief it seems. I'm sorry, Sallie, but because the whole village knows you climbed over the fence into the library garden on Saturday night, they are thinking you had something to do with it.'

'Oh, for pity's sake! It's so unfair!

When they had finished their coffee, Emma went up to the counter to pay and Sallie saw her having a brief conversation with Dolly Sweetman, the café owner.

She felt a pang of sadness. She had known Dolly for years and had always liked her, accepting her eccentric behaviour without question.

Dolly came over to the table with Emma and said, in a silly, babyish voice: 'I'm very sorry, Sallie. Dolly should learn not to listen to silly gossip. I've told Emma it's on the house today and of course you are always welcome in here. I should have known you and Jo wouldn't have had anything to do with those nasty bones.'

'Well, it all seems so childish and silly,' Sallie said rather feebly.

She looked at the garish, shocking pink fascinator bobbing up and down in Dolly's dyed blonde curls as she cleared the table. Her face was caked in make-up and was perspiring in the heat. Everyone was used to Dolly dressing in the 1950s fashions of her youth. Sallie had never really thought about it before and now she felt suddenly uneasy. There were some very strange people living in the village.

*

After doing some food shopping, Sallie toiled up the hill to her cottage in the midday heat. She was thinking about Emma, who was probably the nicest, most decent person she knew. She was beautiful, with her long blonde hair, pale skin and perfect figure. Her features always reminded Sallie of a book illustration she had once seen of a squire's lady in medieval times. She was kind, generous and supportive to people. 'I don't know why she bothers with me,' Sallie suddenly said out loud, but fortunately there was no one nearby to hear her.

She knew from some of the things Emma had said that she was very much in love with her older husband, Howard.

As far as Sallie could tell, Howard seemed to be a kind, decent man. She could tell by the way Emma spent her time that being a vicar's wife was hard work. In all the time they had been friends, she had never known her to be so fed up about something. People just assume Emma and Howard will do everything asked of them without complaint and it's not fair, Sallie thought.

She wondered what had attracted Emma to Howard. He was tall and thin with receding fair hair and always seemed quiet and not particularly interesting whenever she encountered him.

She knew Emma had been a designer or artist in London before she came to live in the village. With her looks, she wouldn't have been short of male interest, Sallie thought and wondered how she had come to meet Howard. Now she had ended up here, having to have arguments with a pompous busybody such as Malcolm Bray in order to protect her husband when he wasn't well and needed to rest. Sallie wondered whether she ever regretted leaving her life in London.

Her thoughts were interrupted when she saw a small figure in the distance with a tiny dog on the lead.

She realised with a sinking feeling she was about to come face to face with Joyce Ferrier, who was out walking Sebastian.

When they drew level Joyce said in a slightly forced way: 'Hello Sallie, have you been in the pub with your friends again?' Then she gave a silly little titter.

'I've been having coffee with Mrs Goodall, the vicar's wife, in Dolly's Pantry.'

'Oh good, as long as you've been enjoying yourself. Only, I was thinking, if you find yourself at a loose end, you could always do some voluntary work somewhere.' Joyce gave her a malicious smile. 'You see, that's going to be the future for our great country in these times of economic crisis. People like us, offering their services unselfishly to work voluntarily.'

'Actually, I've already got another job lined up. But in any case, there's a slight flaw in your thinking. If everyone worked for nothing, no one would pay any income tax.'

'Well, what would that matter?' Joyce sounded a little less sure of herself.

'If no one paid any income tax, the Government would have no money to pay your old age pension, you silly old bat!'

Sallie swept off without a backward glance and the only sound she heard was an indignant squeal from Sebastian as Joyce pulled angrily on his lead.

CHAPTER SIX

Sallie and Jo were sitting in the pretty garden behind Sallie's cottage later that evening, enjoying the last of the sunshine, which was casting a golden glow over the fields in the distance. A pan of Bolognese sauce was simmering on top of the stove in Sallie's kitchen and they were enjoying a glass of the excellent wine Jo had brought with her.

Sallie had been unable to settle to anything after her encounter with Joyce Ferrier in the street and hadn't wanted to be on her own. She had invited Jo round for dinner, telling herself it was only fair to offer Jo a meal in return for her previous hospitality.

'The problem is, I told Joyce I had a job already lined up,' Sallie said, relaxing back in her chair and sipping her wine. 'When she doesn't see me boarding the bus first thing every morning to leave the village, she'll know I made it up.'

'Well, go to the Job Centre first thing tomorrow to see what's available. You never know, you might get something straight away.'

'I've made myself an appointment for tomorrow morning because I do need to start looking. It isn't doing me any good being cooped up in the house on my own. If I could find a job to occupy me three or four days a week, it would be ideal. That's why I've had my hair cut, I wanted to look smart and efficient.'

'Your hair looks great. I'm sure you'll be snapped up quickly. You've got good qualifications and you used to be a journalist before you had your kids.'

'Yes, but that was a long time ago. All I'm hoping for is some kind of clerical or shop work. But I'd take anything to get me out of the house for a bit and earn something towards the bills. Don't you feel every day is the same and boring now you're not at the library?'

'No, because at the moment I'm working flat out on the house.'

'But your house is perfect as it is!'

'Yes, it looks all right but I've got too much clutter. You probably can't tell when you visit, but it bothers me because I know where it's all hidden away. So, now I have time to spare I'm going through every room in the house removing all traces of Despicable Dave. You see, after he left me to go and live with his new woman, I couldn't bring myself to get rid of the things he'd left behind. He took everything he wanted when he left, but I kept finding all sorts of odds and ends he'd missed and just put them away in cupboards. I've been living with them, and not facing up to them.

'Losing my job and having to spend more time in the house has made me think. I love the house and the village and don't want to move anywhere else at the moment. So, part of my plan to get on with my life is to go through every room, getting rid of anything that belonged to him.

'Actually, I want to go even further than that. I'm going to look at all the things we bought together and decide whether

I really want to keep them. In fact, I'm going to get rid of everything I don't like, or don't want around me now. That way I can move on to the next phase of my life.'

'And what will that be?'

'I don't know yet. I need to work out who I am and what I want to spend the rest of my life doing.'

'I'm sure it's all great therapy, but don't go mad and throw valuable stuff away. You could give some of the things to charity or make some money by selling them.'

'I don't need the money. He left me well provided for to ease his conscience. But you're right, I'll give the things to charity and it will be therapeutic. I somehow feel if I can get complete control over the environment I live in, I can start to control other areas of my life.'

'What areas?'

'I don't really know at the moment. What I want to do and where I want to end up, I suppose. But I'm taking it one step at a time.'

'It all sounds very sensible. I wish I could do the same here. But I need to get a job as soon as I can.'

Sallie brought the plates of pasta out from the kitchen to eat at her small garden table. After they had finished and decided they were too full for anything else, Sallie cleared away, and then brought a notebook and a pen out into the garden with her.

'Right, let's take stock. We know we didn't let ourselves in using your key on Saturday and we didn't put the bone on the chair, so let's think who else had access to the library over the weekend.'

'Everyone,' Jo said immediately. 'Anyone could have put the finger in the book and put it through into the drop-box and anyone could have gone into the library on Saturday with a holdall containing the bone, taken it out just before they closed and left it on a chair in a corner where it wouldn't be discovered till Monday.'

'Yes, but there are usually several volunteers on each shift wandering around the library with nothing to do, according to Emma. One of them would have spotted the person leaving the bone, wouldn't they? I think we should concentrate on everyone who has a key to the building.'

'Well, for a start there's Tracy Dolby. Write her name down, because she has a key and lets herself in to clean, when there's no one else around.'

'Okay, for the same reason, there's Clive Fenton, the handyman. He's always had a key to the building.'

Jo giggled. 'Yes, and he's definitely one sandwich short of a picnic!'

'Then there's the awful Malcolm Bray.'

'Yes, but he wants the volunteer-run library to be a success, so why would he cause problems by playing silly jokes on the others?'

'Good point, but I'm going to put him down anyway because even though I don't really know him, I've decided I wouldn't like him.'

They both laughed loudly. 'We're going to have to go inside soon because we might disturb my neighbours,' Sallie said eventually.

Jo said quietly: 'We obviously can't count Emma.'

'No, but I'm going to put her down because we need to think of the names of all 12 volunteers to make sure we don't miss anyone out.'

'Okay, so there's Louise and Don. That makes four so far, even though they only do housebound deliveries. They're not the same as the other volunteers.'

'Then there's that bitch Joyce Ferrier. She makes five.'

'There's Verity and Eileen, the Knit and Stitch ladies, but they've both been the victims of the practical jokes.'

'Yes, but I need to put them down to work out who's left. They make it seven.'

'Well, then, there's George Bloodworthy, the butcher. He's the one who told them it was a bone from a cow. That makes eight.'

Sallie hesitated. 'But he could have put it there himself. He's a butcher so he would know where he could get hold of one.'

'Yes, that's true. Who else is there?'

'One of my regular customers, Mrs Whittaker, told me this morning there was a young girl among the volunteers.'

'Oh, that'll be Alicia Potter. I know her family. She's a bit of a drip, but harmless. She wouldn't play tricks on the others, I'm sure.'

'Did she ever use the library when we were working there?'

'No, never.'

'Then why did she bother volunteering?'

'I've no idea, but she's definitely one of them, so that makes nine.'

'Louise said there was one volunteer who didn't really count because he only wanted to do half an hour every three months.'

'That's ridiculous!'

'I know, but they weren't counting him in the dozen. So who are the others?'

'Isn't Deirdre Carter one of the volunteers? She was a bit shamefaced about it because she's a retired library assistant, but her excuse was that it was an opportunity to work in a library again because she'd really missed it.'

'So she makes ten. Who are the other two?'

'I've just remembered. There's a mysterious young man who no one knows much about. Emma mentioned he's good with computers. His name is Rory, I think.'

'He's the eleventh then, so who's the twelfth?'

Jo giggled. 'You're going to love this. It's your favourite doctor's receptionist.'

'Oh no, not Sandra Thompson! She's got to be the rudest woman in the world. It's a wonder anyone ever manages to get an appointment to see the doctor. She has absolutely no people skills, so why would she have volunteered to work at the library?'

'Like the others, she wants to do her bit, I suppose. So there's your twelve.'

'The Dirty Dozen. Let's go through them and see if we can think of any reason one of them might be behind these silly pranks.'

'All right. So, just imagine the cleaner, Tracy Dolby, is responsible for the practical jokes. Why would she do it?' Jo asked.

'Good question. I've known Tracy for years and the thing about her is that she always seems to end up on the right side financially. She's got three kids and no man supporting her, but she never seems short of a few quid and always drives smart cars. She's good at standing up for herself and insists on doing the hours that suit her and everyone in the village is too scared of her to object, so she comes and goes as she pleases with all her cleaning jobs. I can't imagine her wasting her time playing practical jokes on the volunteers unless it would make her some money.'

'Perhaps she has a hidden agenda and upsetting the volunteers would eventually result in her making some money,' Jo suggested.

'I can't see how and unless there was something in it for Tracy, she wouldn't bother doing it. Clive on the other hand is very strange. I can easily imagine him doing something like that.'

'I've just remembered something,' Jo said. 'An old lady once told me that the cottage the library is housed in used to be owned by the Fenton family, some of Clive's ancestors.

Perhaps he wants to get the volunteers to drop out so that the library closes and he can buy the house back again.'

'That's unlikely. Clive has worked as the odd job man at the library for years and never shown any particular interest in the house, as I recall. Anyway, where would he get the money from?'

'That's a good point. So, we think Emma, Louise and Don and Malcolm Bray are all above suspicion, but what about Joyce Ferrier?'

'I wouldn't put it past her. She's strange and twisted enough to do that sort of thing.'

'We could keep an eye on her and see what else she does.'

'Perhaps you could befriend her and ask her about the library and see what she says. It's no good me trying to talk to her. I think I've burnt my bridges with her now.' Sallie remembered her last encounter with Joyce in the street and felt guilty.

'Okay, I'll launch a charm offensive on Joyce and see how I get on.'

'Moving on, we've already said it couldn't be Verity or Eileen because they were both victims,' Sallie said, writing down their names.

'Unless they were both being very clever.'

'No, Eileen ended up in hospital because of it. I really can't imagine she put the bone there herself and then pretended to faint. She would have made sure she didn't injure herself if she was being devious.'

'What about George Bloodworthy?'

'Yes, he's an obvious suspect because he could easily get hold of a cow bone. But why would he do it?'

'Unless someone is deliberately trying to frame him.'

Sallie laughed loudly again and then stopped herself because of the neighbours.

'It's not a crime story! Why would someone try to make people think George Bloodworthy is playing practical jokes on his fellow library volunteers?'

'Come to think about it why would a busy man like George volunteer to help out at the library in the first place? What's in it for him?'

'Again we need to talk to him and see what we can get out of him. He's always been pleasant enough to us in the past, particularly you, Jo. I think he likes you.'

'All right, I'll try to strike up a conversation with him when I next see him in the pub.'

Sallie made another note and then asked: 'What about the young girl, Alicia? I can't see it being her unless she's a bit of a mental case.'

'Well, actually I think she has had a few issues from what I've heard,' Jo said guardedly. 'Perhaps you could try to get to know her, unless you've fallen out with her as well.'

'No, I don't think I've ever spoken to her, so I can at least try. Like most of the volunteers, she never used the library. Perhaps she's not much of a reader.'

Sallie made more notes and then asked: 'What about our ex-colleague Deirdre Carter? I wouldn't have thought she was the practical joker, unless she's making her own protest about the library being run by volunteers. It would be worth having a chat with her to see what she says about the pranks and also what she can tell us about the others.'

Jo said: 'I always got on well with her when we've been on courses together.'

'So did I. Not everyone hates me you know!'

Jo giggled. 'What about the mysterious young man no one knows anything about?'

'He's definitely worth getting to know. We could look out for him in the pub and try to get into conversation with him. So who's left?

Jo laughed again. 'Your best mate, the doctor's receptionist!'

Sallie groaned. 'Oh no! She's always horrible to me. I'm sure she won't tell me anything.'

'Well, I'll have to see if I can worm my way in with her then.' Jo relaxed back in her chair contentedly. 'I like the fact we've got something to do and a reason for going out and mixing with people again. Trying to find out who's responsible for the jokes could be fun!'

CHAPTER SEVEN

When Alicia put her key in the lock of the back door of the library she knew she was late, but she resented having to get up early to go somewhere to work for nothing.

She would have to move quickly now to get everything ready before the others arrived because she didn't want to give Malcolm an opportunity to tell her off.

Something was making a high-pitched shrieking sound and after a moment she remembered she was supposed to stop the alarm with the fob attached to her library key. She put her bag down on a desk and went back to the alarm and held her key up to it until the noise stopped.

Alicia opened the door to the library and went behind the counter to switch on the lights. Then she remembered she had to fetch all the keys to the cupboards and drawers from a room somewhere at the back of the house. She found the room, opened the door and put the lights on and then took the key from its hiding place to open the cabinet where the library keys were kept. She remembered the stories she had heard about the family who had once lived in this house. The odd job man, Clive, who she had been told was their descendant, gave her the creeps.

She returned to the library remembering she had to switch on all the computers. After the two on the counter she switched on the public computers. Then she unlocked the main door at the front where the customers would come in.

Alicia paused for a moment, thinking about what she had to do next and then realised she was supposed to open up the library management system on both of the staff computers.

She was sure there had been something else to do when Malcolm Bray had shown them all how to open up on their own, but couldn't think what it was.

She shivered as she thought of his horrible, podgy little hands and how he had touched her for no apparent reason when he had been showing her how to work the computers. She thought he was revolting, just like all the others. Well, not quite all the others. Rory was always polite and had never tried to touch her, which was a pity because she quite fancied him.

Then she remembered she had to unlock the cash drawer at the counter ready for when the customers came in. She selected the right key and put it in the lock. When she opened the drawer she saw something inside looking up at her. What on earth was it? It took her a few seconds to realise it was an eye. She suddenly felt sick…

*

Sallie was woken by her alarm but just wanted to turn over and go back to sleep. Then she remembered she was supposed to be going to the Job Centre and forced herself to get up.

She really shouldn't have opened another bottle of wine, but they'd been having such fun sitting in the garden drawing up a list of suspects and motives it had seemed like a good idea at the time.

We're just typical library assistants who've read too many crime novels, she thought, yawning as she headed towards the bathroom.

She was out of the house and at the bus stop in good time and was pleased the bus arrived promptly and she was carried down the hill and out of the village quickly. She had been worried she might encounter Joyce and Sebastian, as they always seemed to be walking along her road when she left the house and was returning to it.

She got off in the centre of Mickleton, the nearest town large enough to have a Job Centre, and made her way down an alleyway off the main square.

Inside the Job Centre she encountered the same stale smell of unwashed people and unwashed clothes she had endured in the past when doing shifts at the larger libraries in the county.

She was told to take a seat and nervously read all the posters on the walls waiting for her name to be called. When it was her turn to see an adviser her spirits lifted. Maybe they would help her find a great new job and all her worries would be over.

'Have you ever had a job before?' was the first question put to her by a thin young woman with long, lank brown hair and glasses, who was mopping her nose with a crumpled tissue.

'Yes, 35 years ago I got a job as a trainee reporter on a newspaper and I've worked in some capacity ever since.'

'What sort of jobs have you had?' the woman asked, making notes.

'Journalist, press officer and library assistant.'

'So, why are you out of work now?' she asked, still mopping her nose, which looked very sore.

'I was made redundant from the last library I worked in because it's been taken over by volunteers.'

'Are you claiming any form of benefit?'

'No, not yet.'

'Take this form away with you, fill it in and bring it back next time you come. Also, take this booklet with you because you'll have to make regular entries in it to prove you're looking for a job.'

Sallie took the form and the booklet and put them in her handbag while the girl blew her nose loudly on the tissue.

'Do you want to go on a course to help you improve your reading and writing?'

'No, as I've just told you I was a journalist and I've worked in a library for years.'

'Well, it's up to you but the courses are free. We can also offer you help with English if it's not your first language.'

'But it is my first language.'

'Yes, I'm aware of that, but I'm supposed to tell you what help we can offer you when you're here on your first visit,' the woman snapped. 'For instance, you need to tell me now if you have any learning difficulties or special needs.'

'No, I don't!'

'Are you now, or have you ever, done any kind of voluntary work?'

'No. I had a permanent job until recently.'

'Well, it might be a good idea for you to volunteer somewhere to learn new skills. It will look good to prospective employers and demonstrate to us that you are genuinely trying to find a job.' Then the girl gave a violent sneeze.

'You seem very poorly, should you be at work?'

'No, probably not, but we're short-staffed at the moment. We have several people on long-term sick. I'd definitely recommend volunteering to work somewhere because it will give you something to put on your CV.'

Sallie felt her cheeks flame with anger.

'I've just told you, until recently I worked at a library. I was made redundant because the place has been taken over by volunteers. It would somewhat go against the grain to go and volunteer somewhere and put someone else out of a job.'

'Well, it would be something to put on your CV.'

'Well, actually, I've never had to do a CV before. Do you have someone here who could help me put it together and advise me about what to include and how to set it out?'

'No, we haven't got time to help with CVs.'

'Well, is there a free course I can go on?'

'No. If you need help writing your CV, go and ask at your local library. The staff there have much more time than us to give people help with their CVs.'

Sallie stood up. She was aware she was shaking with anger, but she had to have her say. ‘I’ve just told you, I’ve been made redundant from my local library and it’s now being run by volunteers.’

She realised she was shouting and that some of the people at the other desks were looking in her direction.

She lowered her voice and continued: ‘They are inexperienced and have had hardly any training. Some of them are old and out of touch with the working world and some of them look as though they’ve never done a proper day’s work in their lives. How in God’s name do you think they would be able to help me write a CV?’

The girl blew her nose noisily. ‘That’s all we have time for today. If you find you need the form, or the booklet, in another format, ring the number on the bottom. Right, who’s next?’

*

After Jo had taken Mutz for his morning walk she settled him down on a rug in a shady part of the garden and began to tackle her large shed, identifying boxes of her ex-husband’s unwanted possessions and dragging them out into the garden to search through them. It was hot, tiring work, and after an hour or so she felt hungry and thirsty.

She looked at her watch. Sallie would still be at the Job Centre. She had asked her to come round and tell her how she’d got on when she returned. But she thought that if, in the meantime, she went to the pub for some lunch, she might bump into some of the volunteers she’d promised to talk to.

It would be great if she had some new information to relay to Sallie when she called in.

After freshening up and changing into smarter clothes, Jo lured Mutz into the cool of the kitchen with some dog biscuits and told him to have a rest in his basket.

She strolled down the hill to the village and walked into the side bar of the pub. The first person she noticed was George Bloodworthy, who ran the butcher's shop just outside the village on the main road to Mickleton. She knew he was a widower and that he lived alone in Upper Mickle in a pretty Georgian house not far from the village green.

George was standing at the bar with a younger man she'd never seen before. There weren't many people in the pub and George spotted her as soon as she appeared in the doorway.

'Well I never, it's the lovely library lady. I say, Rory, it's the lovely library lady!'

Jo forced herself to give a flirtatious smile and went across and joined them at the bar.

'Now, what can I get for you, Jo, love?' George asked, beaming at her. He was tall and broad, in a loud patterned blue and green short-sleeved shirt, completely bald, with very pale blue eyes, a tanned face and a big smile.

'That's very kind of you George, may I have a glass of Sauvignon Blanc please?'

'You most certainly may. Rory, this is Jo who used to run the library. Jo, this is Rory, one of our volunteers.'

Jo smiled at him and studied him so she could describe him to Sallie later. He was about medium height, quite a bit smaller than George, with thick, dark hair cut short, very dark brown eyes and a tanned face. He was slim and wore a tight-fitting, long-sleeved white shirt and blue denim jeans.

Rory stared back at Jo, clearly appraising her in his turn, and she found herself blushing.

'Rory, you go and sit with Jo at a table and I'll bring the lady's drink over,' George said.

Rory carried his pint over to a table a few feet away from the bar and Jo followed him. After an awkward pause, Rory said: 'Are you enjoying having a break now you've given up working at the library?'

Jo said: 'Well, neither of us wanted to give up working at the library. We used to run it between us, single staffing most of the time. There was only one day a week when we were both in there together to do displays and things like that. We worked hard to make it the best it could be, given the limited resources we had, but we both really loved working there and were sad to have to leave.'

'Why didn't you stay on as a volunteer?' Rory asked curiously, still watching her face intently.

'Why should we work for nothing?' Jo asked, deliberately looking directly into his dark eyes.

Rory dropped his eyes and took a sip from his beer. He said: 'No, I don't blame you for leaving. It would have been a bit of a cheek to expect you to carry on working for nothing. I presume you had to take redundancy?'

'Yes, and we now have to find new jobs, probably doing something else entirely, which won't be easy at our age.'

'No one really said anything to us about the previous staff, although I seem to remember one or two of the women saying they were surprised you hadn't been kept on to train us.'

'It would have been a bit cruel to expect us to do that.'

'I suppose it would. I've just moved to the village and don't know anybody around here. I volunteered because I thought it would be a good way to meet people. I didn't know anything about how the library was run before.'

George sat down at the table with them and put Jo's glass of wine in front of her.

'Cheers, George,' Jo said, taking a sip. She put her glass down and continued her conversation with Rory. 'They had no intention of keeping us on, even for one more day, once they had enough people willing to work for nothing.'

George said: 'I must admit that when I volunteered to work at the library I had no idea you and your blonde friend would lose your jobs. No one told us and I think some of the ladies who were regular visitors to the library were disappointed you weren't going to be there We had a bit of training from a very strange woman sent by the local authority that I'd never seen before. But I was disappointed to find I wasn't going to be working with you, I must say.'

'And things aren't exactly going smoothly, despite the best efforts of our leader, Malcolm,' Rory chipped in. 'People don't always turn up to do their shifts and there have been a few incidents.'

'What sort of incidents?'

'Some of the customers have been a bit aggressive towards the ladies, not perhaps understanding they haven't had much training. Once a bloke got cross when he was logged out of the computer and lost what he was working on and he said a few choice words to one of the ladies. He had asked for extra time but she couldn't remember how to do it and eventually he was logged off automatically. When someone helped him to log him back in everything had disappeared.'

'Yes, the computer wipes everything people have been looking at or working on when they log out,' Jo said.

'And then, of course, the police had to be called out once and also one of the older ladies had to be taken to hospital by ambulance.' Jo got the impression Rory was watching her closely as he spoke, perhaps looking for a reaction.

'How is Eileen now?' she asked, turning to George.

'Oh she's all right. They let her out the same day. She's apparently just been left with a bit of bruising. It was a lot of fuss about nothing really. I told the others when I got there that it was definitely a cow's leg bone. I said to them, I can guarantee you, that bone is from a cow, although I have no idea what it was doing there, left on a chair by someone.'

Rory smiled. 'The popular theory, from what I've overheard, is that Jo and her friend have been having a bit of fun at the expense of the volunteers.'

'Absolutely not! We were upset about being made redundant and hated having to leave jobs we enjoyed, but we wouldn't stoop to do something as childish and pathetic as to put a fake finger through the letterbox or leave an animal bone in a chair.'

'Oh, I believe you, of course,' Rory said quickly.

'So do I, so do I!' George said loudly.

'I must admit though, I was intrigued when Verity told us the finger was in Be Careful What You Wish For. I wondered whether the book had been chosen to give us some kind of message,' Rory said cautiously.

'What kind of message?'

'Perhaps telling us we would ultimately regret taking your jobs.'

'But how did we manage to get hold of that particular book to put the finger in?'

'You could have taken it before you left, I suppose.'

'I think you'll find it has been out on someone's ticket and either they, or someone acting on their behalf, put the finger in it before returning it.'

Rory smiled at her and took a sip of his beer.

George said: 'Honestly Jo, no one really believes it was you or Sallie that was responsible.'

Jo said: 'I'm just frustrated no one has bothered to look into it properly and find out who had the book out last. Then you could ask the customer about it and when you find out who returned it, you'll get your answer.'

'I shall do that next time I go in to do a shift.' Rory smiled at her again.

George said: ‘Anyway, how’s that handsome doggy of yours? Don’t forget, if you come into my shop, I’ll always be able to find you a nice bone for him.’

‘Thank you George, I’ll do that.’ She took another sip of her wine. ‘I’m amazed you have the time to be a volunteer at the library. I would have thought you’d be too busy at your shop to be able to spare the time.’

‘Oh well, I wanted to be seen doing my bit for the community, and anyway, I’ve got good staff that I can leave in charge.’

‘Well, I think it’s very good of a man like you to give up his time.’

‘It never does any harm to become involved with these community things, for a businessman like myself. You never know what opportunities might come your way,’ George said, giving her a knowing smile.

*

Jo couldn’t stop laughing when she was relaxing in her garden later and Sallie arrived and told her about her encounter with the woman at the Job Centre.

‘You’re right. I’m sure Joyce, Verity and Eileen have never worked, or if they did it was probably before the Second World War. Alicia Potter’s never done a day’s work either. Emma was some sort of designer and I think Louise once told me she trained as a nurse. But I’m sure a shrewd businessman such as Malcolm Bray would be a good help with your CV.’ She went off into a fit of the giggles at the thought.

Sallie gave her a withering look. 'Anyway, enough about me. You seem to have had a productive morning, judging by all these boxes.'

'Yes, I dragged them all out despite the heat, but I went to the pub at lunchtime and now I can't be bothered to do anything with them.'

'The pub! Jo Pudsey, you're getting as dissolute as me. I hope Joyce didn't notice you going in.'

'It was in the interests of our investigation. I was hoping to run into some of the volunteers. George Bloodworthy was in there with a rather dishy young man named Rory.'

'Oh, is he the computer expert that Emma and Louise have mentioned?'

'Yes, I think he must be. He was very pleasant, but I kind of got the idea he suspects us of being responsible for the finger and the bone and when they were mentioned he was watching me for some kind of a reaction.'

'I hope you put him right!'

'Of course I did. I also explained more about our situation to him. I don't think he knew we'd been made redundant against our will, but he said he understood now why we didn't choose to join the volunteers. George actually said some of them thought we would still be working there and were disappointed to find we'd left. He also said he had no idea we were going to be made redundant. So it would seem people weren't given the full picture when they were being encouraged to volunteer.'

'Did you find out why George volunteered?'

'He said he wanted to be involved for the good of the community, but he also hinted he thought it might be to his advantage in some way because he is a local businessman.'

'That's interesting. What about the handsome young man?'

'Rory said he is new to the area and thought it would be a good way of meeting people, which sounded plausible.'

'Why would a bloke like that not be at work during the day?'

'I don't know. We're going to have to try to find out more about him.'

Then Jo told Sallie what he had said about some of the problems the volunteers had been having.

'There you are!' Sallie said triumphantly: 'Everyone thinks working in a library is an absolute doddle but they don't realise how much is involved. It's not just shelving a few books and gossiping with the customers. There's a lot more to it than that.'

Jo gave a sigh and sat back in her chair and closed her eyes. 'Perhaps two glasses of wine at lunchtime wasn't such a good idea.'

'Well, why don't I help you this afternoon? I've got nothing planned. I'll go home and change into something more casual and then come back and give you a hand.'

'That would be great, if you're sure you don't mind. I'm more likely to keep going with the shed if I've got someone doing it with me,' Jo said gratefully.

*

Back home, Sallie changed into jeans and a tee shirt, had a cup of tea and a sandwich, and refilled Des's dishes.

As she crossed the road to go back to Jo's house she saw Joyce and Sebastian in the distance and congratulated herself on concealing the bottle of wine she was taking with her in a carrier bag.

She put the wine in Jo's fridge and went into the garden. They decided to divide Despicable Dave's possessions into three piles: rubbish, charity and to keep.

But both Jo and Sallie found Despicable Dave's book collection was a big distraction and kept picking up books to look at. 'They're in such good condition we could have added them to the catalogue if we still worked at the library,' Sallie said sadly.

'The thing is, he liked thrillers and adventure stories, so I'm never going to read them. There are loads by the likes of Lee Childs and James Patterson. They'll have to go.'

As the afternoon wore on and the rubbish pile grew bigger they started to discuss how they were going to dispose of everything.

'Is there any part of this beautiful garden where you could have a bonfire?' Sallie asked.

'Yes, down at the bottom there's a patch where Dave used to burn things. We could wait till it gets a bit cooler and then try to start one. His books should help to start it blazing.'

'You can't burn his books!'

'Well, I'm never going to read them so what's the point of keeping them?'

'Let's put them to one side while we think about it,' Sallie said hastily.

Once the shed was empty, Sallie said she could hardly believe how big it was, compared to most garden sheds.

'I'm thinking of turning it into a summer office.'

'I thought you'd already got an office inside the house.'

'Yes, I have, but it would be nice to be able to work outside while Mutz is pottering in the garden so I can keep an eye on him.'

'You could fit shelves all the way round the walls and house all these books and more besides.'

'What's the point if I don't want to read them?'

'I know, but it's a shame because there are a lot of people in this village who would read them.'

'Perhaps I ought to start my own library.'

'Actually that's not a bad idea. I'm sure that a lot of our regulars would prefer to come here for their books than be served by the volunteers.'

Jo paused for a moment. 'It's a nice idea in theory, but I haven't got nearly enough books to satisfy people's demands. I've only got my own books and the ones Dave left behind.'

'Yes, but I've got boxes and boxes of books in my attic. Ones I've bought from library sales over the years or online because I thought I might want to read them one day. We could do it for charity, perhaps. If we ran a library from here we could ask people to make donations to a good cause.'

'We could sell any duplicates we've got to raise money to buy new stock.' Jo was starting to be enthusiastic about the idea.

'Let's do it. It would be a great way of getting our revenge on the volunteers if our library became more popular than the official one.'

'Well, if I reorganised my own books, I'm sure I could free up some bookcases in the house to put in the shed.'

'Yes, and I know I've got some old bookcases out in my shed that would just need a lick of paint,' Sallie said.

'It would be a lot of work. Are you sure you want to be bothered with it? I wouldn't relish doing it on my own.'

'No. I'd love to help you with it. How much would it cost to renovate your shed, do you think?'

'Not very much. We could probably get it done in a few days and be open for business in a week or so.'

'We would have to be businesslike and list all your expenses. We couldn't run it at a loss, it wouldn't be fair to you.'

'But what about your plans to get a job?'

'Well, I could still look for one. I decided this morning that I'm not going to bother with the Job Centre again, I'm going to do it on my own. But I could work in your library until I find one.'

'I've been thinking about your job search. We're close to the borders of three different counties here. You could easily get a bus from Mickleton into Nottinghamshire, Derbyshire or Lincolnshire and work for a different library authority.'

'Yes, I'm going to keep an eye on the local authority websites for job adverts but in the meantime I'd love to help you open a library here and see how successful we could be.'

'Let's go outside and have some refreshments and draw up a plan of action,' Jo said. She brought out some cheese and biscuits and they had a glass of the wine Sallie had brought with her.

'We could have a free magazine exchange and a for sale trolley for worn stock or duplicates,' Sallie suggested.

'Yes, and we could rent out jigsaws.' Jo began making notes on a pad.

'We could have a collection box for a worthwhile charity that people would be happy to support.'

'We could also perhaps charge a joining fee. I'm sure people would be willing to pay a small amount for a library card. We could get some printed by a professional firm with a box for the customer's name and we could number them ourselves and keep a record of all the borrowers.'

When it became cooler, Jo said: 'Let's see if we can get this bonfire started down at the end of the garden.'

She arranged a pile of dry twigs well away from the boundary fences and Sallie rolled up sheets of newspaper to make into firelighters.

They soon had a blaze going and began burning Despicable Dave's old paperwork. They threw cardboard wallets full of computer print outs and his accounts books on to the bonfire.

They both traipsed backwards and forwards, fetching piles of Dave's old files to burn, calling out to each other with ideas about what services their library could provide.

On one of her trips back to the top of the garden Sallie paused on Jo's terrace to take another sip of her wine. Then she became aware of a man's voice shouting. It sounded as if it was coming from nearby so she went round the side of Jo's house to see who was there.

She saw through the wrought iron gate that there was a small, plump man in grey shorts and a black tee-shirt, wearing long white socks and white plimsolls. He had thinning dark hair, combed over to disguise where he was balding, large glasses and a Hitler-style moustache.

'What on earth do you think you're doing? There's smoke billowing all over my garden. You have absolutely no right to light a fire in weather like this, you stupid woman!'

Sallie took a deep breath and was just about to put the little man in his place when Jo came round the side of the house.

'Oh. It's you. What do you want? We're in the middle of something here.'

She turned to Sallie and said: 'This is Malcolm Bray. His house backs on to mine.'

'Malcolm Bray, as in library volunteer?' Sallie asked.

The little man puffed out his chest and stood up straight, doing his best to make himself look taller.

'I'm chair of the Library Volunteers Committee,' he said proudly.

As usual, Sallie said exactly what she was thinking, without considering whether it might cause offence.

'I don't know why they picked you, I never saw you in the library once in all the years I worked there, so what would you possibly know about it?'

'They chose me because I'm a good organiser and I have a proven track record of running committees. Someone has to provide leadership for the village women. But, anyway, I haven't got time for this discussion. You must put that bonfire out immediately.'

'I will when I've finished burning everything I want to get rid of,' Jo snapped.

'You haven't heard the last of this,' Malcolm snarled and turned and strode off back down the side of the house into Jo's front garden.

Both Sallie and Jo immediately collapsed on the other side of the gate, laughing uncontrollably.

After they had finally managed to stop, Jo said: 'We'd better finish burning Dave's things as quickly as possible and then put the bonfire out.'

'I suppose so, but to the best of my knowledge it's not illegal to have a bonfire in the privacy of your own back garden.'

'No it isn't. You would think this garden is big enough for any bonfire not to bother the neighbours, let alone a house that backs on to you that also has a large garden. It's as though he wanted to have something to complain about.'

They toiled back and forth with more of Dave's things and then Jo said: 'I'll leave it to die down now and put it out with a bucket of water.'

While they were standing watching the flames subside, they heard shouting again from round the side of the house.

'Let me deal with him,' Sallie said with relish.

But this time when she reached the gate she saw Tom and Wasim, both in uniform, standing on the other side.

'Are you causing trouble again?' Tom asked.

'Not as far as I'm aware,' Sallie replied as she released the bolt on the gate to let them into the back garden.

The two policemen followed her down the path to where Jo was standing by the bonfire. The flames had almost disappeared.

'I was just about to pour some water on it,' Jo said anxiously when she saw them.

Sallie noticed Tom smiling at her indulgently. She followed his gaze and saw the top buttons of Jo's polo shirt were undone and because of the heat it was clinging to her body, showing off her small, firm breasts.

'We had a call saying that there was a fire out of control and that the people who had started it were being rowdy and abusive,' Wasim said.

'Well, as you can see the fire is not out of control so your complainant is wrong,' Sallie snapped.

'Were either of you abusive to any of the people living near here?'

'No we weren't. However, I was called a 'stupid woman' by the man who presumably complained about the fire. Funnily enough, I've never reacted well to being called a stupid woman.'

'Why had you lit a bonfire on a day like this, anyway?' Tom asked Jo in a more pleasant tone.

'We had a lot of rubbish to get rid of.'

'It was mainly old paperwork left behind by her ex-husband,' Sallie added. Tom immediately looked interested.

Wasim was less easily distracted. 'Every time we're called out to this village it seems to involve you two,' he said severely.

'Yes, but you can tell the fire isn't out of control, so maybe we've been called out by someone overreacting,' Tom said quickly. 'Try not to upset any of the villagers again,' he said, smiling at Jo.

CHAPTER EIGHT

'So we've been threatened by the police twice now,' Sallie told Emma the next day as they were having coffee in Dolly's Pantry.

'Yes, but to be fair to Tom he always listens to our side of the story and uses his judgement about whether to take things any further,' Jo chipped in.

'I think he'd like to take things a lot further, with you, Jo,' Sallie said, grinning. 'He has an ulterior motive for this leniency. I don't think he'd be quite so understanding and pleasant if it was just me he was coming to see.'

Jo flushed but said nothing.

'Anyway, Sallie, you texted and said you had something to ask me.' Emma changed the subject tactfully.

'Yes. We're still keen to find out the name of the last person to have the book out that the finger was found in.'

'Oh I see.' For a moment Emma remained silent, lost in thought. 'I do hope the police told Malcolm Bray off for wasting their time,' she said suddenly. 'He's so officious, it's time someone took him down a peg or two.'

'He's the sort of bloke who thinks he's in the right whatever anyone says to him. The thing is, we're both fed up with being blamed for everything. Couldn't you try to find out who had the book out last?'

'Even if I can get on to a computer next time I do a shift, I don't know whether I'd be able to find out for you. I haven't had chance to learn how to work the system yet.'

Jo said: 'Yesterday, when I was in the pub, I saw George Bloodworthy with a young man named Rory, who said he would look it up for us next time he's on duty. But I don't really know him and have no way of contacting him. We wondered whether you could ask him to look it up when you're on duty together and then let us know the name of the customer.'

Emma looked at her with interest. 'It was nice of Rory to offer to help you. He's very good looking isn't he?'

'He's a bit young for me, but yes, he did seem very nice. Could you ask him to help you, do you think?'

'He's got a reputation for being good with computers, so I'll see what I can do. He's always been very friendly.'

'Also we wanted to ask what you think about an idea we've had. We're thinking of starting a library in my shed in aid of charity. It's a big shed and we both have boxes of books taking up room in our houses that we can donate. We would like to raise money for a good cause. What do you think?'

'I think it sounds a great idea and it will give you something to do while you look for jobs. You know I'm always in favour of anything that will benefit the village, or charity.'

Dolly brought a plate of her chocolate dipped shortbread over. 'It's on the house,' she said, winking at Sallie. Resplendent in a purple, glittery party frock with a full skirt,

Dolly was again so heavily made up she looked as if she was wearing a mask and her thin, pale, mottled arms looked like sticks in the sleeveless dress.

'Thank you Dolly,' Jo said gratefully.

'You're welcome, honey,' Dolly replied in a fake American accent and then pirouetted away from their table holding out her skirt.

'She's completely nuts,' Sallie said.

'But she's very well meaning,' Emma corrected her. 'It shows there are people in the village who don't think you are behind the practical jokes. The others will soon stop talking about you and move on to someone else, I'm sure.'

'Rory told me things aren't going very well at the library, leaving the pranks out of it,' Jo said.

'Yes, I'm afraid there are often too many of us on the same shift and we get in each other's way. Tempers can get frayed. Also, one or two of the volunteers have said it's not as enjoyable as they thought it was going to be.'

'Be careful what you wish for,' Sallie said thoughtfully.

'Do you think one of them could be playing a joke on the others for some reason?' Jo asked.

'Well, here's someone else you could ask,' Emma said brightly and when Jo turned round she saw a small, slim woman, with short grey hair coming towards their table.

'Hi, Deirdre. How nice to see you. Why don't you join us,' Jo said, indicating the empty chair next to Emma.

'I've been wondering when I was going to see you two. I was surprised you hadn't been into the library by now,' Deirdre said, sitting down next to Emma.

Dolly appeared with a cup of coffee for Deirdre and then danced away again.

'We've been warned off by the police,' Sallie said. Deidre looked startled for a moment.

'But apart from that, we made a conscious decision not to go in again after we were made redundant. We thought it would be too upsetting,' Jo added.

Deirdre nodded understandingly and took a sip of her coffee. She was wearing a short sleeved white blouse with a silk scarf in different shades of orange knotted at her throat. She looked tanned and fit and full of vitality. She was another person who seemed to be coping well with the heat, despite not being young, but then she wasn't carrying excess weight, Sallie noted.

'It's a real shame you've had to leave,' Deirdre said. 'I've felt guilty about volunteering, but I've really missed library work since I retired. It just seemed too good an opportunity, to get the chance to do a few shifts occasionally. It gives me something to look forward to and yet it's not like being employed and having responsibility for the library because there are so many of us. I thought it would be just the thing to break up my week.'

'So, are you enjoying it?' Jo asked.

Deirdre hesitated. 'Well, it's not like it used to be when I came in when one of you was on holiday. There are too many people trying to use the two counter computers all the time and the other volunteers don't just let you get on with it when you're dealing with a customer. They keep chipping in with their opinions, which is very annoying. Also, the way some of them speak to the customers is bordering on rudeness. It's been a bit of an eye-opener working with some of them, I can tell you.'

'Who do you think is responsible for the practical jokes?' Jo asked.

'I've no idea. It's obviously someone's idea of humour, but it's unfortunate that they chose occasions when two of our older ladies were on their own.'

'Maybe it wasn't unfortunate. Maybe it was planned that way. Anyone who had access to the timetable would know they were going to be on their own,' Jo said.

'Yes, it could have been deliberate,' Sallie said. 'Out of all of them, who do you think is most likely to be the culprit?'

Deirdre looked cautious. 'Well I don't want to accuse anyone, but it seems to me it would be something a man would do rather than a woman. Using human bones, I mean,' she said in a low voice.

'They weren't human bones. The finger was made from latex and the bone was from a cow,' Emma pointed out.

'But neither Verity nor Eileen knew that at the time.'

'Which of the men do you think would be most likely to have done it?' Jo asked curiously.

'Oh, I don't know, although I have wondered about the young man, Rory. I mean, no one seems to know anything about him and it does seem odd that he has so much spare time and would want to do voluntary work at his age. He doesn't say much either, or at least he doesn't talk to any of us women. He seems happy to talk to George and he always makes a point of having a chat with Don when he comes in, but he obviously can't be bothered with females.'

Jo and Sallie exchanged a glance. 'I met him for the first time yesterday and I thought he seemed very nice,' Jo said.

'Oh, he is nice, of course. I didn't mean anything against him. But we know all the other men, don't we? Malcolm is furious about it, so it can't be him.'

'That could just be a smokescreen,' Jo said, looking sideways at Sallie, who giggled.

'No, honestly, I don't think he would want anything to go wrong because he wants to be seen to be running the library well.'

'That's probably true, we've said that ourselves,' Sallie said.

'What about George or Don?' Jo asked.

'But they're both respectable businessmen,' Deirdre said.

'George could have easily got hold of that cow bone, so I think it's unlikely to be him, because he wouldn't want to be that obvious.'

'Well, why would Don do it? His wife has been a housebound volunteer for years. What possible reason could he have for trying to scare elderly ladies?' Emma asked.

'What about Sandra Thompson? Do you think she's trying to scare the other women off so she's the only woman left and can run the library all on her own? She's definitely got a power complex,' Sallie said eagerly.

'I wouldn't have thought anyone would be keen to get extra shifts,' Emma put in. 'It takes up a lot of time and can be boring.'

'Well, what about Joyce Ferrier? Could she have a strange reason for playing tricks on the other ladies?'

'Poor old Joyce. She can seem a bit weird sometimes, but I don't think she would want to be in trouble with Malcolm Bray,' Deirdre said.

'Why, is he a bit of a tyrant?' Sallie asked innocently.

Emma flashed her a warning look.

'Yes, I'm afraid he has a nasty habit of telling people off in front of other volunteers, which has upset some of the ladies,' Deirdre responded. 'I mean, it's ridiculous! They haven't had enough training. They're bound to make mistakes. There's such a lot to the job they've got to learn. It takes new staff months, even years, to grasp it all and that's when they're working with other experienced people.' Deirdre then flushed as though she regretted being outspoken. She drank the rest of her coffee quickly.

'Anyway, I'd better go. I'm opening up today and I don't want to be late. If I haven't got everything ready I might incur the wrath of Malcolm Bray.' She laughed happily, picked up her handbag and went out of the café.

*

That afternoon, Sallie and Jo worked hard, emptying and cleaning out Jo's shed. They washed down the walls with soapy water and Jo cleaned the wooden floor.

'It will be ready for us to start painting tomorrow, that's if you don't mind helping me.'

'No, I'd be happy to help. I've got nothing else to do. I reckon we could have a nice little library in here and if we get busy we could always offer Deirdre some shifts. She's obviously frustrated about having to work with a load of amateurs.'

'I tell you what, why don't we get cleaned up and changed into something smarter and I'll treat you to a meal at Marco's tonight.'

'No, I couldn't let you treat me. I'm happy to pay for myself.'

'Nonsense. You've worked really hard helping me with the shed and getting rid of Despicable Dave's stuff over the last couple of days. I think dinner should be on me.'

*

That evening Marco looked pleased to see them when they arrived at the restaurant and brought them both a complimentary glass of Prosecco while they looked at the menu.

The only other customers were a couple holding hands across the table and whispering things to each other in a secluded corner.

Sallie glanced at them briefly and then looked back at her menu. Then something made her look again.

'Oh no! The infamous doctor's receptionist turned library volunteer is at that table in the corner with some poor, unsuspecting bloke.'

'Not Sandra Thompson,' Jo said and immediately turned round to look.

'Don't make it obvious we've seen her!'

Jo turned back and made a point of studying her menu.

'Did you see the state of her?' Sallie whispered. 'She's had her hair dyed blonde, although she wears it so short I don't know why she bothered and she's obviously spent too much time in the sun as her face and arms aren't normally that colour.'

Jo turned round again to have a look and this time Sandra looked across at their table but then turned back to her companion without acknowledging them.

They ordered their food and when their starters arrived ate in silence while they were treated to a performance from Sandra, who kept laughing hysterically every time her dinner companion said anything.

'She's showing off for our benefit. Who's the bloke? Have you ever seen him before?' Sallie asked.

'No, he's no one I recognise. He's definitely not one of the volunteers,' Jo said, after glancing casually behind her again.

'He perhaps offered to take her out because he was desperate to get an appointment with the doctor.'

Marco came over to ask if they were enjoying their starters. He was not particularly tall, but although he was lean he looked strong. He had a good head of black curly hair cut short and was dressed as always in black trousers with a white shirt and black bow tie.

'It's very quiet in here tonight,' Sallie remarked.

At that point Sandra let out a shriek of laughter.

'I mean, apart from that,' Sallie said.

'Yes. Well it is very hot and you British are not used to it so you stay inside your houses to keep cool,' Marco answered.

'Apart from us, that is. Your food is so lovely it's worth coming out in the heat,' Jo said.

When he came back to the table with the dishes of pasta they had chosen, he was obviously about to say something, but then Sandra's dinner companion held up his empty wine carafe to attract his attention.

'Please excuse me,' Marco said with a little bow in Sallie's direction and went over to Sandra and her friend's table to take their wine order.

'What an ignorant prat! Mind you, he'd have to be a complete idiot to bother with her.'

'Sallie!'

'Well, you can't see him properly where you're sitting. He's small, fat, bald and wearing silly glasses!'

'Silly glasses?'

'Well, they look silly on him.'

'Look, ignore them and eat your pasta. Let's talk about something else. Do you really think we can run a successful library in my shed?'

‘Well, I don’t see why not. We’ve had plenty of experience and anyway it will be fun trying. If it’s all for charity, then anything we make will be a bonus.’

‘We’ve got plenty of books to start off with and we could put up a poster asking people to bring in their old books as donations. If we end up getting more customers than the volunteers running our old library, it would be a fitting way of getting our revenge, don’t you think?’

‘They do say revenge is a dish best served cold,’ Sallie said thoughtfully. Then a voice whispered in her ear: ‘Would you like to try the tiramisu?’

Sallie nearly jumped out of her seat.

‘I’m sorry if I startled you. It is my grandmother’s recipe. It’s very good.’

‘No, thank you,’ Jo said.

‘What about you, Sallie? Can’t I tempt you? Marco asked, looking into her eyes.

‘No, honestly I’m sure it’s lovely but I know I won’t have any room when I’ve finished this, thank you.’

When he had gone back into the kitchen they both started giggling helplessly.

‘I’ve told you before and you never believe me, he obviously fancies you,’ Jo said.

‘I’m sure he doesn’t, but in any case, he’s too old for me.’

‘I don’t know why you think that. I think he’s probably about our age and anyway, he’s very fit looking.’

A few minutes later, Sandra Thompson and her escort went past their table on their way to pay. He said something to her in a low voice and she shrieked with laughter.

'Oh, you are so naughty,' she said to him loudly and shrieked with laughter again.

'Is she on something, do you think?' Sallie asked loudly.

Jo did not reply until the couple had left the restaurant.

'I think she was just putting on a show for our benefit.'

'Yes, but the dress was definitely for his benefit. Did you see how short it was?'

'Yes, I did. Unfortunately, she's so thin she has really knobbly knees, which kind of spoilt the effect.'

Sallie started giggling again and Jo said: 'Now they've gone let's just relax and enjoy ourselves. I'll order more Trebbiano.'

CHAPTER NINE

The walls were now painted a soft, creamy pink and made the shed look even larger inside. As Sallie stepped back and surveyed her work with pride she heard her mobile phone ping with a text message.

'Emma wants us to meet her in the pub at about six. She's got a couple of things to tell us,' she said, after looking at her phone.

Jo called down from the top of her ladder where she was painting the ceiling the same colour as the walls.

'Great. We've got time to finish off here and get showered and changed. This will be dry by tomorrow and then all I've got to do is stain the floorboards. When they're dry the shed will be ready for us to put the bookshelves in.'

Sallie was glad when she put her brush down for the day. An hour and a half later they were walking down the hill together, all the paint scrubbed off and dressed up for the evening.

They found Emma already in the pub, standing at the bar with George, Rory and Malcolm, with a beer in her hand.

Emma left the men to go and sit at a table with Jo while Sallie waited at the bar to be served.

'What news on the book?' Jo asked after Sallie had brought their drinks over.

'With the help of Rory, I managed to find the book on the system and it's still checked out to someone,' Emma said proudly. 'I don't really understand how the book managed to come back into the library with a joke finger inside, causing all that fuss, and yet still be checked out to someone.'

'I do,' Sallie said. 'It will be because no one has bothered to discharge it. Someone put it in the drop box and Verity took it to the counter. But then she found the fake finger inside and all hell broke loose. Since then, obviously no one has had the sense to discharge it properly.'

Sallie made no attempt to lower her voice, seeming not to worry that the volunteers standing at the bar might hear her. Emma gave her a reproachful look.

'Did you find out who had the book last?' Jo asked in a much quieter voice.

'Yes, it was checked out to old Mrs Jenkins.'

'I don't remember a Mrs Jenkins coming in when I was working there,' Sallie said.

'I know who she is because Howard goes to her house to give her communion.' When she saw that they looked puzzled, Emma explained further. 'Mrs Jenkins lives in a cottage near the church but she is very old and is now bedridden. She used to be a regular church goer so Howard visits her to give her communion once a month.'

'So she's unlikely to have got hold of a latex finger, put it in the book, hopped out of bed, walked uphill to the library and put it in the drop-box,' Sallie said in a much lower voice.

'Very unlikely indeed,' Emma replied.

'So we're not much further forward,' Jo said dispiritedly.

'No, but there's something else I wanted to tell you. There was another weird incident at the library on Tuesday. The young girl who's become a volunteer, Alicia Potter, was opening up and she found a glass eye in the cash drawer at the counter when she unlocked it. So, it seems somebody is still trying to frighten us off.'

'Did it upset her?' Jo asked sympathetically.

'It startled her, because it was so odd for her to see it there but she quickly realised it wasn't a human eye and she was okay about it eventually. I happen to know she had a nervous breakdown last year so it wasn't a great thing to happen to her.'

There was a sudden burst of loud laughter from the men at the bar and when Sallie looked across at them she saw Sandra Thompson had joined them.

'Judging by that outfit she's going in for another knobbly knees contest later,' Jo said, alluding to Sandra's extremely short white skirt.

Sallie noticed Geoffrey and Roger were also at the bar being served by Frank. She watched them give the noisy group a wide berth and retreat to a corner table with their cocktails.

'It was unfortunate though, because Alicia is already nervous about being in the library on her own. She's been a bit spooked by Clive's strange behaviour,' Emma said.

'Well, he's always been a bit weird.'

'Yes, I know, but he's definitely got worse., Something must have happened to him recently, to make him behave the way he does. He's always talking to himself and sometimes you hear him shouting out when he's in the garden at the back. It doesn't really help the morale of the volunteers.'

Sallie was about to say how little she was concerned about the morale of the volunteers but then decided it wasn't a good idea.

Jo started telling Emma about the progress they were making with the shed and asked if she would sound out Howard about conducting the opening ceremony.

Relaxing in the pub with a glass of wine after the exertions of the day, Sallie's eyes were just starting to close when there was another loud burst of laughter from the volunteers at the bar. She heard Rory mention the hairdressing salon on the main street of the village.

'Why is it called Head and Shoulders? I thought that was the name of a dandruff shampoo.'

Everyone laughed raucously. 'It seems a strange name for a hairdressing salon,' she heard him say.

Sallie cringed, remembering Geoffrey and Roger were sitting in a corner of the pub with their cocktails.

She glanced across at them and saw Geoffrey's plump cheeks had gone bright red.

'I mean, Head and Shoulders, what a disastrous choice of name,' she heard Rory say and the others all laughed again.

By now Geoffrey was getting to his feet still holding his cocktail. The paper umbrella was bobbing about in his drink because his hand was shaking.

'It's called 'Head and Shoulders… above the rest' you stupid man. You're meant to read the words underneath '…above the rest', you ignorant cretin.'

She saw George whisper something to Rory, who looked horrified.

'I'm so sorry, I didn't mean to criticise your salon. We just happened to be talking about the local shops. I'm really sorry, but I've never noticed the words underneath. It's my mistake. Please let me buy you both a drink as an apology.'

'We couldn't possibly accept a drink from you!' Geoffrey protested furiously, but Roger said to him in a low voice: 'He's apologised, hasn't he?'

'Oh, go on then, could we both have 'Sex on the beach' again?'

Sandra shrieked with laughter but none of the men joined in.

'Yes, of course,' Rory said quickly, ignoring her. 'Could we have two more cocktails for the gentlemen, please?' he asked Frank. When Frank had prepared the drinks Rory carried them over to Geoffrey and Roger and stood talking to them for a few minutes.

Meanwhile the group at the bar had begun discussing something else.

Sallie was still feeling drowsy and closed her eyes again until she heard the novel, Be Careful What You Wish For, mentioned. She opened her eyes again quickly.

'No, I'm sorry, Malcolm, I've never read it,' she heard George say. 'No, I'm sorry, but I've never read any of his books.'

'Oh, I have,' Sandra said smugly.

'Well, what's it about then? Tell us what the book's about.'

'I seem to recall it was about a couple who couldn't have children and so they adopted a child. But I think he turned out to be a serial killer or something. Anyway, that's why it's called Be Careful What You Wish For.'

Sallie felt something snap. She was hot, tired and profoundly irritated. Her cheeks flamed with anger and she stood up. 'What a load of absolute rubbish. And yet you lot think you can run a library! You've obviously never read any of Jeffrey Archer's books!

'If you're going to tell someone about a book, at least give them accurate information. Be Careful What You Wish For is part of a series. It's about big business and banking and takeovers, all that sort of thing. It's about the rivalry between powerful families. You have absolutely no idea what it's about so I don't know why you think you can work in a library,' she said directing her scorn towards Sandra, who went an even darker shade of pink than she was already.

But Sandra hit back immediately. 'I volunteered for the library to prevent it closing, which would have been a blow to the entire village.' She gave a superior smile.

‘Well how would you like it if I volunteered at the doctor’s surgery to do your job as a receptionist for nothing?’

‘You couldn’t do my job, you’re not medically qualified.’

Jo said: ‘Neither are you. All you’re qualified for is to be rude to the patients. I think anybody could do that.’

Sandra gasped. ‘How dare you speak to me like that!’ She lunged towards their table. Sallie stepped to one side quickly and Sandra stumbled into the table knocking Sallie’s wine on to the stone floor, where the glass shattered into several pieces.

‘Right, that’s it. I’ve had enough of this,’ Frank said angrily. ‘Get out Sallie!’

Emma stood up. ‘That is most unfair, Frank. Sallie was not the aggressor and it is her drink that has been spilt.’

‘Oh, all right, then. But you’d better calm down, all of you, or I’ll close up early tonight.’

Jo said: ‘Give us another glass, Frank, and we’ll go into the garden to finish our bottle of wine. Emma, you go with Sallie to find a table outside and I’ll bring our drinks out on a tray.’

Once out in the fresher air and peaceful surroundings of the pub garden, Sallie apologised to Emma. ‘I’m sorry I behaved like that. I feel foolish now for arguing with them. But when I heard Sandra telling them a complete load of rubbish about that book I felt the red mist descending. But in future I’ll try to ignore them.’

‘It’s not always easy though, is it? But I do feel if you rise to the bait and argue with them it’s just going to make matters worse. Try to be the bigger person.’

'That should be no problem for me. Sandra's just a bag of bones.'

Emma allowed herself a little smile.

Jo came out into the garden followed by George, who was carrying a tray with beer for himself and Emma and a fresh bottle of wine and two glasses.

'Just wanted to let you know there are no hard feelings. I say, there's no hard feelings between us. We're all friends here, aren't we?' he said, smiling at Sallie as he sat down with them.

Soon Geoffrey and Roger came out into the garden and joined them at their table.

'I feel a bit foolish, now,' Sallie confided to Geoffrey in a low voice.

'You feel foolish! Welcome to my world. I completely overreacted. It must be because of the heat.'

Sallie relaxed while chatting to Geoffrey and Roger and felt herself becoming calm again. Meanwhile George was talking happily with Emma and Jo at the other end of the table.

A few minutes later Louise came out into the garden accompanied by Rory, who was carrying a tray of wine and beer for her.

'I'm out on the razzle because my husband's away and I've found this handsome young man to carry the drinks for me.' Louise looked cool and elegant in a pale blue dress with matching sandals, her blonde hair perfectly styled and her face beautifully made up.

'Don's gone to Spain to try to encourage the builders to get on with things, so I'm free to go out and enjoy myself,' she explained to the others, before sitting down next to Jo.

Rory pulled up a chair from another table and positioned himself between Emma and Sallie.

He spoke to Sallie quietly. 'I can see the hairdressers are friends of yours so please don't think badly of me because of what I said about the name of the salon. I should have realised it might cause offence.'

'Oh, don't worry, we've all had a laugh about the name in the past,' she whispered back to him.

They stayed in the pub garden, laughing and talking and enjoying the warm summer evening until it was time for Jo and Sallie to walk home up the hill together.

Sallie reflected afterwards that it had been a pleasant evening with people she regarded as friends and yet quite a few of them were actually library volunteers.

It was only much later that she remembered Sandra Thompson and Malcolm Bray and wondered what had become of them, after they had been left alone together in the bar.

CHAPTER TEN

While Sallie and Jo were hard at work in the shed the next morning, Louise texted them and offered to treat them to lunch in the pub. They walked down the hill to join her in The Gentle Knight as soon as they were able to break off.

After they had all ordered at the bar, Louise led the way to a table in the corner where Frank wouldn't be able to hear their conversation.

'I just wanted to say I've been hearing about how some of the volunteers behaved in the pub last night and I want you to know that I'm ashamed to be one of them. I heard there were glasses flying and some terrible scenes before I arrived.'

'Actually, I made a complete fool of myself before we went into the garden,' Sallie said wearily.

'The volunteers were talking about the plot of Be Careful What You Wish For, by Jeffrey Archer, and it was clear no one knew what it was about,' Jo explained. 'Sallie stood up and told them they were talking a load of rubbish and weren't fit to run a library.'

'Yes, thank you, Jo, I'm embarrassed about it enough, if you don't mind. But it's reminded me about something I wanted to ask you, Louise. I was wondering if while you've been making your housebound deliveries you've taken Be

Careful What You Wish For to Mrs Jenkins, an old lady who lives near the church.'

'No, I'm sorry, I haven't. She's not one of my ladies. But none of them would want that kind of book, anyway. They like their misery memoirs and true crime books. They'll read sagas instead if there's nothing they haven't already read available on the shelves, but none of them would want a Jeffrey Archer.'

Louise took a sip of her wine. 'I just wanted to say that although technically I am one of the volunteers, I want to disassociate myself from them. I've been doing housebound deliveries for years and I've managed to get on well with all the staff that have worked at that library. The volunteers who've taken over the running of the library now seem to have got a bit power crazy. Not all of them, but definitely some of them. I just do my housebound deliveries and try not to get involved.'

'Oh, don't worry, we know you and Emma are nothing like the others.'

Jo said thoughtfully: 'Although, come to think of it, Rory seems a really nice bloke and George is lovely. The two old dears from Knit and Stitch have always been really pleasant to me as well. They're not all power crazy.'

*

Later that afternoon, Sallie caught the bus to Mickleton to go to the newspaper office with a press release she had written about the opening of the shed library. She found the office of the weekly newspaper down one of the alleyways of old shops that went off the main square.

The woman on the front counter offered to ring the newsroom and get a reporter to come down to speak to her. Sallie sat on a comfortable sofa in reception and flicked through the latest edition.

She suddenly became aware of a tall, thin man standing over her and got to her feet.

'Are you Sallie Parker?' he asked.

She nodded and he smiled at her: 'I'm Jerry Halford. It's okay, sit down again. What can I do for you?'

Sallie said: 'I was wondering whether you could send a photographer out tomorrow to cover the official opening of a new library we're going to open in Upper Mickle to raise money for charity.'

Jerry sat down next to her on the sofa and took the press release she was holding out to him. 'We all have to take pictures now. The days when you were either a reporter or a photographer are long gone, I'm afraid,' he said after glancing at it quickly.

'Saturday is actually a good day for us as we put the paper together on Monday mornings and go to press in the afternoon. It will still be news by Wednesday morning when the paper comes out. I'll try my best to cover it.'

Sallie noticed he had dark brown hair that flopped on to his forehead and brown eyes that looked alert and intelligent.

She said: 'Thank you. Any coverage we can get will be great.'

Jerry smiled at her and she thought he looked even more attractive.

If only I was ten years younger, she thought, sadly.

*

Afterwards Sallie did some shopping and then went to wait for the bus to take her back to the village. She noticed a thin, pale girl with limp fair hair and glasses was already at the bus stop.

I'm sure that's Alicia Potter, she thought. She had seen the girl around in the village even though she didn't remember her ever coming into the library.

'I'm glad to see you waiting for the bus as it means I haven't missed it,' she said to the girl cheerfully.

'No, I've been waiting ten minutes and nothing's come yet.'

'It's Alicia, isn't it?'

'Yes, that's right.'

'I'm Sallie.'

'You're one of the library ladies, aren't you?'

'I used to be but I've been made redundant. You're one of the volunteers, aren't you?'

'Yes,' Alicia said without enthusiasm.

'Are you enjoying it?'

'No, not really.'

'Well, what made you volunteer? I don't remember you coming into the library while I was working there.'

'My parents made me volunteer. I didn't get the grades for uni last year and they said they were fed up with me sitting around the house doing nothing. They were really pleased when they read somewhere that the library was looking for volunteers. They said it would be good experience if I ever wanted to get a job in a library.'

'But soon there won't be any jobs in libraries because they'll all be filled by volunteers. Don't they realise that?'

'Oh, I don't know,' Alicia said vaguely.

'But you must find it interesting talking to the customers and looking for books for them.'

'There's usually so many of us on duty you don't get chance to do much apart from putting the books back on the shelves.'

'But at least you can chat to the other volunteers during your shift.'

'Yes, but they're all old women, apart from the pervy blokes that is.'

'Who's pervy?' Sallie asked, trying to sound casual.

'All of them, apart from the young, good-looking one.'

Before Sallie could ask for more details Alicia continued: 'And Malcolm can be really nasty to us as well. When I was asked to make up a four for tennis the other day, I didn't think they would even miss me on my shift because there are always so many of us, but he gave me a right earful the next time I went on duty. There's also the nutty bloke. He gives me the creeps.'

'Who's that?' Sallie was completely fascinated by now.

'The odd job man. He mutters things to himself and if he gets upset about something he shouts things out. Don and George have to calm him down outside.'

'Oh, you mean Clive. He's always been a bit like that.'

'He thinks the library is haunted.'

'That's rubbish.'

'Don told me Clive's ancestors used to live there when it was a private house. You know, in the olden days.'

'It would have been in the last century,' Sallie pointed out.

'Yes, that's what I meant. I hate going in on my own early in the morning to switch everything on.'

'The library is not haunted. I worked there for years and nothing ever happened to me.'

'Well, who keeps leaving all these things in the library then? The other day I found a glass eye in the drawer at the counter. For a moment I thought it was a real eye. It was disgusting. Who could have put that there?'

'Someone who thinks it's funny, I suppose. To begin with people thought it was me and Jo.'

'No, they said it couldn't be you because you haven't got a key to the drawer even if you could get into the building.'

'Who said that?'

'Emma, the vicar's wife. But the two really old ladies said they didn't think it was you, as well.'

'That's something, I suppose. Thank goodness, here's the bus at last.'

*

Sallie's phone began ringing while she was putting her key in the lock of her front door. She dumped her bags of shopping on the floor as soon as she was inside, saw it was Jo's number and answered it.

'You'll never believe it,' Jo said excitedly. 'While I was finishing off the floor of the shed, George left a message on my phone asking me to meet him for a drink in the pub tonight.'

'Great, you can pump him for information. I'm sure he must have some ideas about who could be playing all these childish pranks at the library.'

'But I don't really want to go! He might get the wrong idea and think I'm actually interested in him.'

'Yes, but on the other hand it will give you the chance to talk to him and ask him why he became a volunteer. It seems an odd thing for a self-employed shopkeeper to do. You can always put him right later if you think he's got the wrong idea.'

'Oh, all right. I suppose I could ring him back and agree to meet him. But would you come to be my back-up plan?'

'What do you mean?'

'Well, if you come into the pub and have a drink, I could text you if I need rescuing.'

'Okay. What time does he want you to meet him?'

'He said seven pm in the side bar.'

'All right, I'll come in at about half past seven and look surprised to see you in there.'

Sallie put her shopping away and was preparing a meal for herself when she heard a knock at her front door. As she opened it she was assailed by a familiar smell. ‘Mr Jackson! What a surprise. What are you doing here?’

The middle aged man with receding hair and an unshaven chin standing in front of her was wearing a shapeless dark brown raincoat over his shirt and trousers, despite the heat. He muttered something under his breath.

‘I’m sorry, I didn’t hear what you said.’

‘I said could you help me to attach my CV to an email?’

‘But I don’t work at the library now.’

‘I know, but I thought you might have a computer here.’ He tried to look past her into the room behind her.

Sallie knew her laptop would be visible on the desk in the corner of the room. ‘I’m sorry, but I’m really busy. Can’t you ask one of the volunteers at the library to help you?’

Mr Jackson muttered something again.

‘Sorry, what did you say?’

‘I said they’re all old women.’

‘Not all of them. One of the volunteers is a young man and I’ve been told he’s really good with computers.’

Mr Jackson just sighed.

‘I’m sorry, I really have to go. I’ve got something on the stove,’ Sallie said and quickly shut the door. She put the chain across before returning to the kitchen.

*

When Jo walked into the side bar of the pub later, Rory and Malcolm were standing at the bar with George.

'It's the lovely Jo. I say, it's the lovely Jo,' George said beaming at her delightedly. 'Now what would you like to drink?'

'A glass of Sauvignon Blanc please, George.'

'With pleasure,' he said bowing to her. 'Frank, a glass of your finest Sauvignon Blanc for the lady, please.'

'We're discussing the latest drama at the library,' Rory informed her, grinning.

'Yes, we think our practical joker's been at it again. One of the ladies found a whole cracker biscuit inside a book,' George said.

Jo laughed. 'Oh, I know who does that. She uses a cracker biscuit as a bookmark and sometimes forgets to take it out before returning the book. It's got nothing to do with these practical jokes, I'm sure.'

Malcolm banged his pint glass down on the bar and glared at her. 'Well, I think that's outrageous. When I find out who it is I'll give her a piece of my mind.'

'That's a body part we haven't seen in the library yet,' Rory whispered to her. Jo laughed again and Malcolm gave her a sharp glance.

'She's one of our most loyal customers. Try not to upset her because she's... Oh never mind, it's up to you, I suppose,' Jo said resignedly.

George handed Jo her glass of wine and suggested they found a table. They left Rory and Malcolm at the bar.

'Are you enjoying working at the library, George?' Jo tried to make it sound like she was just making polite conversation.

'Well, it's a bit tedious at times but I'm glad of the company if I'm honest.' He looked at her meaningfully. 'I get lonely in that big old house of mine all on my own every evening.'

'Yes, but you've got your shop. You have plenty of people working there. You must get on well with them and find them good company.'

'Oh, I do. I say, I do get on very well with all of them. But at the end of the day, Jo, they are my employees. It doesn't do to get too friendly with them in case one of them does something I have to take them to task for.'

'No, I suppose it doesn't.' Jo resisted the impulse to look at her watch. How long have I got to sit here making small talk? she thought, with a sinking feeling.

'What particular aspect of library work do you find the most enjoyable, George?'

'Well, I don't really know, it's all much of a muchness really, as far as I can see. I suppose I enjoy chatting to the customers and it's always very pleasant when your friend Emma's there. She's a lovely lady. I say, she's a lovely lady!'

'Yes she is. I'm very fond of her. But I must say I was surprised when I first heard you'd volunteered to help out at the library.'

'Oh, why was that?'

'I suppose, because you have your own business to run. I would have thought the library would have taken up too much of your time.'

'Oh, it does, I suppose. Yes it does. But I've got reliable staff and I trust them to run the shop properly while I'm at the library.'

'Well, I think it's very good of you to give so much time to the library. Did you volunteer because you didn't want it to close?'

'I suppose that was part of it. But I always say it doesn't do any harm to get involved with these community things. It's better to be on the inside than the outside in my opinion.'

'Sorry, but I'm not sure I know what you mean.'

'Well, you never know what opportunities might come your way.'

'Opportunities? What sort of opportunities?'

George tapped the side of his nose and looked at her significantly. 'Well, it's occurred to me if the library being run by volunteers doesn't do as well as when you and your blonde friend were in charge, the local authority might decide to close it and then the building might become available.' He winked at her.

'Available for what?'

'To be put to an alternative use. It would make a very good butcher's shop, in my opinion. It would help all the old folk up here to be able to buy their meat from a handy shop in the village rather than having to get the car out to go to a supermarket.'

'Oh, I see,' Jo said thoughtfully.

*

When Sallie walked into the bar on cue at 7.30, the first person she saw was Jo, who was sitting at a table talking to George. She was surprised to see her friend was wearing a short, black leather skirt that showed a lot of thigh and a thin, lacy short sleeved white blouse with the top two buttons open.

She said she didn't want him to get the wrong idea, Sallie thought, so why on earth had she turned up dressed like that?

She went up to the bar and ordered herself a glass of wine. When she turned away and started looking for a spare table she saw Jo waving to her and gesturing that she should join them.

'Hello, I didn't see you two sitting there,' Sallie lied

'George invited me for a drink,' Jo explained.

'Oh, that's nice.'

'He was just telling me about all the different cuts of meat he can get for his regular customers.'

'Yes, I can get things in specially that the supermarkets don't stock if one of my customers wants to cook something unusual.'

'How interesting! What's the most unusual meat you've ever been asked for?' Sallie asked eagerly.

'Let me get you a chair, you might as well join us,' he said happily. Jo quickly pulled up a chair for Sallie from the next table.

As Sallie was sitting down, Rory came up to the table. 'Malcolm's gone home to work on the library accounts and left me on my own. Can I sit with you lot, please?'

'Yes, of course,' Jo and Sallie said simultaneously.

'I'll get us all some drinks,' Rory said gratefully.

CHAPTER ELEVEN

Jo and Sallie had both enjoyed unpacking all their books that had been hidden away in boxes for years. They had arranged them neatly on the odd assortment of bookshelves they had found to line the walls of the shed.

Sallie had donated a small table and chair to put by the door for the library assistant on duty and Jo had found a rectangular table with four chairs to stand in the middle of the shed, for customers who might want to sit down while they looked at the books.

'It's starting to look like a real library,' Jo said on Saturday morning, looking round proudly. 'I've made some numbered cards, using a programme I found on my computer, to give to customers. I'm quite pleased with them. I've also found one of Dave's unused accounts ledgers, so we can start a hand-written record of who has borrowed what.'

'It will be like going back to the good old days of libraries before computers when customers got personal service. I've even found some date stamps in a drawer at home that I once bought in a cheap stationery shop, so we'll be able to stamp the books,' Sallie said.

'I think we should charge people 50p for a library card so they don't keep losing them.'

'What happens if people ask if they can request a book?'

'We could have a quick look on the internet and if the book isn't too expensive we could order it to add to our stock. Otherwise, we will say we can't get it at the moment.'

'I've still got some children's books that used to belong to my kids. I've been saving them for potential grandchildren, but I can bring some to put in rummage boxes for customers who bring children with them,' Sallie said.

'Yes, I've got some children's books as well, somewhere in the house. We could also spend a bit of money on new children's books to give us a good start. Unlike the village library, we can buy books in bargain book shops and supermarkets and don't have to pay over the odds to some approved supplier.'

'If we get donations from our customers and end up with duplicate books we can list our copy for sale online to make money for buying new stock.'

'Oh, there are loads of things we can do. I'm sure things will keep occurring to us as we go along.'

'And we must stress to everyone that the main purpose of the library is to raise money for charity.'

'But what will we do if it annoys Malcolm Bray and the volunteers?' Jo asked.

'Nothing. We're doing it to raise money for charity and if it takes customers away from them, that's just a bonus.'

'Actually George might be pleased if it took customers away from them.'

'Why's that?'

‘Well, last night when I asked why a busy man like him had volunteered to work for nothing at the library, he gave me the usual line about wanting to do his bit, but then admitted that if the library failed and the building was put up for sale he would be interested in buying it to convert into a butcher’s shop.’

‘The crafty so and so!’

‘He thinks it would benefit the village to have a butcher’s shop up here so that everyone doesn’t have to drive to a supermarket to buy their meat.’

‘But that gives George a very good motive for playing the practical jokes at the library. He might have thought if he managed to scare the volunteers off it would have to close. There’s no way it could stay open if all they’ve got is Malcolm Bray working there.’

‘I’m sorry, I can’t see it being George.’

‘Oh, are you starting to fall for him?’ Sallie asked mischievously.

‘No, of course not! I just think the person playing the jokes on the volunteers must be a bit childish and it wouldn’t be George’s style.’

Sallie looked at the shelves with satisfaction. ‘I think we’ve done as much as we can for now. We’ve actually got books left over and yet the shelves are nearly full. We’ve got to leave a bit of room, so people can get the books out easily to look at them. ‘

They went inside the house to the kitchen where Jo started to prepare the free refreshments promised on the flyers that

Sallie had designed and distributed round the village. Sallie rang the local radio station to make sure they had seen her press release and tried to encourage them to give the library opening some coverage.

Jo put two bottles of Prosecco into her fridge so they could drink a toast after the formal opening ceremony.

They had asked Emma to bring Howard round at 12 noon to perform the ceremony and had persuaded Geoffrey from the salon to pop round to be on the photograph as the first official customer.

Sallie was pleased that Jerry, the reporter from the weekly newspaper, was the first to arrive, well before the opening. He asked for more details about why they had decided to open their own library in a garden shed.

Sallie tried her hardest not to sound too bitter about being made redundant, but Jerry's gentle, but persistent, questioning brought out the whole story about being accused of playing practical jokes on the volunteers and being shunned by people in the village.

Sallie thought Jerry even more handsome than when she had seen him at his office. She noticed again that he was tall and lean, with a tanned face and dark, unruly hair that flopped on to his forehead. He was wearing a tweed jacket, over a grey and white striped shirt and dark grey trousers. She liked the way his face seemed to crease attractively every time he smiled at her.

She couldn't help being aware of this, but then reminded herself he was probably a good ten years younger than her.

While they were waiting for Emma and Howard to arrive, Jerry said: 'You know, your press release was very well written and had all the relevant information in it. We're not used to receiving anything quite so professional, especially when it's about village news or charity events.'

'Well, many years ago, I was a newspaper reporter. I started on a country weekly, just like you.'

'This isn't my first job in journalism, you know. I started on a big regional daily and after a few years I was head-hunted by a national newspaper. I did 15 years in London. The only reason I'm working here now is that I was made redundant. I was glad to get this job in the end, even if it did mean leaving London,' he explained.

'Oh, I'm sorry, but you don't look old enough to have done all those different jobs.'

'Thanks, that's very flattering, or at least I think it is. Let me get a picture of you and your colleague in the doorway of the shed before anyone else arrives.'

Sallie hated being photographed and was sure she must have looked a complete mess by then, but she tried to smile nicely as she posed obligingly in the doorway of the shed with Jo.

Geoffrey arrived, looking hot and bothered. 'Hope I'm not too late, but I've had to leave a woman in the middle of a roots touch-up. I'm having to trust Rog not to leave the colour on too long.'

Howard and Emma walked into the garden hand in hand. Sallie thought Emma looked very beautiful and much happier than the day before, although she was still pale. When Jo popped the cork on the first bottle of Prosecco ready for the toast, Sallie noticed Emma quietly refused a glass.

Howard said a few kind words about Sallie and Jo and then declared the shed library officially open for business.

Jerry took a picture of Geoffrey being signed up for a library card by Jo sitting at the table in the doorway. Alicia Potter was the next person to arrive and ask to join, much to Sallie's surprise and then Tom and Wasim, from the neighbourhood policing team, came to sign up.

By the time they closed at five pm they had several more joiners and had issued a few books.

Walking home happily afterwards, Sallie heard her mobile ping in her handbag. She took it out and saw Jerry had texted her to invite her out for dinner at the Italian restaurant in the village the following evening. She smiled to herself and put the phone back in her bag, deciding she would text him back and accept his invitation when she got home.

She was nearly at her cottage when she found her way barred by an old gentleman she vaguely recognised.

'I thought you should know, I've had a completely wasted afternoon.'

'Why? What's happened to you?' She had no idea what he was talking about.

'I've had my time wasted in that so-called library you used to run. I think you should know the people working there now have absolutely no idea. I asked for extra time on the computer because I was filling in a difficult form, but it took them so long to do it I got logged out and lost everything I'd done previously. It was a complete shambles!' He glared at her and stomped off.

Before the shed library opening Sallie would have found being accosted by him annoying, but she was in such a good mood that afternoon she just smiled to herself as she walked home.

She had arranged to go for a celebratory drink with Jo in the pub before going back to Jo's house for dinner that evening, so after replying to Jerry's text she quickly changed and put on fresh make-up before Jo called for her to walk down to the village.

As soon as they entered the side bar, Frank spotted them and pointed at a table in the corner.

'Can you help me out with this, ladies? She's a friend of yours, isn't she?'

They looked across at the table and saw Deirdre slumped back in her seat, asleep with her mouth open and a full glass of white wine in front of her.

They went across and Jo tried gently to wake her. When she opened her eyes she saw Sallie sitting across the table from her and gasped with shock. Then she picked up her glass and took a gulp. 'I've walked out,' she announced loudly to the whole bar. 'I've told them all to get stuffed.'

'Has something happened to upset you?' Jo asked gently.

'Yes, working with that bunch of amateurs. That's what's upset me,'' she said loudly.

'How much has she had?' Sallie asked Frank.

'That's her fourth, but she hasn't had much of it as you can see,' the landlord answered from behind the bar.

'Yes, but she isn't used to drinking a lot and she doesn't live in the village so she's probably come up here in her car,' Sallie said.

Jo sat down in the seat next to Deirdre. 'What was it that upset you?' she asked sympathetically.

'That obnoxious little Hitler told me off in front of a customer. He had the nerve to question my methods. Me! A trained library assistant with more than 40 years experience! He seemed to want to undermine me in front of the others. I was angry and upset and then I suddenly remembered I wasn't being paid to do the job and I didn't have to put up with his unpleasantness, so I walked out. I came in here to calm down.'

Deirdre took another gulp of her wine and then burst into tears. 'But I love working in libraries. I was so happy to get the chance to do it again. I shall really miss it,' she sobbed. She leant back again and her eyes started to close.

Sallie and Jo looked at each other. 'She can't drive home in this condition. I'll get my car and we'll take her home to sleep it off,' Jo said.

'Good idea. I bet she's left her car in the library car park. It will be safe enough there until she's fit to drive again,' Sallie said.

A few minutes later, Sallie saw Jo's car pulling up outside the pub, half on the narrow pavement and half in the road. 'Come on Deirdre, let's get you home,' she said firmly to the woman sitting opposite her, who was by now fast asleep with her head on the table.

She tried to rouse Deirdre and asked her to stand up. Deirdre tried but then fell forward clutching at the table for support.

Frank came out from behind the bar to help Sallie and with each of them holding one of Deirdre's arms, they managed to walk her out of the bar and down the flagged stone passageway into the sunshine. Together they got her into the back of Jo's car and Frank did up her seatbelt.

Jo knew roughly where Deirdre lived on a country lane near the village of Woodford, just off the main road to Mickleton. Sallie, who was sitting in the back with Deirdre, eventually roused her enough to get the house number.

They managed to get her out of the car and after Sallie had found Deirdre's keys in her handbag, they manoeuvred her into the house and lowered her on to the settee in the living room.

She slumped against the cushions and immediately fell asleep again.

'So what do we do now?' Sallie asked.

'I don't know. We can't stay with her all night, I've got to get back to Mutz and put the finishing touches to our dinner.'

'Yes, and I'll have to feed Des.'

'We could take her keys, lock the front door and then put them through the letter box so she finds them in the morning on the doormat. I'll write her a note to tell her what we've done,' Jo said, rummaging in her bag for a pen and a notebook.

While Jo wrote the note, Sallie looked at the bookcases on either side of the fireplace, curious to see what sort of books Deirdre read.

Among the framed photographs on top of the bookcases, Sallie noticed a picture of a young man in a silver plated frame.

'Who do you think this is? Could it be her son?'

'I'm fairly certain she doesn't have any children. She's been divorced for absolutely ages and I don't think she and her husband ever started a family.'

'And yet, the young chap in this picture looks strangely familiar.'

Jo tore the page she had written on from her notebook and put it on to the coffee table in front of Deirdre.

She held her hand out for the photograph. 'Let me have a look. Well of course it looks familiar, it's Don Bainbridge.'

'Are you sure?'

'Yes, it's Louise's husband, Don. He was a lot younger when this was taken, but it's definitely him.'

'Let me look at it again.'

Jo passed the framed photograph back to her.

'Yes. I can see now that it's Don. But why would Deirdre have a framed photo of him on display in her sitting room?'

'I don't know. We'll have to ask her when we next see her.'

Sallie put the picture back in the exact place she had found it. 'He was very handsome when he was younger,' she said. 'I assume Deirdre lives here on her own.'

'Yes, she's been divorced all the time I've known her.'

'No man in her life since?'

'Not that I'm aware of.'

'We'll have to come and see how she is in a couple of days and see if we can get the conversation round to the photograph.'

*

Later, as Sallie crossed the road to go to Jo's house she saw Joyce coming downhill with Sebastian and quickened her pace so she wouldn't have to speak to her. She climbed up the steps to Jo's front door, noticing a white plastic carrier bag on the top step. When she reached it, she peered inside without touching anything and saw there was a parcel wrapped in white paper with blood oozing from it. 'Oh my God!' she gasped and picked up the bag and threw it down the steps and on to the pavement. There was a howl and then a frenzy of barking. Joyce appeared at the foot of the steps looking furious.

'What the hell do you think you're doing, throwing things at my dog? Poor Sebastian, what's he ever done to you?'

'I'm sorry, but I saw blood coming out of the bag. I thought someone was playing a nasty trick on Jo. I didn't see Sebastian was there.'

Sebastian had pulled away from Joyce and was attacking the bag, dragging out what looked like a piece of raw offal and eating it greedily.

'Stop it! It could be poisonous!' Joyce shrieked.

She snatched Sebastian up and held him in her arms. 'Oh, he's got blood all over his face,' she yelled. 'How dare you do this to him. I'm going to report you to the police.' She ran away, holding the dog, towards her house in the centre of the village.

CHAPTER TWELVE

An hour later Tom and Wasim sat facing Sallie across Jo's kitchen table.

'So, you're saying you thought someone had left a bag of human remains on Jo's front steps as some kind of a joke,' Tom said disbelievingly.

'Well, no, I'm not saying that exactly. I don't know what I thought at the time. I just saw blood coming out of the parcel inside the bag and thought someone was trying to get at Jo for some reason. I threw it down on to the pavement to get it off her front steps.'

'And it just happened to hit Joyce's dog as he was going past,' Tom said, trying to suppress a smile.

'Obviously I didn't see the dog or I wouldn't have thrown it. It was just because all those things left at the library were body parts, even though they turned out not to be real. I thought it was going to be something like that.'

Wasim said: 'It looked like raw liver to me, or at least, the bit of it I could see that the dog hadn't managed to eat.'

'Do you know why someone would leave a bag of liver on your doorstep?' Tom asked Jo. 'It seems a strange thing to do, particularly in this heat.'

'Oh my God, I've just realised. I bet it was calves' liver,' Jo said suddenly.

Sallie and the police officers all looked at her for an explanation.

'The doorbell rang just a few minutes before Sallie arrived. I looked through the spy hole and saw it was George, so I didn't answer it.'

'Who's George?' Tom asked immediately.

'George Bloodworthy, the butcher. I didn't answer the door because I would have had to invite him in and I still had stuff to do in the kitchen before Sallie arrived. Besides, I didn't want him to think he could just drop in any time to see me. I didn't want him to get ideas.'

'What makes you think George Bloodworthy, the butcher, would leave you a bag of calves' liver?'

'Because the other night, when I went out for a drink with him, he asked me whether there was any meat I couldn't easily get at the supermarket that I enjoyed cooking. Just for something to say I told him I sometimes cook *fegato alla veneziana*, Venetian liver, but to do it properly you have to use calves' liver.'

Sallie saw that Tom had gone red in the face. 'You went on a date with George Bloodworthy, the butcher!'

Jo blushed as well. 'Well, it wasn't exactly a date. He asked me to go for a drink with him in The Gentle Knight, that was all.'

'But why did you accept?'

'I wanted to find out more about him.'

'Really? I wouldn't have had him down as your type.'

'No, of course he isn't, but he's a nice chap and good company and, anyway, it's not as though I have a queue of men waiting to ask me out,' she retorted. 'Also, I wanted to talk to him to try to find out who, or what, is behind these practical jokes at the library. I thought he might know something. It's unfortunate the meat was wasted. I don't know what George will think when he hears about it.'

'Well, it wasn't really wasted. It gave Sebastian a good meal,' Wasim said and they all laughed.

Sallie noticed Tom was looking relieved. Suddenly a wave of tiredness hit her and she knew she wouldn't be able to eat anything.

'Jo, if you don't mind, I won't stay for dinner. I'm not really hungry. I suddenly feel exhausted. It's been a long day. I think I'll just go home and have a cool shower and get an early night.'

'Are you sure?'

'Yes, I'm tired out, but if I get a good night's sleep, I'm sure I'll be fine in the morning.'

'Well, I'll see you in the morning at the shed library to work on the cataloguing, if you think you're up to it,' Jo said, getting up to show her out.

Wasim got up too. 'I'll walk you home, Sallie. I'm off duty now.'

Sallie was surprised, but she just wanted to get home and relax in her own cottage so she made light of it.

'I suppose you're worried I might try to throw meat at another dog.'

As they crossed the road towards Sallie's cottage, Wasim said. 'You know he's sweet on her, don't you?'

'Who do you mean, Tom?'

'Yes, that's why I wanted to leave them on their own. We both came up here in our own cars so he won't be stranded. Let's see if he plucks up the courage to ask her out.'

After she had said goodbye to the young police officer on her doorstep and was safely inside the cottage, Sallie locked the front door behind her and then collapsed on to the settee next to the sleeping Des.

'Well, well, well,' she murmured as she stroked the top of the cat's head. Des gave a contented little growl in reply.

*

They spent most of Sunday working in the shed and cataloguing all the stock on the shelves. When Sallie told Jo about her date that evening her friend was really excited and pleased. 'I'm sure you'll get on really well. You have so much in common. This could be the start of something really good.'

'It's probably not going to be the start of anything. But I have to admit, I'm a bit nervous. It's ages since I went out for dinner with a man.'

'Well, why don't we go for a drink at The Gentle Knight first and then all you have to do is leave the pub at the right time and walk across to the restaurant. Would that help?'

'Yes, thank you. I think it would,' Sallie said gratefully.

*

Later that evening, Sallie was sitting opposite Jo in the pub. 'Do I look all right?' she asked Jo for about the fifth time.

'You look great. Your skirt and top are very nice and your hair and make-up look lovely,' Jo said encouragingly.

At that moment the door to the bar opened and Louise and Don walked in hand in hand.

Don looked fit and tanned in a smart suit and Louise looked glamorous in a glittery, silver-coloured, figure-hugging dress. Her blonde hair was beautifully styled and her make-up made her look radiant.

'We're going out to dinner to celebrate Don being back,' she told the girls. 'But we thought we'd drop in for an aperitif in the pub first.'

Sallie's heart sank. She felt plain and ordinary in comparison with Louise.

'Where are you going for dinner?' Jo asked.

'The Feathers at Broadfield,' Louise said, naming an Egon Ronay listed pub restaurant in a nearby village. 'We thought we'd push the boat out.'

At least they're not booked in at the Trat, Sallie thought with relief.

While Don was ordering their drinks at the bar, Louise came and sat with them.

'Don's got everything sorted out with the villa,' she announced proudly. 'We'll be able to go out and stay there in the autumn as planned and I'll be able to supervise the people who are going to be doing all the finishing touches.'

'That's great,' Jo said politely.

Don came over to the table with their drinks and sat down with them. 'Here's looking at you, kid!' he said, raising his pint glass to Louise.

'Oh, don't be so silly!' She smiled at him indulgently.

There was an awkward hiatus and Sallie racked her brains for something to say. She was about to ask them what time their table was booked for when Jo broke the silence. 'Oh look, Emma's come in,' she said.

Sallie turned round and saw the vicar's wife standing at the bar talking to Frank. Then there was the sound of a car hooting its horn outside.

'That will be our taxi,' Louise said. 'It's early, but it doesn't really matter. Come on, Don. Leave the rest of your drink. You can have another pint at the restaurant.'

Emma spoke to Louise and Don briefly as they were leaving the pub and then came over to sit at the table with Jo and Sallie. She was carrying an empty glass and a bottle of sparkling mineral water.

'Didn't you want your favourite beer this evening?' Sallie asked.

'No. I'm so thirsty this is all I want at the moment. Louise was looking very smart, wasn't she? She's so pleased to have Don back.'

'They're going to The Feathers at Broadfield to celebrate,' Jo explained.

'It's all right for some. She's got it all. Money, looks and a devoted husband,' Sallie said sourly.

Emma looked at her severely. 'You should never envy anybody, Sallie. You don't know what other people's lives are really like and in any case it never does you any good to envy people.'

'Oh, I don't really envy her. I wouldn't want to be married to Don. He seems a bit of a prat.'

'Sallie! Please try to be more charitable. I don't know, everywhere I've been today people seem to be grumbling about each other. There seems to be a strange atmosphere in the village at the moment. People are less tolerant than they used to be. It's not very pleasant and it doesn't encourage people to feel responsible for their community or to help each other.'

'I think it's just the heat getting to everyone,' Jo said with a sigh.

*

Jerry hadn't arrived when Sallie walked into Trattoria Marco, which only made her more nervous. How humiliating it would be if he didn't turn up.

Marco showed her to a table and brought her a glass of Prosecco. She sat quietly sipping it and made no attempt to look at the menu. She knew it so well she could probably recite it out loud, she thought. After a few minutes she decided to go to the ladies' and check her appearance.

By the time she returned, Jerry was sitting at the table reading the menu. She felt pleased and nervous at the same time.

He got up politely as she approached the table. 'Sallie, I'm so sorry I'm late. I got held up by a phone call just as I was about to leave the office.'

'Oh, don't worry. It's no problem,' she said, trying to sound casual.

'Have you decided what you would like?'

Sallie said she would have the seafood risotto because it was always very good and Jerry said he would have the same because Sallie had recommended it.

'Shall we have some assorted bruschette to start with?' he asked.

'Okay.'

'What's the house wine like?

'The white is Trebbiano. It's always very good.'

'Right. Let's have some of that and some mineral water,' he said, closing his menu.

While they waited for their wine and bruschette he told her about an argument that had broken out at a local council meeting he had covered a few days ago. Sallie found him very entertaining company and laughed at his imitations of the local councillors.

After Marco had brought their wine, he took a sip from his glass and then put it down. 'Anyway, there was something I wanted to ask you. How would you like to write some village news for the newspaper? I haven't got time to go out and get all the stories myself and the editor has suggested I find people in the villages to send stories in. Would you be interested in covering Upper Mickle?'

'Yes, I would definitely be interested,' Sallie said straight away.

'It's not very well paid, I'm afraid. It would just be our usual lineage rate.'

'Anything is better than nothing, considering I've just been made redundant and I'm working for no pay in my friend's shed.'

Jerry laughed. 'Great. Just keep your eyes and ears open for things going on in your village. The deadline is Monday afternoon each week, so anything at all you could get to me by tomorrow would be greatly appreciated, but if not, look out for stories for the following Monday.'

'Do I just email it to you?'

'Yes, I'll give you one of my cards, which has my email address on it.'

After that, Sallie relaxed and they had an enjoyable meal together. Jerry was great fun and now she knew he had no romantic interest in her, she could just be herself. She was conscious of Marco watching them at times but was quite pleased in a funny sort of way. It might be a good thing for him to think I've met someone, she thought.

Jerry, who had only drunk one glass of the carafe of Trebbiano, drove her up the hill to her cottage afterwards.

'We must do this again some time,' he said to her as she was getting out of the car.

Sallie was relieved to be back safely in the cottage with Des. 'I'm sure he's not interested in me, but it's a good opportunity to get my foot in the door of a newspaper office again,' she told the cat.

After she had locked up and gone upstairs to bed, she lay on top of the quilt for a while reading. The room was still too warm even though it was after midnight by then, so she got up to open another window. Joyce and Sebastian were just going past her house in the direction of the village. She knew Joyce lived right in the centre of the village near the church. What was she doing up here after midnight? Sallie asked herself, especially considering all the unpleasantness of the day before. If she had taken the dog out so he could relieve himself, surely she would have stayed near her home? Sallie climbed into bed still thinking about Joyce but quickly fell asleep.

CHAPTER THIRTEEN

Sandra Thompson wearily put her key into the lock of the back door of the library. Her head was throbbing and she felt queasy. She could have done with staying in bed. It was her day off from the surgery, after all. She wished she had never volunteered to work at the library. But now her name was on the timetable she had to come in to do her shifts even if she had been out late the night before. She didn't want to give Malcolm Bray any opportunities to tell her off. Malcolm had already criticised her for the way she spoke to the customers. How dare he criticise her, a doctor's receptionist! As if she didn't know how to deal with customers, with all her experience, she thought resentfully.

As she put her handbag down on a desk in the back office, she was irritated by a bleeping noise. Of course, the alarm! She had to fob it to stop it making that awful sound.

Really there wasn't much difference between the library and the surgery, she thought, as she put the key back in her handbag. You were providing people with a free service and so you shouldn't be expected to lick their boots as well.

The problem was she had joined the library volunteers in the hope of meeting someone. But all the men were either taken, or by now had shown they weren't interested. So she was fed up with it now, but it was difficult to see how she could get out of volunteering. She certainly didn't want to give people a reason to slag her off behind her back.

Her thumping headache reminded her she should have stopped drinking much earlier the night before and gone home. But she knew her problem was that she had no willpower. She had wanted to try every bar in Mickleton to see if she had any luck.

As she opened the door to go into the library she suddenly stopped as a thought occurred to her. She had met someone last night, she was sure. So, what had happened to him?

She stood in the doorway between the office and the library, still thinking about it. She remembered dancing with a man in a bar somewhere. She remembered him having his hands all over her at one point, so he must have been interested. She had thought her luck was going to change.

She vaguely remembered going home in a taxi. So what had happened to him? To be so drunk as to be unable to remember what happened the night before was frightening.

Then she realised she had to fetch the keys so she could switch on everything in the library. She shook her head impatiently and immediately felt a throbbing pain over her right eye.

She felt anxious. She had really overdone it the night before and yet she was supposed to set an example to people who came into the surgery. If one of the doctors ever saw her out drinking she might lose her job.

After collecting the keys from the safe, she went into the library and switched on all the lights. It worried her that she couldn't remember what had happened with the man she'd been dancing with. She suddenly had a flashback and remembered he'd been quite tall and had dark, curly hair. She had fancied him at the time. So why had she ended up going home alone?

She switched on all the computers and took the books out of the drop box in the porch. She carried the pile of books back to the desk and discharged them all to the date of the day before. Her mouth was dry and she felt as though she might be sick any minute so she went to the kitchen to get a glass of water. She opened the door and walked over to the sink but then turned sharply to look at the opposite wall, having caught a glimpse of something out of the corner of her eye. A man was sitting on one of the chairs watching her.

'What are you doing here?' she asked, startled.

The man didn't move. Sandra felt there was something wrong about the way he looked at her. She forced herself to go up to the chair. The man remained very still, just staring straight ahead. She made herself reach out and touch his hand. It was cold.

Screaming, she turned away and ran through the office to the back door of the library. She grabbed the handle with a shaky hand and let herself out.

She ran down the side of the library through the front garden to the pavement outside, where she was discovered after a few minutes by a woman walking past, who found her leaning against the wall, crying.

*

Jo heard the police sirens as she was about to attach Mutz's lead to his collar in her hall. She decided to walk him down to the village so she could find out what was going on rather than uphill and out into the countryside. As soon as she set off she saw two police cars and an ambulance parked outside the library further down the road. There was a police officer she didn't recognise attaching police tape to the gate. She crossed the road and went up to him and asked what was going on.

The officer said: 'There's been an incident at the library and it's closed at the moment. I'm afraid you won't be able to go in.'

'What kind of incident?'

'I can't give you any more information.'

'Is it another practical joke?'

'No madam, I can assure you, it's definitely not a joke.'

Jo took Mutz for the rest of his walk then got him home as soon as she could so she could get the shed library open for business. She left him happily eating doggy treats in the kitchen while she unlocked the side gate and the door of the shed.

Later that morning, after a customer had been in and then gone again, she discussed the latest drama at the village library with Sallie as they sat having tea and biscuits.

'Can't you ask Tom what's been going on when you see him?' Sallie suggested.

'Yes, I suppose I could, if I happen to run into him.'

'Oh come on, Jo. I know he's keen on you. I'm sure it won't be very long before you see him again.' Jo flushed with embarrassment and quickly changed the subject.

'Anyway, how was your date with the journalist last night?'

'It was great, but it wasn't really a date. He had asked me out for dinner so he could talk to me about writing village news for his newspaper.'

'What a pity!'

'No, I'm not sorry about it at all. Actually, I'm quite pleased. If I make a success of it, I'll be able to earn some extra cash. In any case, he's a lot younger than me. It was ridiculous to even think he might be interested in me.'

Jo laughed. 'Oh, Sallie you are funny. There's no law that states a man has to be exactly the same age as you to go out with you. First you say that Marco is too old and now you're saying Jerry is too young.'

'What about you and Tom?' Sallie asked to change the subject.

'Well, actually we've discovered we're almost exactly the same age. We were born in the same year and our birthdays are within a few days of each other.'

'Well there you are then!' Sallie said triumphantly. Another customer came in at that moment so the discussion stopped.

Later that morning, when there were no customers, they were both browsing on the internet on Jo's laptop, when Emma came into the shed.

'Hi Emma, how are you feeling today?' Jo asked her.

'I'm fine, thank you, just a bit tired. But I've got some news for you both.'

'Not more silly pranks at the library?' Sallie asked.

'No, it's much more serious than that. It's something very sad. I'm sorry to have to tell you, but Don Bainbridge is dead.'

'No! I can't believe it. He looked so well last night,' Jo said.

'Oh, poor Louise. She was so thrilled to have him home again,' Sallie said.

'She's completely devastated.'

'What happened to him?'

'Everybody seems to think it was his heart because that's why he was planning to retire early. Apparently, he's been having problems with it for some time.'

'Was Louise with him when he died?'

'No, she was in bed at home, according to what I've been told. He was discovered in the library first thing this morning. He was just sitting in a chair in the kitchen.'

'What was he doing there?'

'No one seems to know. His body was discovered by Sandra when she went to open up.'

'Did she attempt to revive him?' Sallie asked.

'No, apparently when she realised he was dead she ran out of the library screaming. The police have told Howard nothing could have been done for him anyway. They could tell he'd been dead for some time.'

'Poor Don. I didn't particularly like him but I wouldn't have wished him any harm.'

'That's what everyone's been saying to me this morning,' Emma said wearily.

'In any case, it will be devastating for Louise. She seemed on top of the world last night,' Jo said, giving Sallie a reproachful look.

'I know. She looked positively radiant when she came into the pub. They were going by taxi to Broadfield for a meal. He must have gone round to the library early this morning. Perhaps Louise will be able to tell us more when we see her,' Sallie said.

'Howard's been round, of course, but she isn't ready to talk about it yet, he said. He has told her he will call on her again tomorrow. He will have to try to get her to discuss the arrangements. She's got Tracy with her today, so she's not completely on her own.'

'She needs someone with her at a time like this,' Sallie said.

'Perhaps the three of us should go round tomorrow, just for a few minutes before Howard arrives,' Emma suggested.

'We could take her some flowers,' Jo said.

'Malcolm Bray told me he's going to stay closed for the rest of the day. The body has now been taken away and he's planning to open as usual tomorrow.'

'Oh, jolly good!'

'Sallie! This isn't the time to be resenting the volunteers. In fact, it's a good time to drop your vendetta once and for all.'

Sallie managed to stop herself from reminding Emma that neither she nor Jo had done anything wrong. Instead, she suggested they met at Louise's house the next day. Emma said she would text them a time when she knew when Howard was planning to visit.

After she had gone Sallie and Jo looked at each other. 'I bet you're thinking we should close as well,' Sallie said.

'Yes, I don't think we'll have many customers today and I haven't really got the heart for it after news like that. Poor Louise! Whatever we might have thought of Don, he was her husband and she loved him. Now she will be completely on her own. Both her parents are dead and they never had any children.'

She switched off the laptop and they tidied up and locked the shed for the day.

*

Back at home Sallie sat on the settee thinking about it all, while cuddling Des. She felt oddly detached about Don's death. She hardly knew him, but she felt sorry for Louise. In the meantime she was at a loose end.

Then she saw Jerry's business card on the coffee table in front of her. She picked it up and went over to her desk and switched on her laptop. He had asked her to send him any news from the village and a dead man found first thing in the morning in the village library was definitely news. She would write it up tastefully so no one could take offence.

*

Later that evening, after Sallie had finished dinner, she decided to text her daughter to tell her about the opening of the shed library. She hunted everywhere in the cottage for her mobile phone and went through her handbag twice. She thought back and remembered receiving a text earlier in the day and realised she must have left it in the shed library.

She remembered Jo had said she had plans for that evening but decided to walk across to Jo's house anyway, let herself in through the side gate and into the shed using the keys Jo had given her, to retrieve her phone. She hated being without her phone in case one of her kids needed to get in touch.

Sallie crossed the road, walked down the side of Jo's house and unlocked the gate. Even though it was getting dark she wasn't worried because she knew her way round to the shed. When she reached the back of Jo's house she was surprised to see the kitchen light was on. As she stood watching, she saw Jo appear in full view at the sink. Sallie saw her turn the tap on and could see she was rinsing out a glass. Suddenly a large pair of tanned arms wrapped themselves round her slim body and pulled her away from the sink. She watched fascinated as Jo leant back happily against the bare chest of a man and saw him lower his head and begin to kiss her neck. Jo turned round and the man leant down and kissed her passionately while Sallie stood frozen to the spot. When the man lifted his head again she saw it was Tom, the police sergeant.

She felt her face turning red with embarrassment and was terrified of being caught spying on them. She turned and ran back down the side of the house, locking the gate behind her and abandoning the idea of trying to retrieve her phone from the shed.

She ran across the road and down the path to her front door and unlocked it. She felt calmer when she was inside her own home again and told herself she was being silly. It wasn't completely unexpected, after all. Wasim had told her that Tom had fallen for Jo. She had wondered whether they had started seeing each other, but hadn't expected things to develop quite so quickly. She poured herself a glass of wine and sat down on the settee with Des and told the sleepy, contented cat all about what she had just seen.

*

Jo was walking along in a happy daze in the sunshine the following morning with Mutz on his lead. She was deep in thought as she got close to the village library and did not notice the agitated old lady on the pavement outside until she found her blocking her path.

'Oh, Jo, what a relief it is to see you! I'm on my own in there. Malcolm had a dental appointment and none of the other volunteers have turned up yet. I can't seem to get the computers on the counter to come on. Customers could come in at any time. Malcolm will be furious with me, especially considering we had to close yesterday. Please, can you help me?'

Jo looked at the little old lady who had grey, curly hair and a pretty face. She was wearing powder and lipstick and a blue, flowery patterned dress. She was darting about on the pavement nervously. She suddenly realised it was Verity, one of the knit and stitch ladies, who had come to the library every Thursday afternoon when she was working there.

Jo was in such a good mood that all her animosity towards the volunteers seemed a bit pointless on this lovely, sunny day.

'I'll just tie Mutz up securely outside and come and give you a hand,' she said.

It felt strange being back in the library again, particularly with Verity for company. No one had changed the passwords so she was quickly able to get the two staff computers on the counter to come on. She showed Verity how to discharge the books from the drop-box to the previous day's date. When the first customer came in and approached the counter, she left Verity to deal with her and walked quickly over to the shelves.

She found a hardback copy of Be Careful What You Wish for and took it over to the counter to check its status on the other computer. 'Bingo!' she said to herself quietly. No one had bothered to discharge it after the finger had been discovered in it and someone had shelved it. Every day it stayed on the shelf Mrs Jenkins would be building up a big fine, unless she was exempt from paying fines because she was housebound.

She saw from the computer the book had first been checked out to Mrs Jenkins on a date after she and Sallie had finished working at the library.

She assumed that one of the volunteers must have done it and someone must have delivered it to Mrs Jenkins, unless a family member had taken it out on her behalf. After the old lady had finished with the book, someone must have put the finger inside before returning it through the drop-box. That same person could have left the cow's bone in the chair just before the library closed on the Saturday. However, the glass eye must have been left in the drawer at the counter by one of the volunteers. Library users would have had no access to it.

Jo wanted to jump up and down with excitement but restrained herself. She couldn't wait to tell Sallie about her discovery when they opened the shed library for business again later that day.

*

That afternoon, after two customers had come and gone, there was a lull, so Jo went indoors to make a pot of tea.

Sitting on garden chairs outside the shed, they discussed her discovery at the village library that morning.

'As Mrs Jenkins isn't one of Louise's old ladies, perhaps someone in her family takes books out for her and brings them back,' Sallie suggested.

'But why would they put a fake finger inside one of her books?'

'Perhaps she's got a mischievous grandson, or something like that? It could have nothing to do with the library being run by volunteers.'

'Louise said Mrs Jenkins wasn't one of her ladies, but it's possible some of the other volunteers have been asked by old people in the village to visit them with library books. Mrs Jenkins could have a connection with one of them and for some weird reason of their own, they could have used her library book to play a trick on the others,' Jo suggested.

Sallie sighed. 'It's very annoying that Malcolm Bray didn't bother to look into it properly and immediately assumed it was us. It's caused us so many problems.'

'True, but it all seems a bit trivial now when you consider poor Louise has just lost her husband.'

*

Tracy Dolby opened Louise's front door to them later that afternoon after Emma had rung the doorbell.

Sallie looked at her in surprise. She was wearing her usual leggings and button through shirt with her long dark hair taken back in a ponytail, but her face was without its usual thick make up and she looked really pretty.

As if reading Sallie's mind, Tracy said: 'I decided to stop the last two nights with her. I couldn't leave her on her own. She was distraught.'

'What about your children?' Sallie asked, as usual coming out with exactly what she was thinking.

'Oh, they're all right, you don't need to worry about them. I texted my mate, who lives next door to me, and she's had them staying over at her house. She's been texting me pictures of them and they look like they're having a great time.'

Tracy showed them into the front reception room where Louise was sitting on the settee, wrapped up in a fleecy dressing gown even though it was a warm day. She was almost unrecognisable as she was wearing no make-up. Her eyes were red rimmed from crying and her dyed blonde hair looked lank and wispy.

'Louise, we just wanted you to know that we are all very sorry about Don,' Jo said, handing her the bunch of flowers she was carrying. 'It must have been a terrible shock for you to get such awful news.'

Louise said: 'I keep expecting him to suddenly turn up. If only it was all a mistake.'

'Was he tired after his flight back from Spain, do you think?' Sallie asked sympathetically.

'He didn't seem to be. He wanted to go out and celebrate. It was his idea.'

'Why do you think he went to the library?'

'I've no idea. We went to bed soon after we got back from the restaurant. When I woke up the next morning he wasn't there, but I thought he'd got up early to go down to his study to do some work, as he often did. Before I had time to get ready myself the police were knocking on the door. They said he'd been found dead inside the library. I still can't quite believe it. I just keep thinking he'll turn up again and it will be one of his jokes.'

'Howard is going to be here in a few minutes and he'll help you make all the arrangements,' Emma said to her gently.

'Thank you, that's very kind of him.' She gave a little sob.

'It was good of Tracy to stay with you, wasn't it?' Jo said.

'Yes, it was very kind. There was nothing she could do for me really but she said she didn't want me to be on my own.'

'You're still suffering from shock at the moment but it will get easier for you I promise,' Emma said, trying to sound reassuring.

'I feel so alone now. It was always just me and Don. We could never have any children. So now I'm completely alone. It's a terrible feeling.'

They heard the doorbell ring and a few seconds later Tracy ushered Howard into the room.

Emma got up to go and Jo and Sallie followed her lead.

'Text one of us if there is anything we can do for you,' Jo said.

'Thank you.'

'Or, let us know if you want some company and we'll come round,' Sallie added.

'You're all being so kind. '

'We'll leave you to it then, Howard,' Emma said to her husband and led the way out of the room.

Later, over a cup of coffee in Dolly's Pantry, they discussed their visit.

'I must say it never occurred to me she didn't have any family and that she would have no one to look after her,' Sallie said.

'Thank goodness Tracy stepped in,' Jo said.

'Yes, it shows she's not a bad girl at heart really,' Sallie agreed.

'Louise is going to find it hard getting used to being on her own. She's been married to Don for a long time,' Emma said.

'What a shame Don is never going to get the benefit of the villa in Spain after all the work he's put into it,' Jo said.

'It just shows you never know what's round the next corner,' Sallie said gloomily.

They were silent for a moment, until Sallie said: 'Anything that happened in the library while Don was in there yesterday morning should have been recorded on the CCTV. The police could send someone to view the CCTV and then they will have more idea about what happened to him.'

'I'll mention it to Tom when I see him and he might be able to find out whether they've done that,' Jo said.

It sounds as though they've definitely become an item, Sallie thought, suddenly feeling even more lonely than usual.

Back in her cottage, Sallie went straight to her laptop, hoping to find an email from Jerry about her first village news item.

'Absolutely nothing. I thought he would have at least acknowledged receiving it,' she complained to the cat.

CHAPTER FOURTEEN

The next morning, Tracy Dolby and Clive Fenton were having a cigarette together in the garden in front of the library as Sallie walked down to the village to do some shopping.

'Good morning,' she called out cheerfully. 'What are you two up to on this lovely, sunny day?'

Tracy looked round: 'Oh, it's you, is it? I wouldn't have thought you'd dare show your face round here after your latest stunt.' She turned away again with a toss of her ponytail.

Sallie was taken aback. Only the day before Tracy had been pleasant towards her and Jo when they visited Louise.

'Being as I live only a few yards up the road, I can't avoid showing my face round here. Anyway, what am I supposed to have done now, left a pig's trotter in front of one of the computers, or something?'

Tracy walked across to her menacingly. She was wearing her usual thick make-up again. 'You want to watch out. You've upset a lot of people with that article in the paper.'

'What article?' Sallie asked exasperatedly.

'Don't pretend you don't know. You and your friend had your pictures splashed all over it.'

With a sinking feeling Sallie realised it was Wednesday, the day the weekly paper came out, and that Tracy must have seen Jerry's piece about the opening of the shed library.

'Oh, that was just a bit of publicity for our new venture. We've decided to run our own library from Jo's garden shed to raise money for charity.'

'Well, don't expect people here to be pleased about it. You should hear what they've been saying about you and your friend. You left this place in a right state and caused them to have no end of problems.'

'That's not true. We left things tidy and organised. The reason the volunteers have been having problems is that they haven't been properly trained.'

Clive had been watching their exchange from a few feet away while finishing his cigarette. He threw the end to the ground and trampled on it. Then he picked up his rake, let out a howl like an animal and stomped off down the side of the shed.

'Now look what you've done. You've got him upset again,' Tracy said, but as she turned away to follow him Sallie saw she was trying to suppress a smile.

*

Sallie went straight to Dolly's Pantry, knowing the local newspaper would be available there for customers to read.

She saw Dolly behind the counter, wearing a pale pink ball gown, which had a top covered with sequins. She had a matching pale pink fascinator in her bleached blonde hair.

'Hi, Dolly. Can I have a cappuccino and a look at the weekly paper, please?'

'Sure. Take a seat and I'll bring it over.' Sallie went over to a vacant table, feeling anxious because Dolly seemed less friendly than the last time she had been into the café.

A few minutes later Dolly brought her the newspaper with her cup of coffee and Sallie turned the pages quickly until she found the piece near the back in the village news section. There were some lovely pictures of Howard and Emma and Jo and Geoffrey and a reasonably good picture of her and Jo in the doorway of the shed. Then she saw the headline. 'LIBRARY WARS', it screamed. Sallie groaned.

Jerry had quoted her as saying she and Jo hadn't wanted to be made redundant from the library and missed working there. That's why they'd started to run their own library from Jo's shed to raise money for good causes.

The next blow came further down the page. 'No one has shown us any compassion and some of the volunteers seem pleased to have taken our jobs,' Ms Parker said.

How am I going to live this down? she asked herself miserably.

But there was worse to come with the quote: 'There seems to be a practical joker playing tricks on the volunteers and we are being unjustly blamed for anything that goes wrong.'

Yes, she probably had said that to Jerry. But she didn't think he would use it. He must have realised she was speaking off the record. She had thought he would do a straight news story about the shed library opening and would have realised some of the things she had said to him were just for background and not be to be published.

When Dolly came past her table Sallie handed her the newspaper back and thanked her. Dolly folded it neatly and put it under her thin arm while she took Sallie's empty coffee cup with her other hand.

'I'm afraid your article hasn't gone down very well with some of my regulars,' Dolly said. 'I would have thought you and Jo would have been better off keeping a low profile for the time being, especially after what has happened to Louise's husband.'

Sallie felt near to tears. 'But we've done nothing wrong. We've got every right to open our own library to raise money for charity. Surely it's up to us how we publicise it? Anyway, Don was away in Spain when we opened it. I couldn't have predicted what was going to happen to him.'

'Please yourself,' Dolly said brusquely and skipped her way back to the counter.

*

On an impulse, Sallie went straight from Dolly's Pantry to the bus stop. It was all the fault of that damned journalist in Mickleton and she was going to tell him exactly what trouble he'd caused for her. When she got off the bus in the square she marched down the alleyway of quaint shops with their Georgian-style shop windows and burst into the reception area of the newspaper offices. The girl on duty took her name and telephoned the newsroom to find out if Jerry was there.

'Take a seat. He says he'll come down in a few minutes,' she said.

Sallie sat on one of the settees. There was a copy of the newspaper on the low table in front of her and she picked it up to read the story again. It was the headline and the quotes attributed to her that were the problem.

After a few minutes Jerry appeared in front of her. He smiled and looked pleased to see her.

'I've come to ask you to explain this,' Sallie said, gesturing towards the newspaper, which she had left open at the page with the library feature on it.

Jerry's smile disappeared.

'What do you mean by explain?'

'Well, you've made matters worse for me and Jo now. We're going to be even more unpopular in the village.' Sallie could feel herself flushing and felt tearful again.

Jerry said: 'Come on, we can't talk here. Let's go for a drink in the square and you can tell me what's upset you about the piece.'

*

In one of the pubs, Sallie took a large gulp of the wine Jerry had bought her. 'The headline is inflammatory and there are quotes from me that I would have preferred you not to use. I thought you would just report the story in a straightforward, factual manner. You could have just said when we were going to be open and what services we are offering.'

Jerry looked serious. 'Well firstly, can I say that you know only too well that reporters don't write headlines. It was just one of the sub-editors trying to make it sound more exciting. Also, you never told me you didn't want me to quote you exactly. You said all those things and I quoted you verbatim. You must also know the newspaper might not have been willing to give it a good show, or use the piece at all, if there hadn't been a bit of a story behind it.'

Sallie was taken aback and felt annoyed with herself for not thinking it through, as someone who knew how newspapers work.

'Yes, of course I understand all that. It's just that Jo and I are even worse off than we were before. We were just starting to think we had managed to convince people we had nothing to do with the practical jokes.'

'But you must have realised that starting your own library in a garden shed is bound to put the volunteers' backs up, especially if they lose customers to you,' Jerry said.

'I suppose so. But then, surely we have some rights? We should be allowed to continue doing something we both enjoy doing. Who has the right to say we can't open our own library?'

'No one has. You've both got to keep your heads up and carry on doing what you want to do, which is running your own library. This will soon become last week's news and be forgotten by everyone.' His face crumpled with the grin that Sallie was beginning to find more and more appealing and she felt foolish. She wished she had not gone to his office and complained to him without thinking properly about what she was going to say first.

He looked at his watch. ‘Look, I’m sorry but I’ve got to get back to work. I’ve got a meeting with the editor in ten minutes. But I’ll text you later.’

‘Oh, okay.’

‘Sorry to have to leave you but I really have to get back.’ He smiled at her again and then left the pub.

*

‘So, as usual, I went steaming in there without thinking things through and made myself look stupid.’

‘Oh, I shouldn’t worry too much. I bet he gets complaints like that all the time. It must be part of the job,’ Jo said, trying to be comforting, as they sat in the shed that afternoon waiting for customers.

‘Yes, but I ought to know better, having been a journalist myself. The reporter never writes the headline and they always have to find some angle to justify using things like charity events and opening ceremonies when space is limited.’

‘Well, I’m sure it will all blow over in the village and you’ll be able to make it up with him when you see him again.’

Sallie looked at her in disbelief. ‘You surely don’t believe he’ll contact me again? I’m quite sure I won’t ever hear from him again. He definitely won’t text me.’

Jo just smiled at her. But, all the same, when Jo got up to do something in the library, Sallie found her phone and checked it eagerly before putting it safely back in her handbag.

*

Later in the afternoon, Alicia Potter wandered into the shed and looked round at the shelves vaguely.

'Can I help you?' Sallie enquired.

'Yes, I'd like to volunteer here,' the girl replied.

'We don't take volunteers here, and anyway, I thought you were already volunteering at the village library.'

'I am, but I hate it there. I'd like to work with you two instead.'

'But we don't take volunteers!'

'Oh okay, but just so you know I would much sooner work here than at the village library.'

Sallie opened her mouth to tell Alicia exactly how unrealistic her idea was but Jo stepped in swiftly.

'Sallie, can I have a word outside please?'

Jo led the way out of the shed into the bright sunshine.

'Why don't we just humour her and let her come and watch the way we operate here. It will be a good opportunity to find out from her what Malcolm Bray and his band of volunteers are up to. Also, she might be able to shed some light on the practical jokes if we talk to her in a more relaxed way.'

'I suppose so, but it still goes against the grain to let her volunteer here.'

'Well, we'll just have to think of something else to call it. Let's say she's on work experience.'

They went back into the shed and Jo said: 'The thing is Alicia, we haven't got nearly as much work for you to do here as they'll have for you at the village library, so you ought to carry on doing your shifts there. But you're welcome to come and spend time with us when you're not doing a shift and watch the way we do things. Is that okay?'

'Yes, that would be great. I just think because you were trained to do the job properly you'll be able to teach me more than that bunch of geriatrics.'

'But you will carry on doing your shifts at the village library, won't you?'

'Yes, I suppose so,' Alicia said without any enthusiasm.

'Good girl! I'll go and make us all a nice cup of tea.'

Left on her own with Alicia in the shed, Sallie said: 'Let's sit down at the table to have our tea. Tell me, why don't you enjoy working at the village library?'

'I suppose it's because the men are all horrible and they're all really nasty to the odd job man, who's extremely weird. He thinks the library is haunted and he gets very worked up. They're even nasty to the customers sometimes. There was this poor old man who had taken some books out about improving his memory, but he brought them back really late because he'd forgotten about them and Malcolm Bray had a right go at him.'

'Oh, I see.'

'Don was a bit strange, too. I feel sorry for him now he's dead, of course, but he once put a whoopee cushion on the seat at the counter and when one of the old ladies sat down, it made this sound like a fart. She was really embarrassed and upset, but he thought it was ever so funny. The old ladies are okay, I suppose, but they talk about really boring things like sewing and knitting all the time. One of them is crocheting new cushions for all the chairs at the library and they spend ages talking about what sort of wool she should be using. It's all so boring.'

'Fair enough,' Sallie said. 'It was nothing like that when we worked there.'

*

Later that afternoon when Sallie was sitting on the sofa with Des reading a novel, she received a text from Jerry asking if he could call on her that evening to discuss the story about the dead body found in the library with her. Her heart pounded, but then she told herself not to be so silly.

Even so, she tidied up everywhere and went upstairs to freshen up and change into something smarter.

When Jerry arrived Sallie offered him tea, coffee or a glass of wine and he asked for a glass of wine.

She poured them both a glass and they sat on the sofa together, drinking their wine and discussing Don's death.

Eventually Jerry said: 'We've managed to get a paragraph in this week's edition and we've got till next Monday to file the full story so we can afford to wait and see if you find out anything else.'

He smiled at her. 'Anyway, you've made a very good start with coming up with stories for me.'

When Jerry had finished his wine he looked at his watch and said: 'Do you fancy going out for dinner? Only I haven't eaten anything for hours.'

'Why don't I cook something for you here? I could make you an omelette and some salad. That's what I was planning to have.'

'Well, that's very kind of you. Thank you, that would be great.'

While Sallie was in the kitchen preparing the food, she saw through the open door that Des had jumped on to the sofa with him. The cat stood looking at him quizzically and then Jerry reached out and stroked her soft, furry head. Des climbed on to his lap and sat there purring happily.

After they had finished their meal they moved back to the sofa and had another glass of wine. Des immediately came and sat on Jerry's knee again. When Sallie reached out to stroke the cat, Jerry took her hand in his and raised it to his mouth and kissed it, looking directly into her eyes. The next moment his arms were round her and they were kissing.

*

Sallie was on duty at the village library while a knit and stitch session was going on. Suddenly, Verity came up to the counter crying and told her she needed first aid but before Sallie could do anything the lights went out and she was alone in the dark...

Sallie turned over in bed feeling hot and thirsty and reached her hand out to her bedside table for her water. She realised she must have been dreaming, but it was rather disturbing to dream something like that. She sat up in bed. There was no glass of water on her bedside table. She looked at her watch, which she always left near the water, suddenly worried she was going to be late for work. Then she remembered she didn't work at the village library now.

The events of the previous evening with Jerry came back to her and she turned slowly to look at the pillow next to her. There was no one there. She felt relieved and got out of bed and put on her towelling robe and slippers and went downstairs.

Des was in the kitchen at her food bowl, eating happily. 'So he fed you, then, before he left,' she said to the cat. Des did not even raise her head to look at her.

Sallie went into the sitting room. There was a page torn out of his notebook on the table.

Jerry had written: 'Sorry, have had to leave because I had an early appointment. Thank you for a lovely evening. Will text you. Love, Jerry xxx'

She felt embarrassed and ashamed and wondered why she had slept with him. She hardly knew him. She hadn't given it any thought. She started to cry.

After she had stopped, she began to wish she could confide in someone. She knew there was only one person she could talk to about this.

She went to her desk, picked up her phone and scrolled down till she found the number. It rang for a while and then she heard a familiar voice. 'Hi Sallie, sorry for the delay. I'm out taking Mutz for his walk and didn't hear my phone ring straight away. Stop doing that Mutz!'

'It's okay, Jo, but I need to talk to you. Can you come over to me?'

'Of course I can. Is everything all right?'

'No it isn't. But I need to talk to you in person.'

'Okay, I'll be with you in about ten minutes.'

*

When Sallie opened the door to Jo, Mutz started barking at her angrily.

'I'd better let Des out into the garden,' Sallie said hastily.

While she was shooing the reluctant cat out through the back door she could hear Jo yelling at Mutz and telling him to sit on the mat by the front door.

When she came back into the room, Mutz uttered a low growl when he saw her but stayed where he was.

She told Jo what had happened in a few words without going into any detail.

'What do you think of me now?' Sallie asked.

'Honestly, Sallie, all I want to say is: 'Good for you!' Why shouldn't you have some fun?'

'But I feel I've made a fool of myself. I've only just met him. And anyway, he's far too young for me.'

Jo laughed. 'Oh dear, not that again. Look he must have fancied you and you must have fancied him. What is there to stop you? You're single now. It's time you met someone else, just like your ex did. I don't regret getting together with Tom. I couldn't stay moping about Despicable Dave forever. I'm starting to have some fun for the first time in ages.'

'I know, but Tom's different. You've known him for a while and it's obvious he has feelings for you. I don't know

Jerry at all and God knows what he must think about me now. That's probably the last I'll ever see of him.'

'But he said he'll text you and anyway, if you send him news items for the paper, he's bound to get in touch with you again at some stage.'

'But I still wish I hadn't slept with him. I feel terrible about it now.'

'Look, the best thing for you now is to get dressed up in something smart and go out. It's a lovely sunny day out there. It's nearly lunchtime, why don't we go to the pub? I'll take Mutz home and sort him out while you get yourself ready and I'll call back here for you in about half an hour.'

*

She knew Jo was right of course. Getting dressed up and putting on perfume and make-up helped Sallie feel better. There were only a few other people in the pub and Jo and Sallie were able to sit in a corner and talk privately. They had a nice, relaxed lunch together, although Sallie sneaked a look at her mobile every time Jo went to the ladies' or up to the bar. But there was never any text from Jerry.

An afternoon at the shed library dealing with customers and keeping everywhere looking tidy was a welcome distraction.

After Sallie returned home she made herself a meal and sat in a garden chair reading a novel before deciding to go for a walk as it became cooler.

She headed up the hill out of the village, towards the open countryside, thinking about everything that had happened.

All the gardens were riots of colour with valerian flowers tumbling over the stone walls and roses and wisteria perfuming the evening air. She met Joyce, who was coming back down the hill with Sebastian. After all that had gone on recently, her feud with Joyce seemed petty and ridiculous.

'How are you?' she asked Joyce, bending down to pat Sebastian.

'I'm okay, I suppose. I just wish it would cool down.'

'What a terrible thing to have happened to Don.'

'Yes, it's shocking. The poor man.'

'What do you think he was doing in the library at that time of day?'

'I've no idea. Doesn't Louise know why he was there?'

'No. She says she woke up in the morning and he wasn't in bed with her. She doesn't know why he left the house and went to the library.'

'Oh well, I dare say it will all get sorted out in the end, but it's been an awful shock. Did you know I was once engaged to him, years ago?'

'No, I didn't. How extraordinary. What happened?'

'My father thought he wasn't good enough for me and wouldn't give us his consent to get married. He said he would cut me off without a penny so I had to break it off. Don didn't speak to me for years afterwards. Eventually he met Louise and married her. She was younger than me and it was said at the time that her father had put a lot of money into his business. I don't know whether she ever knew we were once engaged. When we've been at the library together, recently, he has shown no sign of remembering me at all. Oh well, it was all a long time ago,' Joyce said sadly. She tugged on Sebastian's lead and continued walking down the hill.

*

Back home again, Sallie slumped on the settee with Des and thought about Joyce's revelation. 'I can't believe those two were once an item,' she said out loud.

The cat opened one eye and looked at her.

'Don't look at me like that. All this is your fault. You started it by going and sitting on his knee,' she told the cat sternly.

CHAPTER FIFTEEN

Jo had a tray with coffee and biscuits ready when Sallie arrived at the shed library the next morning.

'Sit down and have a cup of coffee. I've something to tell you.'

They sat on either side of Jo's hall table in the middle of the shed and Jo poured the coffee.

'Tom came round last night…' she began.

'It sounds like he's getting serious!'

'I don't know about that, but listen to me for a minute. This is important. He told me there is to be a post-mortem examination carried out on Don Bainbridge.'

'But why? Everyone knew he had a bad heart.'

'I know, but according to Tom he hadn't seen his doctor recently because he'd been feeling well and his condition was under control because he was on medication. They are treating the death as unexplained and therefore, they have to have a post-mortem. He looked in the best of health when we saw him in the pub, didn't he? Also, what was he doing in the library so early in the morning? They obviously think it's not straightforward and that there are grounds for a post-mortem.'

'Poor Louise. It's bad enough he's dead. How will she feel if the death is treated as anything but natural causes?'

'I know. It will be horrible for her. Promise you won't tell anyone else about it. Tom probably shouldn't have told me so I don't want it to get round the village.'

Sallie spent the morning looking at the stock and compiling a list of the titles by popular authors they didn't have, while Jo worked outside, painting designs on to terracotta plant pots. They were to contain plants she had grown from cuttings that she was planning to sell to raise money for the shed library.

As soon as she could, while Jo was inside her house seeing to Mutz, Sallie quickly texted Jerry to suggest he asked his police contacts whether they knew the cause of Don Bainbridge's death, or could confirm that there was to be a post-mortem.

The girls locked the shed at lunchtime and walked down to the village to have lunch in the pub.

On the way down, Jo cautioned Sallie again about not revealing to anyone else that there was going to be a post-mortem on Don Bainbridge.

While they were at the bar ordering their drinks and food, George invited them to sit with him and Rory.

As soon as they had sat down at the table, George said dramatically: 'Have you heard the news? Apparently they're going to have to do a post mortem on Don Bainbridge!'

'Really? But why, I thought he had a bad heart?' Jo said.

'He did have a heart problem, but he's on tablets for it and anyway his doctor told the police he was doing really well and that he'd said Don didn't need to see him for another six months.'

'I suppose a heart problem can suddenly get worse,' Sallie suggested tentatively.

'Yes, I suppose so.' Rory said. 'But it was also odd he died in the library. What was he doing there so early in the morning?'

'You're assuming he did actually die there and not somewhere else,' Sallie said enthusiastically. 'Have you ever read the crime novel, The Body in the Library by Agatha Christie? In the story, the person has been murdered somewhere else and taken to the library of a big country house to be discovered there.'

Realising she had used the word 'murdered', she felt embarrassed, remembering what Jo had said to her on the way down to the pub. She took a sip of her wine and forced herself to stay quiet for a few minutes.

Rory broke the silence. 'I've never read any of Agatha Christie's books but I've seen some of the stories on television. There's usually a large number of suspects all with different motives, isn't there?'

'Yes, and it's usually the least likely person who's done it, someone you didn't realise even had a grudge against the victim,' Jo said.

'Right, well I can take my name off the list. I can take it off straight away. I always got on well with young Donald when I was doing a shift at the library,' George said.

'Well, so did I. Although I didn't actually see him very often or speak to him much,' Rory said to George.

'Is there anyone he didn't get on with?' Jo asked casually, picking up her glass and studying her wine.

'I don't think Clive the odd job man liked him,' Rory said. 'I think he was a bit scared of him. Don was always going outside, interfering with whatever Clive was doing and telling him off.'

'Mind you, Clive often became upset and Don was really the only one he would listen to when he got worked up,' George added.

'Why did Clive get so upset? He was always all right when we worked there.'

'Well the library is in a house that used to be owned by Clive's ancestors,' George explained. 'Apparently there was a lady who disappeared. I think it was Clive's great-grandma. Everyone thought she'd left her husband and children. But after Clive's great-grandfather died the house was sold. The next owners found a trunk buried in the ground next to the shed, full of her body parts. He'd murdered her and chopped her up, it seems. After that, the story went round that the house was haunted by her.'

'Yes, I remember an old lady telling me all about it a few years ago,' Jo said. 'She said the new owners only stayed for a short time and then put the house up for sale again. There weren't any takers to begin with, but then the local authority bought it to convert it into a library for the village.'

'But Clive has worked there for ages. Why is what happened suddenly bothering him now?' Sallie asked.

'I've no idea. Perhaps you two lovely ladies were a reassuring presence when you were there and now there are so many volunteers it has upset him.'

'Also, Malcolm seems to really annoy him,' Rory added. 'He keeps asking him to do little jobs.'

'What sort of little jobs?' Jo asked.

'Repairs to the building and that sort of thing.'

'He should be phoning the helpdesk at Mickleton Library and asking them to book the repairs with the council's property department. He shouldn't be expecting Clive to do things like that.'

'He's told us not to ring the helpdesk.'

'Why?' they both asked at the same time.

'He's had quite a few arguments with the women who answer the phone on the helpdesk,' Rory explained. 'There was one occasion when he rang them and said none of the computers were working. He became angry when the woman who answered just said she'd log a job request with the IT department. He expected them to sort it out straight away. Then when I tried to put on the lights I realised there was no power at all, it wasn't just the computers that weren't working. It turned out Verity had been so conscientious the night before when she went round checking everything was off that she switched off the electricity supply.

'Of course, once he realised what the problem was he felt foolish because he'd been so aggressive with the woman on the helpdesk. Since then, he's told us not to ring them, but to try to work things out for ourselves.'

'What a prat! Clive isn't supposed to do anything apart from gardening and very basic jobs,' Sallie said.

'No wonder he gets shirty then,' George said. 'I remember on one occasion when he wasn't there, Malcolm went down to his shed to see if he could find a screwdriver and when Clive caught him in there rummaging around he practically went berserk.'

'I remember that, it took Don and Tracy ages to calm him down afterwards,' Rory said.

'Did Tracy get on all right with Don?' Sallie asked.

'Yes, I think so, because she cleans for him and his wife as well,' George said.

'Yes, I've noticed them having little chats when they've both been in the library,' Rory added.

'It's always a good idea to keep on the right side of your cleaning lady, take it from me,' George said.

'Was Malcolm on good terms with Don?'

'Yes, on the whole,' George said.

'They had the odd argument about the running of the library, though. Don was a housebound volunteer and did his own thing so Malcolm couldn't really boss him about. But there were occasions when Malcolm was laying the law down about something and if Don happened to be there at the time he would stick his oar in and then they would clash,' Rory added.

'I don't think some of the ladies were all that keen on Don either. They didn't really get his sense of humour. He made Sandra laugh. But the older ones would give him a wide berth. He seemed to enjoy embarrassing them,' George said.

*

The next morning Sallie started thinking about Jerry as soon as she woke up. He had said she had until Monday to try to find out more about the body discovered in the library. After that, the newspaper would go to press and any more information, or any different stories she uncovered, would have to go in the following week's edition.

Whatever happened between her and Jerry, she was determined not to lose the chance to write village news for the newspaper. She wanted to earn extra money to boost her pension and perhaps make it possible for her to carry on working at the shed library with Jo.

Also, she knew she would do it well and it might lead to other journalistic opportunities. She felt it was vital she didn't lose her big chance because of becoming involved with Jerry and was determined to put all romantic ideas about him to one side and focus on what was important.

Today she needed to ask around and try to find out as much as she could about Don's death so she could send something to the newspaper before the next deadline.

After showering and dressing in a smart outfit, she carefully did her hair and make-up and walked over to Jo's house, determined to speak to everyone she encountered about Don's death so she could find out something new.

After they had opened up, Sallie asked Jo if Tom had been able to tell her any more about Don's death.

'Tom said he has been told unofficially there will be a murder inquiry because there are suspicious circumstances, but he doesn't know yet what they are.'

'Have they got any ideas from the forensic evidence they gathered?'

'Tom said forensics weren't able to get much when they went over the crime scene. He said that apart from Sandra, other people had trampled all over it before they got there.'

'That's very odd behaviour,' Sallie said thoughtfully. 'You'd think these days, with so many crime dramas on TV, everyone would know they had to leave things exactly as they are when a body is discovered.'

'I suppose so.'

'Don't they have any idea how he died, yet?'

'Not officially, and Tom said even if they did have some idea, they won't put it out to the media until after they get the results from the post-mortem.'

'Have they been able to find anything out from the CCTV?'

'No, nothing. The evening before he was found dead, the only thing of interest apparently was Tracy Dolby cleaning. Or not cleaning, in fact. Apparently she moved all the chairs in the middle of the library and vacuumed for about thirty seconds and then got a call on her mobile. She sat down in one of the chairs, had a five-minute conversation with someone and then after she ended the call, she put all the chairs back in their original positions and took the vacuum cleaner to put it away in the back, out of the range of the cameras.'

Sallie laughed. 'That sounds like our Tracy. But just suppose for a moment that Don was murdered by someone, why did that person leave his body in the library?'

'Well, perhaps he was killed there and the killer left him exactly where he was, sitting in that chair.'

'Possibly, although I've been thinking it all seems a bit staged. His body may have been placed there by someone, just as the bone was placed in the other chair, to make some kind of point.'

'Yes, I see what you mean. But I've been thinking along slightly different lines, although I haven't said anything about it to Tom yet.'

'Go on.'

'Well, what if the practical joker had been Don Bainbridge himself? Several people have told us he had a silly sense of humour and, if you think back a few days, after he left for Spain, the practical jokes at the library stopped. Also, he had started to do housebound deliveries and if old Mrs Jenkins was visited by him, he would have had access to her book when she had finished with it to put the finger in it. The only thing I can't explain is why he would bother doing any of it.'

'The most obvious explanation is that he was a silly prat,' Sallie said.

'Yes, I agree. But I can't see that being a reason for someone to want to kill him,' Jo said thoughtfully.

*

Sallie had texted Emma and asked if they could meet her in Dolly's Pantry for lunch, so after they shut the shed library they walked down to the village together.

On the way she remembered her encounter with Joyce on the road on Thursday evening and told Jo about Joyce being engaged to Don.

'That's amazing because she must have been quite a bit older than him.'

'Not necessarily. She has probably aged quicker than him. I would say she is probably in her late fifties or early sixties now, like Don and Louise, but years of being a dried-up old spinster and dressing like a frump have made her look older.'

'I wonder if Louise knows they were once engaged.'

'I've no idea. It was all a long time before I came to the village. It will have been before Emma's time, too.'

After they had all ordered coffee and something to eat from Dolly, who was wearing a shiny, purple dress with a matching purple fascinator, Sallie asked Emma how Louise was getting on.

'I called to see her this morning and she's still very upset. She says she can't understand what he was doing in the library. They went straight to bed after they arrived home from the restaurant and she says she slept soundly. The next morning when she woke up he wasn't there. She doesn't know when he went out to the library, or why he went there.'

'Is there anyone you can think of that he might have arranged to meet in the library, who could have killed him?'

Emma looked at her steadily and Sallie felt herself going red. 'You surely don't think someone deliberately killed him, do you?'

'I just wondered…' Sallie began awkwardly.

'If you are thinking along those lines you must be very careful. Please don't talk about it in front of Louise. It would make her even more upset than she is already.'

Sallie felt ashamed. As usual, Emma had pointed out the error of her ways to her.

'You're right, I'm getting carried away and I'm being thoughtless. I promise I won't do, or say, anything to upset Louise.'

CHAPTER SIXTEEN

The next day was Sunday but Jo was keen to keep things in order in the shed and had suggested they spent a couple of hours tidying the stock. While they were working, Jo said: 'I've had a thought. If we want to get to know more about Don Bainbridge, why don't we speak to Deirdre? Do you remember, she had a photo of Don as a young man on top of one of the bookcases in her sitting room?'

'Yes, but I feel a bit bad ferreting round for information after what Emma said to me yesterday.'

'I know what you mean, I feel the same. But it's one thing going round talking about murder and blatantly trying to get information out of people and another thing to visit an old friend and colleague to see how they are. Your trouble is you say exactly what you're thinking all the while but sometimes it doesn't go down well with people. It's better to be a bit more subtle. Why shouldn't we go and see how Deirdre is? After all, the last time we saw her she was drunk and upset and we still don't really know why she'd got like that. If everyone Malcolm Bray was unpleasant to went to the pub and got drunk, Frank would be a very rich man.'

'Actually, it's possible Deirdre may not have heard about Don's death yet, so we could say we wanted to let her know about it. But it might be better if you contact her. She seems to like you more than me.'

Jo went outside into the sunshine with her mobile, while Sallie made a small display with some hardback crime novels on top of one of the bookcases.

When Jo came back in she looked triumphant. 'She was ever so pleased to hear from me, although she says she doesn't want to come up here again. She asked if we could meet her for lunch today at her local pub. She said Verity had rung to tell her about Don's death. She didn't sound particularly upset about it, but just said she would like to see us.'

As Jo drove them down the hill to Woodford, where Deirdre lived, she said: 'I feel a bit sorry for Mutz, the poor old sausage. I feel I've been neglecting him ever since we opened the shed library. I must take him out for a good long walk after we get back to tire him out before Tom arrives.'

'How does Mutz get on with Tom?'

'Oh, Mutz adores him. Tom used to be a dog handler so he knows all about German Shepherds. He knows exactly how to handle him.'

'It seems Mutz isn't the only one Tom knows how to handle,' Sallie couldn't resist saying, but Jo didn't dignify it with a reply.

Deirdre's local pub was very different from The Gentle Knight. It had stripped wooden floorboards, square pine tables and modern prints on the white walls. It was nearly empty and every movement made by the staff setting tables echoed round the large, minimally furnished room.

They all ordered fish and chips after Deirdre had recommended them. As soon as the wine had been delivered and poured, Jo went into action. 'Why did a little nonentity like Malcolm Bray cause you to get so upset the other day?'

Deirdre blushed. 'Well, it wasn't just him. I'd been at a low ebb for a few days. I'd begun to wonder whether I'd been wise to go back and work in a library.'

'But I thought you loved working in libraries.'

'I did when I was properly employed, but just recently I've been thinking perhaps I shouldn't have tried to recreate the past by volunteering.'

Sallie couldn't wait any longer. 'Were you upset because of something to do with Don Bainbridge?'

She saw Jo close her eyes and give a sigh.

Deirdre would never have made a good poker player. Her face displayed various expressions before ending in one of anguish. She looked down at her wine glass and went even redder.

'What made you ask about Don?'

'When we took you home the other night we noticed you had a framed photograph of Don in your sitting room,' Sallie answered.

'Oh, I see.'

There was an uncomfortable silence.

Jo was the first to break it.

'You don't have to tell us anything you don't want to, but you might find it will help you to talk to us about him.'

Deirdre sighed. 'It was all such a long while ago.'

At that moment the waitress showed a couple to the table next to them and Deirdre's next words were drowned out by the sound of them pulling their chairs back from the table, scraping them on the wooden floor and sitting down.

'Did you have an affair with him?' Sallie asked bluntly as soon as the noise stopped. She noticed Jo sigh again.

'Yes, I did. For a while we were in love. But then he ended it because he didn't think he was being fair to his wife. It was years ago, but I've never met anyone who could measure up to him since. I think he was worried I was getting too fond of him and he didn't want me to get hurt.'

'But it sounds as though you did get hurt,' Jo said gently.

'Yes, but it was only what I deserved. I don't know what you two must think of me for having encouraged advances from another woman's husband, but he could be very charming.'

'I bet he could,' Sallie muttered.

Deirdre didn't seem to hear her. 'He was like a lost little boy when I first met him. He said Louise didn't understand him…' She broke off as the waitress delivered their plates of fish and chips to the table.

'In what way didn't Louise understand him?' Sallie prompted her when the waitress was out of earshot.

'He said she had no sense of humour and they didn't have much in common. But he couldn't leave her because of the way their money was all tied up. Her father was a businessman who had invested in Don's shops, more or less in return for him marrying Louise. She had apparently given up her job and come back to live with her parents and they were keen to see her settled.' Deirdre paused for a few seconds to eat some of her food.

'But the big disappointment for Don was they weren't able to have any children,' she continued. 'When he met me he told me he had started to think it was time he did something for himself rather than just trying to make her happy. I think he eventually realised I was getting too attached to him and told me he couldn't leave her because she was too fragile. He said it would be devastating for her if she was left on her own.'

Deirdre took a sip of wine and Sallie could see she had tears in her eyes.

'What happened after that?' Jo asked gently.

'Well, I didn't meet anyone else, obviously, and since I retired I've been very lonely. But then I ran into Don quite by chance in Mickleton and he told me he'd had a heart scare and was taking early retirement. He said he was going to be a housebound volunteer at the library like Louise. She'd told him to take a back seat at work and get other people in to run his businesses for him. He told me about the villa they were having built in Spain and how they were hoping to have long holidays there. I suppose that would have been that if I hadn't seen in the local newsletter that the library in Upper Mickle was going to be run by volunteers and they were looking for recruits.' Deirdre paused again while she ate more of her food.

'So that's the real reason you volunteered,' Sallie said.

Deirdre nodded. 'I must admit I was ridiculously excited about working in a library again and being able to see Don regularly, so I couldn't wait to volunteer. I even held on to the fantasy that seeing me regularly might ignite things between us again.'

'But you must have found it painful seeing him with Louise,' Jo said.

A big tear ran down Deirdre's cheek. 'I used to hear Louise talking to the others saying things like, Don and I are going out to this restaurant, or to that party. They were obviously a happy couple and she would have had no idea he'd had an affair with me. That's why when Malcolm told me I was incompetent in front of a customer, all my pent-up emotions got the better of me and I yelled abuse at him and stormed out.'

'Good for you! That man needed someone to tell him what a pathetic, little pompous nobody...'

'Sallie!' Jo stopped her.

'Sorry, I was getting carried away.'

'No, you're right. He's insufferable,' Deirdre said, smiling through her tears.

'How did you feel when Verity told you Don was dead?' Jo asked gently.

'To begin with I couldn't really take it in. But then I thought it must have been because of his heart and that perhaps it was better for him to go suddenly. Knowing him, I'm sure it was the best thing for him, rather than having to put up with hospital treatment and operations. He would have hated to have lived like an invalid, looked after by a wife who didn't understand him.'

'Do you still have a key to the library?' Sallie asked suddenly.

Deirdre looked startled. 'Yes, I do. It's still in my handbag. I was so angry with Malcolm the day I walked out I never thought about giving it back to him. I just stormed off and went to the pub.'

'Did you know Don was discovered dead in the library by Sandra Thompson?'

'Yes, Verity did tell me that.'

'We understand the police are now treating his death as suspicious,' Jo added.

'Do you mean he didn't die of a heart attack, after all?' Deirdre asked.

'We don't know at the moment. He may have done, but the police haven't revealed the results of the post-mortem.'

'Have you got anyone who could vouch for your whereabouts the night before, or early in the morning, the day he was found dead?' Sallie asked.

'No. I would have been at home on my own. I'm always at home on my own these days. But I don't expect I will even be asked about my whereabouts. Who will be interested in me? After all, our affair was over and done with.' Deirdre sounded bitter.

*

When they arrived back in Upper Mickle, Sallie invited Jo in for a cup of tea. They sat in the garden to drink it and Sallie found the notebook she had used to make notes about the library volunteers a few nights before.

'So, who would have thought our Deirdre would have had an affair with Don Bainbridge?'

'I felt really sorry for her,' Jo said sadly. 'She loved him and then he dumped her and then she had her hopes raised again, but he was obviously devoted to Louise. I can understand why Deirdre found it too painful to work at the library. But now he's dead, she has no hope left at all.'

'I'm sorry, but we can't afford to take what she said at face value. She might not have told us everything and she still has a key to the library. Suppose she'd arranged to meet him in the library and he made it clear he wasn't going to leave Louise for her. She might have flown into a rage and hit him and killed him accidentally.'

'I don't think Deirdre would do anything like that. It's not in her nature.'

'You don't really know that. She lost her temper with Malcolm Bray and hurled abuse at him before storming out and getting drunk. She's not as meek and mild as she looks, is she?'

'I suppose we don't know her that well, really. But then, if she knew she'd killed him, she wouldn't have told us all about their affair.'

'Maybe she thought it would all come out eventually anyway, so she might as well tell us, making herself look as innocent as possible.'

'You may be right, but I still think there are other people who have stronger motives.'

'Such as?'

'Well, we've been told Clive was frequently upset by Don. He's definitely unstable. What's to say, if Don was bossing him about that morning, he didn't pick up an implement and hit him over the head with it and kill him? I think he's a much more likely candidate than Deirdre.'

'Yes, but no one has told us Don had a head injury,' Sallie pointed out.

'Well, it might not have been visible and we don't know that the post-mortem examination won't reveal something like that,' Jo suggested.

'Anyway, we can't overlook Joyce. She told me she had been engaged to Don once. If he didn't show any signs of recognising her, she might have felt humiliated and scorned and wanted to kill him.'

'I was supposed to befriend Joyce. But she's never been in the pub when I've been there and so I haven't had the chance to talk to her yet,' Jo said.

'I've just remembered something.' Sallie was excited. 'The night before Don's body was discovered, I saw Joyce go past here in the direction of the library with Sebastian. It was after midnight and I remember wondering what she was doing up here at that time. I was getting ready for bed and it was so hot I went to open another window. It was then that I saw her. I remember thinking that it was a strange time for her to be up here walking that poor little dog.'

*

Sallie spent a restless evening alone in her cottage. Every time she walked past her desk she checked either her emails or her phone, which she had left next to her laptop, but there was never a message from Jerry.

She hadn't sent him any news items, so if he was busy at work he had no reason to contact her, she reasoned with herself.

It made her even more determined to be the first with any news about Don's death, which would mean trying to talk to everyone she met to find out what they knew. But remembering what Emma had said to her, she resolved to try to be more subtle.

When it became noticeably cooler she decided to go out for a walk to see if she met anyone who could tell her something useful. Ironically, she managed to walk all the way down to the village without encountering a soul. She looked across at the pub but realised it was too early in the evening for there to be many people in, so she turned round to walk home again. It was funny, all the while she had been trying to avoid Joyce, she had bumped into her with Sebastian regularly on the road near her house. Now she was looking out for them, there was no sign.

Just as she was about to reach her cottage she saw a tiny figure higher up the hill with a dog on a lead.

She slowed down deliberately so that she didn't reach her garden gate too quickly, not wanting it to look as if she was lying in wait for Joyce.

When they got closer to each other she called out cheerfully to Joyce. 'It's a bit cooler this evening, isn't it? I bet it's much more pleasant for dog walking.'

'I always wait till it's cooled down before I take Sebastian out. I wouldn't dream of taking him for a walk when it's really hot.'

'Quite right too! We can't have our young man upset. Actually, I'm glad I've seen you as I wanted to ask you something.'

'Oh, what's that?'

'It's just that the night before Don's body was found in the library, I went to open a window in my bedroom and saw you going past my house in the direction of the library with Sebastian. It must have been well after midnight. You would have passed the library on your way home, so I just wondered whether you saw anything unusual that night.'

Two bright spots of colour appeared on Joyce's normally pale cheeks.

'I wouldn't have been up here after midnight. It can't have been me.'

'No, it was definitely you. I just wondered whether you saw anything out of the ordinary when you passed the library.'

'I'm sorry. I don't know what you're talking about.' Joyce jerked on Sebastian's lead and carried on walking downhill.

Sallie let herself into her cottage thinking about Joyce, wondering why she had become agitated at being asked about her movements and had denied being on Sallie's road the night before Don's body was discovered. All she had to say was she wanted to take Sebastian for a longer walk than usual, or something, Sallie knew she had seen Joyce go past her house and so she wondered what Joyce was trying to hide.

She went over to her desk and picked up her phone out of habit. To her surprise, there was a text from Jerry. *'Sorry not to have been in touch but have been up to my eyes in work. I'm preparing a special feature in addition to doing my day job. Thinking about you. xxx.'*

CHAPTER SEVENTEEN

'Joyce denied having been up here the night before Don's death. I asked if she'd noticed anything unusual when she went past the library, but she was adamant she hadn't been anywhere near my cottage that night.' Sallie was updating Jo about her encounter with Joyce, as they sat outside the shed in the sunshine during their coffee break the next morning.

'I know I saw her, so why did she bother to deny it? I thought she seemed upset when she walked off.'

'How strange! If Joyce had nothing to hide, all she needed to say was she'd been taking Sebastian for his last walk and hadn't noticed anything unusual about the library. It's a bit odd to pretend she wasn't up here at all.'

'Yes, and I can rely on my eyesight, I promise you. It's probably the only thing about me I can rely on these days.'

'I can't imagine Joyce killing him any more than I can imagine Deirdre for that matter.'

'Well, apart from Clive, who else could have done it, then?'

'How about Malcolm Bray? We can't overlook him.'

'No, I don't think so. Just because Don sometimes clashed with him doesn't mean Malcolm would want to kill him. It's not enough of a motive, unless there was something going on between them we don't know about.'

‘Yes, you’re probably right. Everyone says he’s power crazy but I can’t imagine him harming anyone. He’s the sort of person who would always want to play by the rules.’

‘George, on the other hand, had both the means and the opportunity.’

‘Oh no! George is a sweetheart. He wouldn’t hurt anyone.’

‘But George wanted to turn the library into another butcher’s shop. It would be easy for him to get hold of a cow’s leg bone to play that joke on Eileen. Also, he had a key to the library and could have let himself in if he’d arranged to meet Don there for some reason…’

‘No! I don’t believe it was George. I think Don Bainbridge was the practical joker and someone caught him in the act. There may have been a struggle and then Don died of a heart attack. But I don’t think it was Malcolm Bray. I think he would have told Don off, but not fought with him.’

‘Your theory rules out all the ladies as well.’

‘Oh, I don’t know, Sallie,’ Jo sighed. ‘Until we know what the police think caused his death we’re working in the dark. Let’s look for some new books on the internet to take our minds off it.’

A few minutes later, while they were both looking at Jo’s laptop, a slim, young woman with short, blonde hair wearing a mini skirt and vest top wheeled a double buggy containing identical twin boys into the shed library.

‘Hello, Julie. How nice to see you in here. Gosh, Freddie and Felix have grown!’ Jo said.

'Yes, they're nearly two now, so they're into everything. I can't take my eyes off them for a second,' Julie said proudly.

'Do you want to join our library? Sallie asked. 'We've just got some new children's books in.'

'Yes, I want to bring them here from now on, rather than going to the library in the village. I'm fed up with the way the volunteers treat me. Every time I go in one of the blokes tells me I've got overdue books and yet I know I've returned them. I'm sure some of them don't know how to do it properly on the computer. It seems whenever I take a pile of books back, some of them end up staying on my ticket.'

At that moment Freddie filled his nappy noisily. The resulting smell soon permeated the shed, while he leant back in the pushchair smiling happily.

'Even when I find the books on the shelves, which prove that I haven't still got them at home, they look at me suspiciously. I never used to have any problems when you two worked there. You know I can't afford to run up fines as a single mum so I'm always on time bringing their books back. It was Tracy, who lives next door to me, that told me to come here.'

Sallie said: 'You've been looking after her children for her, haven't you?'

'Yes, while she was staying with that Mrs Bainbridge she works for. She felt sorry for the poor lady and wanted to make sure she was all right, what with her husband dying so suddenly.'

'It's very good of Tracy to help her, isn't it?'

Julie smiled and tapped the side of her nose. 'Well, Mrs Bainbridge isn't short of a few quid and she always sees Tracy's on the right side, without involving the tax man, if you get my drift.'

*

At lunchtime, after they locked up the shed, Sallie suggested they walk down to The Gentle Knight to see if any of the volunteers were in the pub.

When they passed the village library they saw Clive digging in the front garden. Jo called across to him. 'Hello, Clive. It's a bit cooler today, thank goodness, isn't it?'

Clive put his spade down and came over to the wall to talk to her.

'What a shocking thing to have happened. You must all be terribly upset about Don's death,' Jo said.

'It's unbelievable. He was no age and, in any case, he always looked as fit as a fiddle,' Clive said.

'Did you get on with Don all right?' Sallie asked bluntly, but Clive didn't seem to mind.

'Yes, he was a decent bloke, was Don. He was always all right with me. I'm sorry for his poor wife because she's a nice lady and she was so devoted to him.'

'It's very sad for Mrs Bainbridge,' Jo agreed.

After they had walked on a few yards and could talk without Clive hearing them, Sallie said: 'He seems to have calmed down a bit. He was more like his usual self just then, wasn't he?'

'Yes, he was. It's true he was always a bit of a loner and I did sometimes hear him muttering things to himself when we used to work there, but he never had the sort of outbursts people have been telling us about recently,' Jo said.

'Curiouser and curiouser,' Sallie said thoughtfully.

*

The pub was busy and there were no spare tables so they sat with Malcolm and Rory, who both seemed pleased to see them, to Sallie's surprise. Jo asked politely after Sandra, suggesting it would have been a shock for her finding Don dead in the library.

Malcolm said: 'She's not been into the library since, so it's obviously upset her because it isn't like her to miss her shifts.'

'Oh poor Sandra,' Jo sympathised. I hope she's got someone in her life she can open up to because they say after a shock like that it helps to have someone to talk to.'

'I don't really know her that well and I don't feel I should be ringing her or going round to her house in case she wants to be left on her own,' Malcolm said.

'Was she friendly with any of the women volunteers?' Jo asked.

'I don't think so. She didn't seem to have a great deal in common with the likes of Verity and Eileen,' Rory said with a smile.

'I'll ask Emma next time I see her whether she'll call on her,' Jo said.

'Footfall's down,' Malcolm said suddenly.

'Do you mean fewer people are using the library?' Sallie asked, trying to sound innocent.

'Yes, it seems to have put people off.'

'It'll soon pick up again, I'm sure,' Jo said.

'Can I get you two ladies another drink and one for you, Rory?' Malcolm asked unexpectedly, rising to his feet with his empty pint glass in his hand.

They all accepted Malcolm's offer and while he was at the bar, Rory said: 'There's something I want to talk to you about but we can't discuss it here. If you two ladies are free this evening, would you like to come to my place for dinner?'

Sallie looked at Jo.

'Yes, I'm free this evening. How about you Sallie?' Jo asked.

'I don't have anything planned,' Sallie said.

'Good. I've bought the Old Manor House. Do you know it?'

'Yes, of course, it's a lovely house and I've always admired it. It's only a short walk from here,' Jo said.

'Great, well come to my house at about 7.30 and I'll cook dinner for you both. It's about time I had some guests.' Rory stopped talking abruptly when he saw Malcolm was on his way back to their table, carrying a tray of drinks.

After they left the pub, they discussed their dinner invitation on the way to the shops.

'I wouldn't have agreed to go if you hadn't been available. After all, we don't know anything about him. I wouldn't have wanted to be alone with him in his house,' Sallie said.

'Nonsense! He's very sweet. I'm sure you would have been fine. But Tom's working tonight anyway so it will be nice to have somewhere to go. I'm curious to see his house and find out more about him.'

'He said he wanted to talk to us about something. He might know something that will throw some light on Don's death,' Sallie said eagerly. 'It still seems vaguely unreal to me that the police are treating the death as suspicious. I can't bring myself to believe anyone we know could have done him any harm.'

'But how well do we know the volunteers? For example, all we really know about Sandra Thompson is that she's rude to the patients at the surgery. We don't know anything about her background. And she was the one who found him. The police always treat the person who finds the body with suspicion.'

'Did Tom tell you that or did you get it from reading crime fiction?'

'I think I've got it from reading detective novels. I wonder if I could persuade Emma to call on her and take me with her. I've never had a problem with Sandra until the other night in the pub and it would be good to talk to her. But how well do we know the other ladies? Eileen is a big, strong-looking woman, isn't she?'

'Not big enough to be able to overpower a fit bloke like Don.'

'Also, don't you remember, Verity used to have anger management books out when we were working there. We sometimes had to order them from other libraries and you used to giggle when you wrote V. Galling on the request slips we put round them.'

'You know I find things like that entertaining. I don't get out much,' Sallie began, but Jo interrupted her. 'Oh, look, here's Emma!'

The vicar's wife looked cool and elegant in a white cotton dress, her blonde hair taken back in a neat ponytail.

'Hi, you two. I was planning to come and see you at your library but I've been rushed off my feet today. I thought you should know the police have told Howard to postpone the funeral indefinitely while they make more enquiries. So it seems Don's death is being treated as suspicious. I'm sorry I was short with you, Sallie, when you were talking about it the other day. I just felt so sorry for Louise and didn't want it to be true for her sake.'

'Have you seen Louise?' Jo asked.

'Yes, I went round with Howard when he told her what the police had said to him.'

'How did she seem?' Sallie asked

'She became very distressed. Obviously she's still grieving and is all on her own. The thought someone might have been there and had something to do with Don's death was too much for her to bear. I felt desperately sorry for her,' Emma said.

'We've just been talking to Malcolm Bray in the pub. He says Sandra hasn't turned up for any of her shifts since discovering Don's body in the library. It sounds like she's still upset. I wondered whether you and I could go to see her together. After all, you're one of the volunteers and I've never had any problems with her when I've been to the surgery. It might help her to talk to us about it and to know people are thinking of her.'

'All right, let me know when you're free and we'll give it a try,' Emma said. 'I've never had any problems with her either.'

'It would probably be a good idea to leave me behind to run the shed library,' Sallie said.

*

Like Jo, Sallie was glad to have somewhere to go that evening and some reason for dressing up and making herself look pretty. None of this is for Jerry, she told her reflection in the mirror, after she had put on her make-up. Even so, she still felt excited because of the text he had sent her with three kisses on the end. Yet she was determined not to get her hopes up and she certainly wasn't going to tell Jo, who would be wildly optimistic if she knew he'd made contact, and Sallie didn't want to be disappointed all over again.

She had texted Jerry to tell him she had it on good authority that the police had asked for Don's funeral to be postponed while they made more enquiries. She hadn't had a reply, but she knew from his last text he was busy with work. She had resolved to go out and enjoy herself and not keep looking at her phone.

As they walked down the hill to Rory's house, Sallie said: 'We don't know anything about Rory, or why he came to live here. Why do you think he invited us for dinner tonight? He hardly knows us. Just suppose he killed Don?'

'Don't be silly. Having dinner with him tonight will give us chance to find out more about him. I've told Tom we're going there and he's going to ring me after his shift. If I don't reply he'll come looking for us, I'm sure.'

'Fair enough,' Sallie said. 'Let's see whether Rory knows anything we don't.'

The Old Manor House was a Georgian gem, well set back from the road behind an immaculate front garden with a large lawn and carefully shaped bushes in the borders.

'Wow, this is even more impressive than your house,' Sallie said as they crunched their way down the gravel path to the front door.

'It's a lot bigger than mine, although it was built in the same period and has similar architectural features. It's the most expensive house in the village,' Jo whispered.

'How could he afford to buy it then?' Sallie asked, cringing when she realised she had made no attempt to lower her voice and Rory was standing in the open doorway smiling at them both.

He really is very good looking, Sallie thought as they got nearer to the porch. Rory was wearing tight denim jeans and a fitted pale blue shirt, which was open at the neck revealing his tanned chest.

'Your house is amazing. I've never been inside it before,' Jo said to him, looking round with interest as he led the way through the large, oak-panelled entrance hall.

They followed him into a huge, modern kitchen, furnished with smart, dark blue painted units with wooden work surfaces.

'I seem to spend most of my time in here,' he said, indicating they should sit at the light oak dining table. He leant back against the island unit and his grin became broader as he looked at Sallie.

'Go on then, ask me anything you want to.'

'Did you win the lottery?'

He chuckled. 'Not quite, but sometimes it feels as though I did, because I'm not used to having money. It still feels a bit unreal, to be honest. I'll get us all a drink and tell you what you want to know.'

He placed three tall champagne flutes on the table and produced a bottle of champagne from the fridge. He popped the cork and carefully filled the three glasses.

'To friendship,' he said, raising his glass.

'To friendship,' they both echoed and they all clinked glasses.

'This is lovely,' Jo said appreciatively after her first sip.

Rory sat down opposite them at the table and put his glass down.

'Okay, you deserve a proper answer, so here goes. Two years ago I was living in a small, rented flat in London with my girlfriend and I had a job in IT with a London bank.

'One day my girlfriend came home and told me her company had offered her a job in New York and she had decided to take it. She never so much as suggested I might go with her. By the end of the week she'd moved all her stuff out and gone back to live with her parents while she sorted herself out before moving to the US. So that was that. I was suddenly on my own.'

'Were you very upset?' Jo asked.

'You'd think I would have been upset, but actually I didn't really know how I felt at the time. I think I was in shock more than anything. Suddenly my whole life had changed. I accepted the relationship was over. I didn't put up a struggle, which looking back must have meant I wasn't devastated by her going. Maybe we weren't in love at all. I don't know. I think now I was probably suffering from depression afterwards.

'I went to work every day and threw myself into what I was doing there to take my mind off everything. I was working on information security and in the evenings when I came home I would carry on working at my laptop trying to design a better security system than the one the bank had already. There had been a couple of worrying breaches and I tried to come up with something that couldn't be hacked into. I kept myself busy so I didn't miss her. But then I started to think perhaps I hadn't loved her that much after all. It was all very confusing

'I had some old University friends I still saw occasionally and one of them, who was a barrister, told me how to register my new security system as my own intellectual property, which turned out to be very good advice.

'As a result, the bank paid me well for my system. Once I had the money safely invested in my account it seemed a bit pointless going to work every day. There was nothing left to aspire to and I was fed up with living in rented accommodation in London. I decided to take some time off while I thought about what I wanted to do with my life. It seemed pointless commuting to a job on the tube every day when I had so much money.

'One day I saw this house advertised in a magazine. I liked the look of it and so I came up here to view it. It turned out to be my dream home, the sort of house I'd always fantasised about living in. For what I paid for it, I would struggle to get a two bedroom flat with a tiny bit of garden in a good area of London. So, I decided to come and live here, enjoy some country air and think about what to do next.'

'So you became a library volunteer,' Sallie said, with a hint of sarcasm.

'I've already told you, that was just so I could get to know people in the village.'

'So now you can sit with Malcolm and George in the pub every evening. How exciting!'

'They're all right when you get to know them. In fact most of the volunteers are, to be fair.'

'But one of them killed Don.'

'What makes you think that?' Rory asked.

'Well, the police are treating his death as suspicious. If he was killed in the library before it opened, it would have to have been done by someone who had a key to the building. So it's either one of the volunteers or Clive or Tracy.'

'Or, one of you two.'

Rory looked her straight in the eye.

'But we no longer have keys,' Jo pointed out.

'But you could have had copies made before you handed them back.'

'Why would we do that?' Sallie asked.

'So you could let yourselves in whenever you wanted to.'

'For what reason?'

'To play tricks on the volunteers.'

'I've already told you we had nothing to do with any of the practical jokes.'

'I believe you. I was just winding you up,' Rory said with a smile, topping up their glasses. 'Anyway, Don could have let someone in. It doesn't have to be someone with a key to the library.'

Rory stood up. 'Let me serve you some food. I've had a catering company prepare it all, I have to admit. I decided in the end not to try my cooking on you. I'll just put out their selection of antipasti.'

He laid the food out, set the table and opened a bottle of Italian white wine.

When he had sat down again, Sallie said: 'Just say it was one of the volunteers, who would you suspect?'

'It's difficult without knowing the cause of Don's death but I would say that the odd job man, Clive, sometimes behaves very strangely. It might be that he has mental health issues.

If Don had upset him for some reason he could have snapped and hit him. On the other hand, I suspect Don had an eye for the ladies. He could have paid unwelcome attention to one of the female volunteers.'

'That's an interesting idea. Who do you think he might have been after? I mean none of them are exactly glamour girls, are they? He always seemed devoted to Louise and she's very attractive.'

Rory looked embarrassed. 'That's true of course, Louise is very attractive, but she's no longer young and things may have cooled between them. He may have fancied a younger woman.'

'I suddenly feel very depressed,' Sallie said.

'Oh, don't be silly, you're a very attractive woman,' Rory said, smiling at her as he refilled her glass.

'If he fancied a younger woman that would rule out Verity, Eileen and Joyce,' Jo pointed out.

Sallie remembered what Joyce had told her about being engaged to Don when she was young, but decided not to tell Rory about it because it wasn't her business to share.

'Don was sometimes not very nice to the older women, so I doubt he was after any of them,' Rory continued. 'However, Emma is very beautiful, isn't she?'

Sallie rounded on him, but saw immediately he had a mischievous smile on his face.

'Yes she is, but Don would probably have thought twice about hitting on the vicar's wife, who happens to be a close friend of his own missus,' Jo said severely.

'Very true,' Rory conceded.

'Alicia Potter!' Sallie said suddenly.

'What about her?' Jo asked.

'She told me all the male volunteers at the library were pervy.'

'Thanks a lot,' Rory said.

'No, now I think about it she said they were all pervy apart from the young, good looking one.'

'Oh, that's a relief.'

'But you don't know for sure she was talking about you,' Jo said, laughing.

'You know how to undermine my confidence, don't you?'

'No, but Don could have made her feel uncomfortable if he fancied her,' Sallie said excitedly.

'Yes, but she could also have been implicating George and Malcolm,' Jo said.

'Have you considered Sandra?' Rory asked.

'Are you thinking that Don pestered her or that she pestered Don?' Sallie asked, laughing.

'Well she may have led him on,' Rory said. 'She sometimes made me feel a bit uncomfortable, by standing really close to me behind the counter and saying things with a double meaning and then looking at me to see how I reacted. I promise, I never gave her any encouragement.'

'But Don may have lapped it up,' Jo said.

'But why would he prefer Sandra to Louise?' Sallie asked.

Rory looked uncomfortable again. 'Well from the male perspective it's not always a question of looks. Sandra is younger than Louise. She might have made Don think she was up for it. If they had arranged a late night assignation in the library, Don might have thought his luck was in. But she may have had second thoughts and fought him off, accidentally killing him.'

'That's not a bad theory, actually,' Sallie said. 'Sandra would have known she was going to be first in the next day and that she would be able to let herself into the library and pretend to discover him.'

'It's a possibility, isn't it? Remember the night we saw her in the Trat with that pathetic little bloke with glasses. She was drunk and all over him. He probably thought his luck was in that night.'

'So, am I being a help with your investigation?' Rory asked eagerly.

'What do you mean, our investigation?'

'Well, I know you two don't come and sit with me and Malcolm in the pub just for our sparkling conversation.'

'To be fair, it started out with us trying to prove we weren't responsible for the practical jokes. But now Don is dead and the police think his death is suspicious, we can't help wanting to know the truth. Louise is one of our friends. We want to do anything we can to help her.' Sallie responded to him quickly, before Jo could mention her new work writing village news for the local weekly.

'Of course I can understand that,' Rory said. Then he leapt to his feet and raced to the oven. 'Sorry, I almost forgot the main course!'

After he had served up *saltimbocca alla romana*, veal with ham and sage, served with a selection of vegetables, they ate in silence for a few minutes.

'This is absolutely delicious,' Jo said appreciatively.

'What did you both find so great about working in a village library?' Rory asked suddenly. 'I mean look at the two of you. You're both attractive, intelligent, with a good sense of humour. You could do anything, go anywhere.'

'Well, it's lovely of you to say so, but we really enjoyed working at the village library,' Sallie answered. 'We both love books and reading and we also like dealing with the public. There's never a dull moment when you work in a library. You won't believe some of the hilarious things that have happened to us over the years, or some of the strange people we've met. But the best thing is talking to customers who like particular authors and helping them find books by other writers to try. It's really satisfying when they come back and say how much they've enjoyed a book you've recommended.'

'Also, we've had people who've been out of work for years, who we've helped with their computer issues week in and week out, and then they finally get a job. That's when it's really rewarding,' Jo added.

'Until they give it up after a few weeks because it's too much like hard work.'

'True.'

'Some of the people we've dealt with have been a complete pain, but some have been lovely.'

'Some of them have been mildly eccentric, while some of them have been completely mad, but it all adds to the hilarity,' Jo said.

'But I wouldn't recommend it to you as a career plan. Remember, we've just been made redundant and replaced by volunteers. There's no future in it,' Sallie said sadly.

There was an awkward silence. Then Jo said. 'The food has been lovely, Rory, but I couldn't eat another thing.'

'So, I can't tempt you with dessert?

'No, sorry, I'm totally full.'

Rory looked at Sallie. 'Same here, I'm afraid.'

'Let's sit in the lounge and have more wine,' Rory suggested.

Jo and Sallie relaxed on a huge, comfortable dark grey sofa facing Rory across a coffee table, who was sitting on a matching sofa. His large, sitting room was painted blue and white, and had white painted French doors looking out on to the huge, beautifully landscaped back garden.

'This is gorgeous,' Jo said looking round appreciatively as she sipped her wine.

'You're obviously a big fan of blue,' Sallie said.

'Yes, I am. Even though I had dark blue kitchen units put in, I wanted this room to be decorated in blue as well.'

After a few moments, Jo asked: 'Do you enjoy doing shifts at the library?'

'I'm beginning to get a bit fed up with it, to be honest, but it's somewhere to go each day, I suppose. Quite apart from having to put up with Malcolm, I find some of the customers trying.'

'I understand only too well. They expect you to do everything for them sometimes, don't they? You wonder how they manage when they go shopping, because I'm sure they don't get the same level of service in supermarkets.'

Sallie said: 'And, you wouldn't believe some of the things people leave behind in the library. We've had a chair, a headboard for a double bed, an entire sheet of first class stamps, full bags of shopping, passports, keys, wallets, coats, and walking sticks, the list is endless.'

'Not forgetting that enormous, scary-looking doll!' Jo chipped in.

'Just tracking down the owners and getting them to come in and fetch their things can take up a big part of your shift.'

'Amazingly, some of them aren't even aware they've left anything behind.'

'Then there are the things people leave inside the books. I've found a cooked rasher of bacon, a piece of toilet paper - unused thankfully - a £5 note, a hair bobble, there's no end to it. You wouldn't believe what people use as book marks.'

'Yes, do you remember that very personal letter we found?'

'Well, I've seen the plastic finger and the cracker biscuit,' Rory said. They all laughed.

'So now you're here, living in this pleasant village, in this beautiful house you've had completely refurbished to your taste. But is it a case of be careful what you wish for?'

'You're very perceptive, Sallie. Yes, I'm lonely here, even though I've made an effort to get to know people. I've no desire to go back to working in IT, but at the moment I can't see any clear future for myself, which is worrying. I now know money can't buy you happiness or a fulfilled life.'

'But without money and some security, it's difficult to be able to relax and enjoy life,' Jo pointed out.

'That's very true,' Sallie said, with feeling.

'Do you have much family?' Jo asked.

'No, my father died while I was at university and my mother only lived for a year afterwards. I was an only child and my aunts and uncles are all dead now as well. I've got a few friends still in London, but they're all busy with their own lives.'

'That's really sad,' Jo said. 'But I'm sure you'll meet another nice girl one day.'

'But how will I ever know if she loves me for who I am, or for the money that I have?' Rory asked. 'Sometimes I worry that I'll always be on my own.'

Later, Rory insisted on ordering a taxi to take them home, even though it was still light and they were both sure they could walk back.

'After all, it's the longest day on Saturday,' Jo reminded him. Rory kissed them both on the cheek and said how much he'd enjoyed their company.

They had all got increasingly merry as the evening had gone on and Jo and Sallie had regaled Rory with more anecdotes about their time at the library.

'Ah, he's so lovely. Some lucky woman out there will get him in the end and she doesn't even realise it yet,' Jo said as the taxi carried them up the hill away from the centre of the village.

'I wish I was 30 years younger,' Sallie said sadly.

'There you go again. I'm sure he's not 30 years younger than you. You are absolutely hopeless at judging men's ages.'

CHAPTER EIGHTEEN

'Now the effects of all that wine and champagne have worn off, I'm wondering again why Rory invited us for dinner last night. It seemed as though he wanted the opportunity to tell us about how he made his money. Don't you think that's a bit odd?' Sallie asked Jo the next morning.

'I've been thinking about it too. He's lonely, living in that big house and he's decided he'd like to get to know us better because he thinks we're fun people.'

'Well, we haven't got much competition round here!'

'He'll have realised everyone is bound to be curious about how he could afford to buy a lovely house like that,' Jo said, stepping back to look at a display of non-fiction books she had arranged on top of a bookcase.

'But how do we know this story about him inventing a computer security programme is true?'

'It's a bit of an elaborate story to tell if it isn't true. Why would he lie to us?'

'To cover up something dodgy, possibly. Suppose the money he bought the house with is the proceeds of a crime.'

'Oh, Sallie! You have such a suspicious mind…' Jo stopped talking when she saw Alicia appear in the doorway of the shed.

'Do you mind if I hang out here with you two for a bit?' Alicia asked nervously.

'Not at all. I was just about to make coffee. I'll go and make a pot for all of us,' Jo said, walking to the door.

Sallie and Alicia sat down at the table in the middle.

Alicia sighed. 'I'm not looking forward to going in for my shift at the library later. I hate it there even more now. Everyone's been acting strangely since Don's body was found.'

'What do you mean by acting strangely?'

'Verity and Eileen are even more nervous and easily upset by people than they were before and Sandra has given up doing her shifts completely.'

'Oh dear. She must have been very upset about finding Don's body.'

'I can understand that. But I think people are being a bit weird because I don't think any of them liked him that much really. They were getting fed up with the silly jokes he played on them.'

'I didn't know that.'

'Yes, I don't think he was very nice. Poor old Joyce brought her little dog in with her one day. I'm sure he wouldn't have been any trouble but Malcolm ordered her to take him home and come back and do her shift without him.

'She looked upset and even I felt sorry for her, but Don just laughed at her. She looked at him as though she could have killed him as she was leaving with the dog. I'm sure most people didn't like him, so I don't know why they seem so bothered about him now.'

Sallie thought quickly about what she could say that would be helpful. 'It's always the same after someone dies. People tend to remember all the good things about the person and are reluctant to admit there was anything bad. The best thing to do is just go along with them.'

Jo came in at that moment carrying a tray of coffee and biscuits. 'Oh good, here comes Jo with the coffee,' Sallie said with relief.

After Alicia had gone off to do her shift, the girls worked on, tidying the books and adding new ones to the shelves. They did not sit down again for a break until Emma came in to see them.

'I've just seen Sandra Thompson going into The Gentle Knight on her own. She looked weird and didn't seem to hear me when I spoke to her.'

'Oh dear, she's obviously still upset about finding Don's body,' Jo said.

'I'm a bit worried about her. She doesn't seem to have any close friends. I mean, she probably does have some friends, but they don't seem to live anywhere round here. It's difficult to know how to help her, really.

'Anyway, I've got some good news for you as well. I went round to see Louise earlier and she seemed a bit calmer. She said the police have told her they think Don went into the library early in the morning and surprised the practical joker about to set up another trick. She says they think there must have been a struggle and poor Don ended up having a heart attack.'

'Everything points to the practical joker being one of the volunteers then. Otherwise, how would he, or she, have got into the library?' Sallie asked.

'Unless it was Tracy or Clive,' Jo added.

'Anyway, I've heard you two were seen going into the Old Manor House all dressed up last night,' Emma said. 'No one else has been invited there so the village is very excited about it.'

'We were invited for dinner,' Jo said proudly. 'Poor Rory is very lonely now he has moved up here. He's an only child and his parents and his uncles and aunts are all dead. He told us his girlfriend left him to take a job in New York so he decided to move away from London to try to make a new life for himself.'

'But he's got cousins and some old school friends just over the border in a village in Nottinghamshire. That's where he was born and brought up,' Emma said.

'He never mentioned them to us. He gave us the impression he doesn't know anyone round here.'

'He told me all about his family when we were on a shift together at the library. Apparently his father used to run the village shop, but he went out of business when someone set up in competition with him.'

'I've just been thinking,' Sallie interrupted excitedly. 'I wonder whether Sandra remembers anything about what the library was like when she let herself in that morning. It could be she noticed a tiny detail that indicated someone else had been there earlier. Why don't you two go round to the pub and talk to her now?'

'We could try I suppose,' Jo said hesitantly.

'I hate to think of her bottling it all up and having no one to talk to about it,' Emma said. 'We can at least try to get her to tell us what she's so upset about.'

'You know, it's strange that with all her supposed medical knowledge she didn't attempt to give him first aid, but ran out screaming and now seems to have gone to pieces,' Sallie pointed out. 'There's perhaps a lot more to this than we first thought. See what you can find out. I'll be fine on my own here if you two want to go and speak to her now.'

Emma looked at her thoughtfully. 'I mean, I don't like to think of her being upset and not having someone to confide in,' Sallie said hastily.

Jo said: 'We could ask if we can sit at her table in the pub and try to get her to talk to us. There's obviously something still upsetting her.'

'All right, we'll give it a try,' Emma said, getting up from the table. Jo quickly picked up her handbag and followed her out of the shed.

*

Later that morning, after Sallie had done some tidying and listed more of their duplicate books for sale online, she was surprised to see Verity and Eileen enter the shed together.

'We were just finishing our shift and Alicia came on duty and told us how marvellous your new library is, so we decided to come and see for ourselves,' Eileen said enthusiastically.

Sallie looked at her closely. There had been no edge to her voice and her smile seemed genuine, but it was difficult to read the expression in her eyes behind the thick glasses.

'Well, we both had so many books that we'd read and didn't need any more we decided to make them available to people in the village by setting up a library. We also wanted to raise money for charity.'

'You've made a lovely job of decorating it. I like the colour,' Verity said, looking round admiringly.

'Verity and I are crocheting new cushions for all the chairs at the village library,' Eileen said smiling happily at the thought of them. 'Unfortunately, one of our group of volunteers, who shall remain nameless, wanted to paint the walls bright orange, but she was outvoted by the others, thank goodness.'

'The cushions we're making are in different shades of pink,' Verity explained.

'Oh lovely,' Sallie enthused, privately wondering why they thought pink would go with the bright blue library chairs.

She realised this was a good opportunity to ask about Don. 'Sit down and we'll have a cup of coffee. There's still plenty left from when Jo made a pot earlier and the jug keeps it hot. I'll just get our guest mugs out for you.'

She bent down behind the table near the door and rummaged in a basket containing crockery Jo had donated from her kitchen.

Verity and Eileen sat at the table with Sallie and she poured them all a cup of coffee.

'Alicia was telling me how upset everyone was at the library about Don's death,' she said, somewhat disingenuously.

'Oh yes, it was a terrible shock,' Verity said, looking serious.

'He was such a good man, giving up his time to take books to the elderly. He was a self-made businessman and successful, but he didn't mind helping others by volunteering. I feel so sorry for his poor wife. They were such a nice couple,' Eileen said.

'But not everyone got on with him well, as far as I understand,' Sallie probed.

'Well, most of us did,' Eileen protested.

Verity pulled a face. 'That ridiculous odd job man used to have a tantrum if Don so much as suggested he did a little job on the building.'

'It isn't really his job, though, to do maintenance work on the building. If something needs doing the council's property department should be asked to send someone who's been properly trained. Also poor Clive has mental health issues,' Sallie said.

'He comes from a very strange family.'

'Yes, I know all about that,' Sallie said hastily. 'I was just wondering what Malcolm thought about Don. Malcolm seems to like being in charge of everything. Perhaps he felt threatened by him.'

Eileen said firmly: 'Well, someone has to take the lead, otherwise a big group such as ours would spend all the time having ridiculous arguments. I mean take for example that woman….'

'Eileen, we've been told not to talk about library business to outsiders,' Verity said swiftly.

'You're right, of course, Verity. In answer to your question, Sallie, there were sometimes disagreements over minor things, but that was to be expected. We all respected Don because of the contribution he was making to the running of the library. He was entirely unpaid, of course,' she said pointedly.

Sallie was tempted to remind her that Don had no relevant qualifications for running a library and hadn't had the training or years of experience she had. This was why she had been paid a small salary for doing the job before being made redundant. But for once she managed to restrain herself, remembering that she was acting in the interests of her investigation.

'One of you can't have liked and respected Don all that much because it looks as though whoever he was with in the library that morning killed him,' she said bluntly.

'What? That's a terrible thing to say,' Eileen reproached her.

'That's what it looks like. The police think there are suspicious circumstances relating to Don's death and have asked the Reverend Goodall to postpone his funeral indefinitely,' Sallie said calmly.

'I know that, but I still can't imagine any of our group of volunteers wanting to harm him. Just because he was found in the library doesn't make it anything to do with us.'

Verity said: 'No, of course not and, anyway, most of us are women. But I suppose, on the other hand, when you get strong businessmen working together there are bound to be disagreements.'

Eileen flashed her an angry look.

'What do you mean? Did you ever see Don clash with any of the other men?'

'Not clash exactly, no. But there was some friction between him and Malcolm occasionally. Also, I once went into the little office at the back, and Don was talking to George and they were both raising their voices and looked angry with each other.'

Eileen put her coffee mug down and glared at her.

'You're incapable of discretion, aren't you? After everything that's been said. Talk about making something out of nothing.'

*

Meanwhile, Jo and Emma had joined Sandra at her table in the pub garden. 'Do you mind if we sit with you? We wanted to know how you are because we've all been worried about you.' Jo put her drink down on Sandra's table and sat down.

'Why?' Sandra asked, sounding puzzled.

'Well, you haven't been going in to do your shifts, have you? You must have had a nasty shock when you found Don's body in the library.'

'Oh, that!' Sandra said dismissively. She laughed harshly, but then began to sob.

Emma went round to the other side of the table and sat down next to Sandra and put a consoling arm round her. Sandra leant against Emma and continued to cry. Eventually she became calmer and pulled a crumpled tissue out of her bag to wipe her eyes.

'Sorry about that.' She looked down at her full glass of wine, clearly embarrassed.

'You're bound to be upset. It's probably good for you to have a bit of a cry every now and then,' Jo said, trying to sound reassuring.

'A bit of a cry? What's that?' she asked bitterly

Jo looked at Emma helplessly, not knowing what to say next.

Sandra took a gulp of her drink and then put the glass down again.

'Whenever I close my eyes I see him sitting there dressed in his suit in that chair. I dread going to bed at night. I can't sleep.'

'But that's only to be expected,' Emma said. 'You found a man dead and you were all on your own with no one to help you. You've had a terrible shock.'

‘No, that’s not the problem. I’ve seen dead bodies before and I’m used to dealing with things on my own. I don’t need other people.’

‘Why do you think it’s upset you so much then?’ Jo asked.

‘It’s confusing. I’ve only got hazy memories of the night before, but I’m sure I was with him. With Don, I mean.’ Sandra began sobbing uncontrollably again.

‘Oh, Sandra, do try not to be so upset about it. It will all be okay in the end.’

‘But how can it be okay? How can it be okay ever again? It must have been my fault. I can’t stop thinking about it. I think I might have killed him!’

CHAPTER NINETEEN

Sallie tidied up and locked the shed library at one pm. Coming out of Jo's garden, she considered crossing the road to return to her own cottage, but then decided to join Jo and Emma at The Gentle Knight. She decided she would sit at another table if it looked like they were making progress with Sandra. She wouldn't go storming in and spoil things, but she was eager to know what they were finding out.

Her thoughts turned back to George as she walked along in the sunshine. Jo wouldn't hear a word said against him. On the surface he seemed to be a kind, decent man. But Verity had seen him have an argument with Don, and now Don was dead. It would be great to find out what the argument had been about. She hoped the matter could be cleared up and George would turn out to be blameless. But it was odd how Verity had insisted on telling her about the argument between the two men even after she had revealed that they had been told not to gossip about the library. Normally Verity would have been too scared of Eileen to say anything out of turn. But she hadn't taken much coaxing to mention George's name.

Ironically, the first two people she saw when she pushed open the door into the side bar were George and Jo, together at a table.

'Where's Emma?' Sallie asked.

'She's gone home with Sandra Thompson. We were talking to her in the garden earlier and Sandra got a bit upset so Emma offered to take her home,' Jo said, making it sound innocuous. 'The poor woman is exhausted. She has hardly slept since finding Don's body in the library.'

'Oh, I see,' Sallie said casually, sitting down in one of the empty chairs.

'Do you want your usual wine, Sallie, love? George asked.

'Oh yes, thank you, George. That's very kind of you. '

'No problem,' George said, getting up to go to the bar.

'Well, what did you find out?' Sallie asked as soon as he was out of earshot.

'It's a bit complicated. I'll tell you all about it later,' Jo said in a low voice.

When George returned with Sallie's glass of wine she sat quietly, thinking about how she could raise the subject of his argument with Don.

Jo was chatting to George and she could see he was looking at her friend admiringly. Surely he didn't still think he was in with a chance with her? He must have heard about her relationship with Tom.

'You're very quiet today, Sallie, love.' George suddenly directed his booming voice in her direction.

'Oh, sorry. I was just thinking about Verity and Eileen. They came into the shed library to have a look round and they were saying how upset all the volunteers have been about Don's death.'

'Yes, it's been a big shock to us all. We really liked young Donald. He was always giving us a laugh. I've heard that the police think he disturbed the person who's been leaving these bones and things in the library and there was a bit of a tussle. He had a weak heart, you see. It was probably too much for him. The crackpot must have left him there dying. It's a terrible thought isn't it?'

'Well, I hope no one thinks either Jo or I had anything to do with it.'

'No, of course not. The very idea! I mean to say, as if anyone would think that!'

'Can you think of anyone among the volunteers who might not have been all that keen on Don?'

'No, I think everyone got on well with him.'

'It's just that Verity was saying earlier she remembers going into the back office one day and finding you and Don having an argument.'

'Did she indeed? Well, you shouldn't listen to tittle-tattle, Sallie.'

'Do you remember having an argument with him, George?' Jo asked him, looking into his eyes innocently.

George sighed. 'Well, I wouldn't exactly call it an argument, but he did get a bit shirty with me when he found me looking at files in the back office to do with the maintenance of the building. I wanted to see what work had been done in the last few years with regard to the electrics and boiler and so on.

'Don asked me what I was doing and I said I was just having a look at the paperwork to see how up to date it was. He asked me why I was interested and I said I'd been thinking that if the volunteer-run library closed, I might be interested in buying the building and converting it into a butcher's shop.

'You should have heard him! He got really angry and told me I had no right to be snooping. I said it wasn't really snooping. I just wanted to know how well the building had been looked after over the years.

'Anyway, he told me the library definitely wasn't going to close so I could forget all about buying the building. He was obviously very committed to making it a success. I'd never seen him so serious. He wasn't having a laugh that day!'

*

On their way home the girls discussed what George had just told them.

'It's almost as though Don had mentally put himself in charge and didn't want George getting any ideas about the library closing,' Sallie said.

'I'm surprised he'd become so keen. He'd only just started being a housebound volunteer and he and Louise were planning to have long holidays at their villa in Spain. He wouldn't have been around to keep the library going,' Jo pointed out.

'Yes, it's a bit unrealistic to have expected an ill-assorted band of people to keep it going when they're working for nothing. I'm sure Rory and Alicia will get fed up eventually and Emma is far too busy with parish business to be expected to do much. I don't really understand why Don had become so determined to keep the library open.'

'I'd love to be able to ask Louise about it but it might be too upsetting for her at the moment,' Jo said thoughtfully.

'I know. It's so frustrating not to be able to talk to her properly.'

When they reached her gate, Sallie invited Jo in for a cup of tea so she could bring her up to date about what Sandra had said.

Jo relaxed on the settee and stroked a sleepy Desdemona while Sallie made a pot of tea. After she had poured them both a cup, Jo leant back against the cushions, sipping her tea and explained what she had found out.

'Sandra obviously had a bit of a thing about Don,' she began.

'Not another one! What did they all see in him?' Sallie exclaimed.

'I don't know. But she said he made it clear at the start that he wasn't interested so she stopped trying. Poor Sandra, she's obviously desperate to get a man so she regularly tours round the pubs in Mickleton hoping to meet someone. She said on one occasion recently she ran into him in a bar and he bought her a drink and was quite friendly. She says they shared a taxi back to the village and had a bit of a snog in the back. When it dropped them off he suggested they went into the library. I won't attempt to go into the details she revealed to us, but she made it clear they had sex in the library.'

'In the library! Oh my God!'

'But of course after that he didn't want to know her and hardly spoke to her when he came into the library and she was working there. However, on the night before Don's death, Sandra went round the pubs in Mickleton again and remembers being with someone tall and dark who, to quote her, 'had his hands all over her.' She had drunk a lot and can't remember how she got back to the village but says she woke up at home alone in her own bed the next morning. She made herself get up and go to open up the library, even though she wasn't feeling well, because she was too scared of Malcolm to phone in sick.

'It was then she found Don, dressed in his suit, dead in the chair in the kitchen. She says since then she's been having flashbacks about what happened to her the night before. She feels sure she was with a man in Mickleton and wonders whether it was Don and whether she went into the library with him again. She's worried they might have 'got it on', as she referred to it, for a second time and that he might have had a heart attack. She's terrified because she can't remember exactly what happened but thinks she might have caused his death.'

'Oh my God, what a mess. Poor Louise!'

'Fortunately, Emma was brilliant with her. She said it might not have been Don she was with in the pub, but someone else. She said it was possible they slipped something into Sandra's drink, because Sandra says she can usually remember what happened the night before when she wakes up the next day, even after she has been drinking a lot. Emma suggested she should go to the police and tell them what was worrying her and have a test to see if she has any trace of a drug still in her system, but I don't know whether she will.'

'But if it turns out it was Don, it will be awful for Louise to have to deal with the fact he had a heart attack while having sex in the library with Sandra!'

After Jo had gone home to check up on Mutz, Sallie made herself a sandwich for lunch and poured herself a glass of lemonade. She sat in a shady part of her garden, reflecting on everything she had learnt that day. She decided not to tell Jerry about George's argument with Don, or about the possibility that Don might have been with Sandra in the library the night before.

However, she thought it was worth passing on that Louise had been told by the police Don may have surprised the practical joker up to mischief in the library and got into a struggle that caused him to have a heart attack.

She went back into the cottage, found her phone and tried Jerry's mobile number. It went to voicemail almost immediately so she left a brief message asking him to ring her.

After washing and putting away all the dishes she had left soaking in the sink, she tried the number again. Still it went straight to voicemail. The same thing happened when she tried again half an hour later.

Tidying and dusting her living room helped her to pass more time. Then she went to check her emails, wondering if he had got in touch with her that way, but there was no message from him in her inbox. She went out into the garden again and sat in the shade trying to read a book but found she couldn't concentrate. She decided to have one more try at contacting him, but the phone went to voicemail once again. This time she didn't bother to leave a message.

What kind of a journalist was he, to have his phone switched off for such a long time? He could miss out on good stories, she thought angrily.

She found the number for Jerry's newspaper on the internet and rang it. After she was put through to the newsroom the phone rang for a couple of minutes and she was just about to give up when a woman answered.

'No, sorry, Jerry's out on a job at the moment,' she was told.

'I've been trying to contact him for a few hours now, but his phone keeps going to voicemail.'

'Does it? Oh, I bet I know where he'll be. He'll be up at the riding stables at Upper Morton. The signal's rubbish there. He's very friendly with the woman who runs the stables. She's one of his contacts so he's up there a lot.'

Sallie just about managed to say: 'Okay, I'll try later,' and hung up before collapsing on to the settee next to Des. She stroked the cat absently while her mind went into overdrive. She could feel her cheeks burning with anger.

Friendly with the woman who runs the riding stables, was he? How friendly? Did he have a woman in every village? The bastard! It gave a whole new meaning to the term 'village contact', she thought angrily.

CHAPTER TWENTY

It took Sallie a few hours to calm down. She tidied upstairs, chuntering to herself all the while. She did some washing and put out more food for Des. Eventually, she cooked herself a meal, but didn't eat much of it.

When the evening became cooler she sat in the garden with a glass of chilled white wine. She resolved again to forget about any kind of romance with Jerry and concentrate on supplying village news to the paper to make extra money. The village show was on Saturday and she was sure she would be able to find some stories if she went round the stalls talking to people. Also, she would make sure she had the latest news on Don's death ready for the Monday deadline.

Just like Jo, she couldn't bring herself to contemplate that George might have killed Don. It was bizarre to think he might have murdered Don because he saw him as an obstacle to his plan for opening a butcher's shop in the library building.

It was possible Don had breathed his last while having sex with a drunken Sandra, but it would be terrible for Louise if it turned out to be true.

For Don to have died in the library while struggling with the practical joker would still be upsetting, but at least preferable to being unfaithful to her with one of the volunteers.

But there was something else niggling away at the back of her mind. It was something she had known for a while but infuriatingly she had forgotten what it was.

After running through the list of library volunteers in her mind she laughed out loud as it came back to her.

She looked round nervously, hoping her neighbours hadn't heard her if they were out in their garden. They already thought she was a bit odd, she was sure.

Joyce and her dog, Sebastian, had passed her house late on the night before Don's death, which meant they would have had to go past the library to get home. When she had asked Joyce about it she had denied being there, but Sallie was certain it had been Joyce she had seen that night while she was opening another window in her bedroom.

In Sallie's mind it all added up: Joyce had once been engaged to Don. She had told Sallie he seemed to have forgotten about the relationship. Alicia had said Don laughed when Malcolm told Joyce to take her dog home. She had said Joyce looked as though she could have killed him. Joyce was not only a woman scorned by him but a woman he had laughed at and that must have hurt her a lot.

She stood up quickly. It was time to confront Joyce and make her tell the truth.

Sallie grabbed her bag, went outside and locked her front door. It was still light, but most of the villagers were indoors, probably watching television or eating dinner, so she didn't meet anyone she knew on her way down the hill.

She began to feel less sure of herself as she approached the village green. Was it really likely that skinny, little Joyce could have fought with a large bloke like Don and killed him? But then Joyce was an embittered person whose whole life had been a disappointment. It must have hurt if he had seemed not to remember they had once been engaged. Also, he had been cruel to laugh when Malcolm told her to take her dog home. Could Don's behaviour have tipped Joyce over the edge?

She knew where Joyce lived, even though she had never been inside the house. It was a substantial, period property, close to the village centre, which she had inherited from her parents.

Sallie pushed open the old, creaking, wooden gate. The large front garden was full of weeds and looked neglected. The window frames looked as though they needed repainting as well, leading Sallie to suppose that Joyce either lacked the money to maintain the property, or couldn't be bothered any more.

She pushed the front doorbell and waited but no one came to the door. Surely Sebastian would have heard it and barked if they were at home? She lifted the old, brass door knocker and banged it down a few times. There was a high-pitched yapping from the back of the house and after a few seconds she could hear someone approaching the door. She heard the rattling of a chain and eventually the door opened a few inches and Joyce peered out at her.

'Oh, it's you. What do you want at this time of night?'

'I just need to ask you something. Please can I come in? It will only take a few minutes.'

'Oh, very well. Just let me take the chain off.'

Joyce unhooked the chain and pulled the door open, standing back to allow Sallie to enter the hall. It was a long, dimly-lit passageway, lined with anaglypta wallpaper painted a mustard colour.

'You'd better come in here,' Joyce said rather grudgingly, opening the door to a front reception room.

The room was furnished with a large, round dark wood dining table surrounded by chairs and a dark green velvet settee with two matching armchairs. There was an upright piano against one of the walls. The dark green, leafy wallpaper looked like it hadn't been changed for a long while. It had probably been the entertaining room and Sallie had a vision of a young Joyce and members of her family gathering round the piano to sing together.

Joyce motioned to Sallie to sit down on the sofa and took one of the armchairs opposite.

'It's late, so tell me what you want, as quickly as you can.'

'Am I holding you up from taking Sebastian for his walk?'

'No, he's had his walk and I've settled him in his basket in the kitchen.'

'It's just that I know you sometimes take him out late at night.'

'I only take him round the block if he needs to do his business. Look, just say what you want to say.'

'I'm still wondering why you were out with Sebastian so late on the night before Don was found dead in the library. I saw you go past my house and you must have passed the library on your way back down to the village.'

'I've already told you it wasn't me you saw. You were mistaken.'

'No, I wasn't mistaken. I definitely saw you walk past my house with Sebastian when I went to open a window in my bedroom. I have very good eyesight and I don't need glasses. I know it was you I saw.'

'Well, what does it matter if I took Sebastian on a later walk than I usually do? What's it got to do with you?'

'You must have passed the library on your way back down to the village. Were there any lights on, or any signs of activity?'

'I'm afraid I can't help you.'

'Look Joyce, I know you were there. Why don't you just admit it? What have you got to hide? All you need to say is you took Sebastian out later than usual. You must be able to remember if you saw any lights on, or if anything seemed unusual, when you passed the library.'

'I have nothing to hide and in any case I am not answerable to you about my movements in this village.'

'No, you are not answerable to me. But if you continue to deny passing my house on the night in question I will have to inform Sergeant Cleaver about it and he will pass the details on to the detectives who are investigating Don's death.'

A furtive look came into Joyce's eyes. Sallie could see her weighing up the situation.

'I had nothing to do with Don's death and did not set foot in the library that night. Why do I have to explain where I took Sebastian for a walk to anyone?'

'You should explain because you passed near the scene of the crime and might have some information that will help the police.'

'The scene of the crime! Who do you think you are? Sherlock Holmes? You're just a nosy woman with too much time on her hands and you have no authority over anyone.'

Sallie got up to go. 'Right, have it your own way, but I will pass the information on to Sergeant Cleaver.'

Joyce stood up as well. Her sallow skin was starting to look flushed and there were red patches on her thin neck.

'No, wait a minute. If I tell you why I was there you will see it has nothing to do with Don, or the library. But I want you to give me your word that you will not tell the police about it.'

'But why, if it has nothing to do with Don's death?'

'Because it's embarrassing.'

'All right, try me with it.'

Joyce thought for a moment as though she was trying to buy herself time to come up with a good excuse.

'Well, it was Verity and Eileen's fault really. They were gossiping about your friend, Jo, and wondering if she was having an affair with Sergeant Cleaver. They said his car was parked outside her house all night. I didn't like to hear Jo's reputation being tarnished by two spiteful old women.'

'But both Jo and Tom have been divorced for a long time and they both have grown-up children who have left home. What they do now is entirely their own business.'

'But it doesn't stop women like Verity and Eileen from gossiping about them. I just decided to take Sebastian for a walk up there late at night to see if Sergeant Cleaver's car was there or not. They were saying he only spends so much time in the village because he has a lady friend here. I thought they might be exaggerating and I didn't want the gossip to spread if it wasn't true, so I thought I would go and see for myself.'

'And what did you see?'

'His car was parked outside her house when I went past.'

'But that's his business and her business and nothing to do with Verity, Eileen or you. More importantly, when you passed the library did you see anything unusual?'

'No, I did not. It was late and I wanted to get home so I didn't even look at the library as I went past.'

Sallie felt hot and uncomfortable in Joyce's musty front room and knew she wouldn't get to know any more.

'I need to get home now,' she said, standing up abruptly.

Joyce followed her to the front door. 'Please don't tell Sergeant Cleaver why I was up there that night. It's embarrassing.'

'I'll have to think about it. If it's not necessary to tell him I won't. I wouldn't want to make either him, or Jo, feel uncomfortable.'

She opened the door and let herself out and walked quickly back up the hill to her cottage. She was glad of the fresh, cool air after being in Joyce's front room.

She remembered Joyce's furtive expression and wasn't sure whether the woman had been telling the truth or not. Had she come up with a plausible excuse to avoid being questioned by the police about Don? Or, was she being painfully honest when she revealed to Sallie she had nothing better to do with her time than to go out of her way late at night to spy on Jo and Tom?

Sallie decided not to tell Jo about her visit to Joyce's house in case it made her feel uncomfortable to discover she was the subject of village gossip.

CHAPTER TWENTY-ONE

In the pub at lunchtime the next day, while Jo and Sallie were finishing off their salads, Rory came to their table and asked if he could join them. Sallie waved to an empty seat, unable to speak because she was eating, and he sat down next to her with his pint.

'What are you two up to this afternoon?' he asked.

'Oh, I think I'll just sit in the garden and read a book for the rest of the day,' Sallie said.

'That would suit me very well too, although I will have to take Mutz out for a good, long walk when it gets cooler,' Jo said.

'I'm stuck in the library all afternoon,' Rory said gloomily. 'I'm down to do the two till seven shift.'

'Be careful what you wish for,' Sallie said. She looked at him pointedly.

'Aha! So you do think that book was chosen to be a warning to the volunteers.'

'Not that again! I don't know, because I didn't choose it. But it does seem a fitting title considering the situation you now find yourself in.'

'What do you mean?'

'All I mean is that people are bound to get fed up eventually, giving their time for nothing to do what is actually a complicated job, if they do it properly, which involves having to deal with the general public and all their charming ways.'

'Yes, and there are so many of you that some volunteers might never get the chance to sit at a computer and learn about stock management,' Jo added.

'I suppose that's a pretty accurate assessment of what my afternoon will be like.'

'Emma said she would join us for a drink soon, which means she can't be doing a shift. So, who will you have for company in the library this afternoon? Just Malcolm?' Sallie asked mischievously.

Rory looked even more fed up. 'You know what, I might just skive off this afternoon and stay and have a drink with the lovely Emma.'

'She's taken,' a gruff voice said from behind the bar.

Rory turned round in surprise. 'Yes, I know she is.'

'Her husband, the Reverend Goodall, is a very nice gentleman,' Frank continued.

'Yes, I'm sure he is. Honestly Frank, I didn't mean to sound impolite. It's just that I always enjoy Emma's company when we're on duty at the library together.'

'He's only winding you up,' Jo said.

'Anyway, whether the book title has any significance or not, what do you think the body parts were meant to represent?' Rory asked, keen to move on with the discussion.

'Well, they weren't really body parts, were they?' Sallie pointed out.

'None of them was. I think it was someone just having a laugh,' Jo said.

'But maybe the fake body parts were chosen to represent the dismembering of the library service.'

Sallie wondered why Rory was so keen to provoke a debate about it all again. She was about to answer him, but then Emma came into the bar and Rory leapt to his feet and offered to buy her a drink.

'Just a sparkling water, please,' Emma said with a smile and came over and sat down in Rory's chair at the table with the girls. She looked pale and tired.

'Are you okay?' Sallie asked.

'Yes, I'm just wilting a bit in the heat and there always seems to be so much to do.'

'You could do with giving up volunteering at the library,' Jo said bluntly.

'Yes, I know, but I don't want to make more work for the others by dropping out, especially since they're without Sandra at the moment. Anyway, I wanted to ask Jo a favour. The police want to speak to Louise again tomorrow and she asked me if I could be there to support her, but I have a medical appointment I really can't cancel. So she asked me to see if Jo would mind sitting in with her.'

'Of course I don't mind. I'll be happy to help. What time are the police coming?' Jo asked.

'She said they'll be there at 10 am.'

'Right, I'll text her and tell her I'll get there a few minutes before that,' Jo said.

'Do you know why they want to speak to her again?' Sallie asked, but Rory came back to the table carrying Emma's drink and she just shook her head. Sallie could tell she didn't want to say anything further in front of Rory.

*

The next morning, after helping to open the shed library, Jo left Sallie to run things on her own and went to support Louise while the police spoke to her.

Sallie did all the jobs that needed doing and then sat down at the table and looked at a book while she waited for customers. She was pleased when Eileen came in after a few minutes because she hoped it would give her the chance to find out more about the volunteers.

'Would you like a cup of coffee? Jo has kindly made some for me and left it in a jug that keeps it warm because she's had to go out to see someone.'

'Thank you very much. That's very kind of you,' Eileen said, sitting down at the table in the middle of the shed.

Sallie brought mugs of coffee to the table for them both and sat down opposite Eileen.

'No Verity today?' Sallie asked.

'No, I went to call on her but she said she didn't feel well and wanted to stay in. Neither of us has a shift at the library, so she said she couldn't be bothered to get ready to come out. She sometimes has what she calls her 'down days'.'

'Do you think she's still upset about Don being found dead in the library?'

'I wouldn't have thought so. Verity has her own issues anyway. Her father was a dreadful man. He was a tyrant and used to rule her life. That's why she never married. As a result she still suffers from low self-esteem. Or, at least that's what she's been told it is. She had to nurse him when he was ill and nothing was ever good enough for him. Then she had to nurse her mother, although she wasn't quite so bad. When her mother died it was too late for Verity to make much of a life for herself, which was a terrible shame.

'I got to know her when I moved into the cottage next door to her a few years ago and I try to look out for her. If she's pushed too hard she lets out her pent-up rage, but she's seen a counsellor to try to deal with her anger issues and she's been a lot better recently. However, I think the pressure of working at the library and being scared of Malcolm and finding herself the butt of people's jokes has set her back again.'

'Did Don upset her?' Sallie asked bluntly.

Eileen hesitated. 'I think he was beginning to get to her. I was going to tell him to back off and leave her alone, because he didn't intimidate me. But as soon as he got back from Spain…' Eileen stopped talking abruptly when she saw that a customer had come in and was waiting by the table at the door. She got up to go.

'It's all right, stay and drink your coffee while I serve this lady.'

'No, I can see you're busy and I've got shopping to do anyway.'

After Eileen had left the shed and Sallie had served the customer, the morning seemed to drag, although she kept finding herself jobs to do, just as she used to when she was employed at the village library.

She was about to have another cup of coffee when Alicia came into the shed. Her eyes were red and she was blowing her nose.

'Hello, Alicia. How are you? You look a bit upset.'

Alicia sank wearily into a chair. 'Oh, I'm all right, really. I'm just dreading going into the library to do my shift. I hardly slept last night. I'm so worried. I'm afraid I've done something really stupid and I'm going to be in big trouble.' She burst into tears.

'Oh, Alicia! Don't cry. I'm sure it's nothing that can't be sorted out. Why don't you tell me all about it?'

Sallie sat at the table, opposite her. Alicia stopped crying and dabbed at her eyes. 'I can't tell you about it. I can't tell anyone what I've done. I'm sorry.'

'Well, have a cup of coffee and let's talk about something else,' Sallie said, going to fetch the coffee pot.

'No, you're very kind, but I think I'd better go.' Alicia got up from the table and as she left the shed, Sallie could tell she was crying again.

*

Jo was sitting on a settee next to Louise in one of her immaculate reception rooms, which was decorated in pinks and creams and had a luxurious beige carpet. Everywhere was spotless so Tracy was obviously doing a good job, she thought.

A middle-aged man in a grey suit with a bald head and a long, thin, clever-looking face was sitting on one side of the fireplace facing them and a younger woman in a black dress and jacket, with her long blonde hair worn loose, was sitting in the chair on the other side.

'Now, Mrs Bainbridge, when my colleagues came to inform you that your husband had been found dead in the village library you were obviously very shocked and you were not well enough to answer many questions. Because some time has elapsed and we hope you're now feeling stronger we wanted to speak to you again to see if you can add anything to your original statement,' the male detective said.

'I see,' Louise said in a faint voice.

'I believe you told my colleagues you'd been out for a meal with your husband on the evening of Sunday, June the eighth.'

'Yes, that's right.'

'I understand you said you'd come home from the restaurant in a taxi.'

'That's correct.'

'Can you remember what time it was?'

'No, not exactly.'

'Can you give us an approximate time?'

'Well, it was probably about 10.30, or it may have been a bit earlier, I'm not sure. We'd been having such a lovely evening, I never looked at my watch.'

'That's okay. We can check with the taxi firm that picked you up from the restaurant. I believe you told my colleagues you'd been to the Feathers at Broadfield.

'Yes, that's right. We were celebrating because Don had just got back from Spain. We were finally going to see some progress with the villa we're having built. He'd been to visit the site.'

'Had either of you had a lot to drink?'

'What a strange question! We'd been out for a meal celebrating. We'd had some drinks, but not a lot, in my opinion.'

Jo intervened. 'I saw them both earlier in the pub in the village and they didn't even get chance to finish their drinks there before the taxi arrived to take them to the restaurant.'

'Okay, thank you, Mrs Pudsey,' the woman detective said, speaking for the first time. Jo thought she was warning her not to butt in again.

'All I'm really trying to establish is whether you would be in a state to remember everything your husband said. For example, while you were coming home in the taxi and when you first got back to the house, did he mention going to the library to meet someone for instance?'

'No, he never said anything about going to the library.'

'What did you talk about in the taxi?'

'I seem to remember we were saying how much we'd enjoyed the meal. He said how much he'd missed me while he was in Spain. He said he was glad to have sorted things out with the villa company and to be home and able to deal with his businesses again.'

'What happened when you got home?'

'Nothing really.'

'Well, did you sit and have a cup of tea for example.'

'No, we didn't.'

'What did you talk about?'

'Nothing. We just went straight to bed.'

'So you entered the house in silence, walked upstairs in silence and got into bed together in silence,' the detective said with a hint of sarcasm in his voice.

Louise burst into tears and Jo reached out and held her hand sympathetically.

'I'm sorry, Mrs Bainbridge, but you must remember something he said to you before you turned the lights out.'

'No, I don't.

'Why not?'

'Well, whatever he may have said, it was nothing that you need to know about.'

'Allow me to be the judge of that.'

'But it's private,' Louise said blushing.

'You can still tell us about it.'

'It's too embarrassing.'

'What's so embarrassing about it?'

'Oh, I'm sure you won't understand.'

'Let me be the judge of that. You can tell me anything.'

'It's all very personal, but if you insist, I'll try to explain. I remember we were both so happy that evening. We kissed in the hall as soon as we'd closed the front door. Then, we both knew what we wanted to happen next. After all, we've been married long enough. We went straight upstairs, undressed, and got into bed and made love. Now do you understand why I was embarrassed to tell you about it?' Louise began to cry again.

*

'So, the next day, when Louise woke up, she says she reached her hand out to touch him and realised he wasn't there. She said she wasn't worried about it, because Don often got up early and went down to his study to work, so she just went back to sleep. The next thing she knew, Tracy was knocking on the bedroom door telling her the police were downstairs waiting to speak to her.' Jo was bringing Sallie up to date over a cup of tea in her kitchen later that day after they had closed the shed library.

'Well, well, well!' Sallie said.

'But it's ever so sad. They were so happy that night and now she's on her own. She swore me to secrecy about what she told the police and I'm not even going to tell Tom about it, but I thought it only fair to tell you. But you mustn't pass it on to anyone else. She was embarrassed about it.'

'I promise I won't mention it to anyone. Poor Louise. It's not something you want to talk about with someone you've never met before.'

'She said afterwards she thought she had shocked the detective. She said she was sure he would have thought that people of their age didn't behave like that. But I didn't like to tell her he'd probably heard all sorts over the years and that nothing would surprise him. He asked her a few more questions afterwards but she still couldn't shed any light on why Don went to the library the next morning, or who he might have met there.'

'He must have been meeting one of the other volunteers. Who else would be there with him so early in the morning?'

'You're probably right, but I don't know how we'll ever find out who it was.'

'Eileen came in while you were round at Louise's house. She was on her own because Verity didn't feel like coming out today. She admitted that Don used to make Verity the butt of his jokes and upset her. She said she had been planning to stand up to him and tell him to leave Verity alone. Also, the day before, Verity was keen to point the finger at George, even though she'd been told not to gossip about the library. It has made me wonder whether Verity thinks Eileen met Don in the library and had a go at him and perhaps caused his heart attack. That could have been why she wanted to implicate someone else as a distraction.'

'Maybe, but I can't imagine Eileen getting into a scuffle with Don! She's an old lady.'

'I know, but if he had some weakness, he might have just keeled over.'

'Well how did he end up sitting on a chair in the kitchen?'

'Perhaps he dragged himself there after she'd left.'

'I suppose he might have done,' Jo said doubtfully

'Also, Alicia came in crying and said she was very worried because she had done something stupid, but she said she couldn't tell me what it was. She was obviously frightened about something. It seems to me we've got too many suspects now!'

Jo laughed. 'Yes, and don't forget, there's also Joyce who used to be engaged to him but has been ignored and humiliated by him.'

'And there's Deirdre who had an affair with him and still has a key to the library. She might have asked him to meet her there early, before the library opened. She could have turned on him and lashed out at him if he knocked her back again.'

'That's without Sandra thinking she might have finished him off by having sex with him on the floor. I find it quite shocking to think of them at it late at night next to Large Print.'

'Who mentioned Large Print?'

'Well, no one, but I've been thinking about it, and the only part of the floor where there would be enough room is next to the Large Print section.'

'You're seriously weird! But, anyway, it seems unlikely that they were at it again the night before he died, in the light of what Louise told the police this morning, so at least Sandra's off the hook.'

'That's true.'

Sallie helped herself to another biscuit. 'So, who do we have left?'

'There's just Malcolm Bray, George and Rory.'

'Actually, I've been thinking about Rory. We need to talk to him again. He seemed very keen to talk about Be Careful What You Wish For and the fake body parts in the pub yesterday. But actually we need to ask him why he gave us the impression he knows no one round here, when he was born and brought up in a village just over the border in Nottinghamshire. He definitely told us he came to live in South Yorkshire simply because he'd seen a house in a magazine that he liked. But he must have wanted to be near his cousins and his old friends as well. And I've had another thought. He blames the deaths of both his parents on the fact his father went out of business. Somebody opened a shop in competition with his father, he said. And who do we know who has opened lots of his convenience stores in villages near here?'

'Don Bainbridge! But it would be a bit of a coincidence if Rory had joined the library volunteers and then recognised him as the man who'd put his father out of business.'

'Not if Rory had already found out where Don lived and that's why he bought a house here.'

'We'll have to see what he has to say about it.'

'Also, he once told us he didn't talk to Don much, but Deirdre said a few days ago that although he didn't talk to the women much, he would happily chat to George and always made a point of having a word with Don when he came in.'

'That's right.'

'Why don't we go for a drink in the pub tonight? If he comes in we can somehow try to work the conversation round to his house purchase to give him the chance to explain himself. Also, we can ask him again about how well he knew Don while they were both working at the library. If he still says he hardly ever spoke to him we can tell him what Deirdre said and ask him if it's true.'

'What a good idea.'

*

After spending a quiet afternoon pottering in the garden and thinking about all the people she had spoken to about Don's death, Sallie went upstairs to get ready for an evening in the pub. She put on a smart skirt and top and made her face up carefully.

'I'm out boozing again tonight, Des,' she told the cat cheerfully when she heard Jo knock at the door.

They walked down the hill to the pub discussing interview tactics. When they got there they saw a little old man sitting on a bench outside while his dog drank from a bowl of water.

'Aye up, Charlie, it's Cagney and Lacey,' he said to the dog as they went past.

Jo stopped in the doorway of the pub. 'Who are they?' she asked the old man.

'Ignore him. They were on the telly years ago but they weren't as good looking as us,' Sallie said, ducking under the low beam above the doorway as usual.

They entered the side bar but found it was empty. Frank served them with their usual order and they went to sit at a table together.

'If Rory doesn't come in soon we'd better go round to his house and see if he's in. We can't sit here drinking all night in a deserted bar,' Jo said.

'Good idea. Let's give him half an hour and if he doesn't turn up, we'll go and see him at home,' Sallie said.

They made their drinks last while they talked about the shed library. After half an hour they got up to go to Rory's house.

They crunched their way down the gravel drive again and rang the doorbell of the Old Manor House.

Rory came to the door quickly. 'Oh, hi!' he said, surprised to see them.

'Sorry to turn up uninvited but there are a couple of things we wanted to ask you,' Sallie said.

'Then you'd better come in,' Rory said cheerfully.

He led them into the sitting room overlooking the garden and Jo and Sallie once again sat on one settee, facing Rory on the opposite settee.

'We were talking to Emma the other day and she said you had told her you were born and brought up in a village near here and you still had family and friends living there,' Sallie said.

'Yes, that's right.'

'But we formed the impression that you had no family and that your friends were all in London.'

'I have three cousins in the area but they are all older than me and married with families. I have a couple of old school friends as well that I'm planning to get back in touch with, but I'm sure they're probably all busy with jobs and wives and kids as well.'

'You also gave us the impression you didn't have much to do with Don, but we remembered our friend, Deirdre, who was a library volunteer for a while, mentioned that you used to chat to him whenever he came into the library.'

Rory's face changed. 'Did she? Well I suppose I must have done then.'

'Did you like Don?'

'Not particularly, no.'

'Well, then why did you make a point of talking to him?'

'I've told you before, I wanted to get to know people.'

'When you lived in Nottinghamshire before, when you were still living at home with your parents, did you ever meet any of the current library volunteers in your village?'

'No.'

'So it wasn't Don who set up a shop in your village years ago that put your Dad out of business?'

Rory took a deep breath. 'All right, I might as well tell you the truth. Yes, Don did set up one of his convenience stores in our village.'

'And your father ran a grocer's shop, didn't he?'

'Yes, but his shop was more of a delicatessen. He stocked a wide range of cheeses and cold meats. He gave people good, old-fashioned service and would order things in for them specially.'

'And his business was badly affected after Don set up his shop?'

'Yes, Don undercut him on everything and took trade away from him.'

'How did you feel about that?'

'Well, I didn't really understand how serious it was at the time. But it forced my Dad out of business and he was so ashamed of being short of money after having to close up and sell the shop that he became ill.'

'In what way did he become ill?'

'He started to suffer from depression. I'm sorry to say that he ended up taking his own life.'

'Oh, Rory, I'm so sorry. Did you blame Don for what happened?' Jo asked.

'Yes, I did at the time. Don deliberately undercut my father so most of his customers deserted him to shop at Don's convenience store. But I've realised now he would probably have said it was just good business, if anyone had asked him about it.'

'You must have been devastated when your father killed himself.'

'Yes I was, but it also affected my mother badly. She became ill and died herself about a year later. In effect, Don robbed me of both my parents.'

‘Is that why you moved back up here?’ Sallie asked.

‘No, I told you I moved here to buy this house and make a new life for myself. But it was also nice to be close to the area where I grew up and where my few remaining family members live.’

‘Did you know that Don was living in Upper Mickle?’

‘Honestly, I never knew where he was from when he set up shop in our village. But of course when I joined the library volunteers here I went to a meeting and recognised him straight away. He didn’t seem to know me. I was only a teenager at the time he set up in opposition to my father. Look, Sallie, I can see where all this is going. So I’ll tell you what you want to know. I still bore Don a grudge and was angry that he didn’t even remember me, despite putting my father out of business and causing the early deaths of both my parents.

‘But I’ll answer the question you clearly want to ask. No, I didn’t kill him. I was planning to confront him and tell him what he’d done to my family. I wanted to see if he showed any remorse at all. But I never got the chance to have my showdown with him because someone else got to him first.’

As Sallie and Jo made their way back down the drive of Rory’s house, Jo glanced over her shoulder. ‘Is he watching us leave?’ Sallie asked, making a conscious effort to stop herself from turning round to look back as well.

‘Yes, he’s still standing in the doorway and he looks worried.’

CHAPTER TWENTY-TWO

'Oh, brilliant,' Jo said on Friday morning, as she was checking the shed library's email account. 'A couple of those duplicate books we listed online have sold.'

'Excellent. Every penny helps,' Sallie replied. They spent the next half hour happily wrapping the books and attaching address labels to the packages, pleased that their idea for raising funds for the shed library was already paying off.

While they were working, they discussed their visit to Rory's house the night before.

'I think he was being honest when he said he was waiting to see if Don recognised him as the son of the man he'd driven out of business,' Jo said.

'But Don wasn't exactly the sensitive sort, was he? It was all just business to him and after he moved on to the next village and the next convenience store he probably never thought about Rory's family again.'

'Rory has said pretty much the same as the other volunteers. He didn't particularly like Don and he had a grievance against him, but he hadn't had chance yet to have his say. Someone else got there first,' Jo said.

Sallie offered to walk down to the Post Office in the village to post the books, leaving Jo sitting outside the shed, painting designs on more terracotta plant pots for her cuttings that she was planning to sell in aid of the library.

Even though the sky was overcast, it was still very warm and humid as Sallie walked along with her books. When she got to the village library she saw Tracy in her leggings and baggy tee shirt about to get in her car in the parking area at the front.

Sallie stopped and called across to her. 'Hi there, Tracy, how's Louise doing?'

Tracy closed the car door and came over to talk to her.

'She's better, I think. She's obviously still upset and sheds a few tears occasionally, but she's looking after herself now, getting dressed properly and doing her hair. She's eating better as well. It's just such a shame that she has no family because she's completely alone in the world now.'

'Poor Louise, it must be terrible to lose your husband and have no children to comfort you. It was always just the two of them, wasn't it? They must have been a very close couple.'

Tracy pulled a face. 'Well, they weren't exactly love's young dream. They had their ups and downs. You couldn't tell what was going on with them sometimes. She'd be grumbling about him one moment and lovey dovey with him the next. But that's marriage, I suppose. What would I know about it, never having had a husband?'

'I thought I might go and see her again, if you think she's up to it.'

'Yes, I think visitors would do her good now. I think she'll be all right once everything's settled, you know, the funeral and the money side and everything.'

'She'll still miss him dreadfully though.'

'Yes, I'm sure she will, but they didn't live in each other's pockets when he was alive and well. She had her own life. You know, shopping, ladies' lunches, the gym, the hairdresser, and so on. Meanwhile he looked after the business and made the money.'

'The last time I saw them together Louise seemed very devoted to him.'

'Devoted? Yes, I suppose she was, but more to his money, than to him, I'd say. She liked nice things and having the money to buy whatever she wanted '

'Tracy!'

'Oh, I'm sorry. Don't listen to me. I'm probably cynical because I've never had a bloke who's stayed around long enough for me to know what it's like to be part of a couple. I do like Louise, you know. She's always been very good to me, so I want her to be all right. I'm sure she'll get over it in time.'

Tracy laughed suddenly. 'Anyway, at least she can have whatever tiles she wants in the Spanish villa now.'

'Why, was there a problem over the tiles?'

'Oh yes! The tiles would have probably caused a big row between them. The day he was due to come back from Spain, Louise had a phone call from the villa company. I wasn't listening on purpose but she started shouting down the phone so I couldn't help but hear what she was saying. She shouted: "Green tiles, of course I haven't picked green tiles. I haven't picked any tiles for the bathrooms yet".

'She listened and then said: "What do you mean you were there when I chose them? I've never looked at any tiles".

'Then a bit later she asked them to describe her. When she heard what they said at the other end she said: "You've obviously got me mixed up with someone else." She slammed the phone down and I could tell she was furious. I thought, oh dear, Don will be in big trouble when he gets home, for not having sorted this out.

'But then a couple of hours after the phone call she started getting ready to go out for dinner with him and went to no end of trouble to look nice. She put on a new outfit and made herself up really well and she looked lovely.'

'Yes. I saw them in the pub together before they went to the restaurant and she looked fabulous.'

'Well, that's what she's like. She's the sort of person whose mood can change really quickly.'

At that moment Clive came round to the front garden from the back of the library with a rake in his hand and gave Sallie a friendly wave.

'He seems to have calmed down a lot. He's much more like his old self now,' Sallie remarked.

'Oh, he was always all right really. He's another one who manages to be on the right side financially, lucky so and so.'

'What do you mean?'

'Well, he told me the other day that someone was slipping him a bit of cash to keep having his little tantrums when he was working here. Apparently they wanted to scare off the old dears so the library would have to close because there weren't enough people working here to keep it open.'

'Did he say who was paying him?'

'No, I asked him, of course, but he wouldn't tell me who it was. I also asked him if he'd left the bone and finger and eyeball in the library but he said it had nothing to do with him. But I must say, whoever was paying him could have kept their money because I think the library will close anyway. The way some of the volunteers treat the customers, they won't have any left soon. I wanted the volunteers to be a success so I could keep my job here, but even I'm prepared to admit they aren't running the library as well as you and Jo used to do.'

'Thank you for saying that, Tracy.' Sallie was surprised and touched by her honesty.

'Anyway, I can't stay around here gossiping any longer, I'd better get home to see what the kids are getting up to with Julie.' She gave Sallie a friendly smile, climbed into the driver's seat of her smart red car and started the engine. She drove out of the car park and in the direction of her home on the outskirts of the village.

After posting the books, Sallie toiled uphill again thinking about everything Tracy had told her. If it was all true and someone had been paying Clive to have his outbursts, it made things even more complicated. It was obviously someone who wanted the volunteer-run library to fail, but was it the same person who had played the practical jokes, or someone else entirely?

The only person she knew who had admitted he wouldn't mind if the library closed, was George.

She was convinced Don must have had a reason for being in the library that morning and the only person likely to be able to shed light on that reason was Louise. It was vital to see Louise now and get some of her questions answered.

When Sallie arrived back at the shed library she told Jo all about her conversation with Tracy.

'Who do you think wore the trousers in the marriage? Louise or Don?' she asked after she had finished.

'Louise,' Jo answered, without a moment's hesitation.

'Exactly, so if Don had arranged to meet someone early in the morning in the library, you would think Louise would have known about it.'

'Yes, but she told the police she didn't know why Don was in the library.'

'But I'm not sure they asked her the right questions. I think it's time I went to see her and asked her about it myself.'

'I'm not sure Emma would approve of you going round there asking questions when she's in such a vulnerable state.'

'But it's really frustrating not to be able to talk to her. I need to get answers.'

'Why don't you wait here and talk to Tom about it this afternoon? He's coming over after he's finished his shift.'

'No, I don't want to wait till then. I'll go round after we've closed.'

'Why is it so important to talk to Louise today?'

Sallie didn't want to say she was looking for a new development in the case so she could write about it for next week's newspaper. 'I'm conscious we haven't been to see Louise for a few days and Tracy was saying she thought Louise would be glad to have visitors now. I don't want her to think we've abandoned her.'

Jo suddenly sat up straight, staring open mouthed at Sallie. 'Oh my God! The wrong trousers!'

'What do you mean?'

'You asked me who wore the trousers, Don, or Louise?'

'Yes, and you said you thought it was Louise.'

'Don't you see? He was wearing a suit when Sandra Thompson discovered him on that chair in the kitchen. He was also wearing a smart suit when he came into the pub before they went for the meal at the posh restaurant.'

'Yes, I see. You're thinking it was unlikely he got up and put a suit on the next morning as well.'

'He was more of a jeans and polo shirt sort of bloke. He wouldn't have bothered putting a suit on just to go and meet someone in the library.'

'So he must have gone there late at night, still wearing his smart suit.'

'Yes, but surely not to have sex with Sandra Thompson, not after he'd made love to Louise?'

'Well, he could have got out of bed when Louise was asleep and put his suit back on, rather than disturb her looking for other clothes. What kind of man must he have been to do that? It's disgusting!''

'I know. It doesn't bear thinking about. I'm still finding it shocking that two of the volunteers were meeting up to have sex in the library. At least, when we locked up at night, we knew no one would let themselves in later. It just shows how dangerous it is to give all the volunteers a key.'

'Yes, you're right,' Sallie agreed absently. 'Anyway, I've just been thinking. Suppose they had a row, or something, and he went off to Mickleton for a drink and ran into Sandra there.'

'But Louise would have told the police that he'd gone off on his own after they got home.'

'Perhaps she was too embarrassed to admit it to them. Also, it's occurred to me that although Louise said she didn't know why he was in the library so early in the morning, she may have known what his plans were for later in the day. That might tell us something. You see, that detective didn't ask her the right questions. I'm sure if I go round to see her this afternoon, I'll be able to find out more.'

'All right. But just don't let on that you know what she said to the detective about how their evening ended. She swore me to secrecy about it!'

*

After they closed the shed library at one pm, Sallie went straight down the hill to the village to call on Louise.

Jo said she would wait at home until Tom arrived and tell him what she and Sallie had been discussing. She would ask if he had heard whether the police thought it significant that Don had been found dead wearing his suit.

When Sallie got down to the village green, she saw Alicia was sitting on what the villagers had dubbed the 'Bench of Sighs', because it was where people tended to go to sit and think if they had something on their minds. It was positioned in front of a copse of trees and had a view of the village green and the main street.

When she got closer she could see Alicia was sitting staring bleakly into space and looked as though she had been crying again.

'Hello, Alicia,' Sallie said, sitting down next to her. 'Is everything all right?'

'Not really,' Alicia said, dabbing at her eyes with a tissue. 'My parents have had a letter from my old school telling them I never turned up to retake any of my A Levels. My dad is furious with me.'

'Oh dear! But why didn't you go and retake any of your exams?'

'Because there was no point. I knew I wouldn't pass them again. I just get worked up and anxious when I sit exams and then I do badly. Last year, I had to be treated for stress by the doctor while I was taking them, but I failed them all anyway. I didn't want to go through all that again.'

'But surely your parents understand and are sympathetic with you?'

'No, they aren't. My father says I need to get good qualifications if I want to marry someone decent. He says if I don't go to university, no one who has any prospects themselves will want to marry me.'

'Well, I wouldn't say that was entirely true, but I agree with him that it does help to have good qualifications if you want to get a decent job.'

'But that's just it. I know now what I want to do and I don't need any qualifications to do that.'

'Oh, what do you want to do?'

'I want to work in a library like you and Jo.'

'But I thought you didn't like library work.'

'I hate working at the village library because of the other people who volunteer there. In any case they don't know how to do the job properly themselves. But I'd like to help out at the shed library. I think I could learn a lot from you two. I want to apply for a library that's got proper trained staff, not one that's run by volunteers.'

'But Alicia, there's not much of a future working for libraries. They're all either being closed, or having their opening hours cut to save money. I'm afraid it's not a very good career plan for a young woman like you.'

'I'd never really thought about it like that.' Alicia looked crestfallen.

'Also, it's not really true to say you don't need any qualifications to work in a library. You have to be well read. The more you know about the different genres of fiction and about history and languages and travel, the more help you can be to the customers. A lot of people who end up working in a library have done another job first, such as teaching, or nursing, or art and design, which has given them an area of expertise they can bring to the job. Jo used to be an accountant and I used to be a journalist. The more work and life experience you've had the better.'

'Oh, I see,' Alicia said, looking disappointed.

'But there are lots of jobs out there and sometimes you can study while you're working. So, dry your eyes and cheer up. It will all work out eventually for you, I'm sure. I'm going round to see someone now, so I haven't got time to talk to you about this properly, but why don't you come into the shed library one day next week? We'll go on the internet and look at different jobs, see what opportunities there are for training and find out how to apply.'

'Oh, thank you. That would be really helpful.'

'I'll see you next week then. Try not to worry too much. It will be all right in the end, I'm sure.'

CHAPTER TWENTY-THREE

Large drops of rain were beginning to fall from the darkening sky as Sallie hurried along the main street of the village in the direction of Louise's house.

The rain will do the garden good, she thought, but then smiled to herself at the thought of how old and boring she was becoming.

She opened the gate and let herself into the front garden and as she approached the front door she saw Louise through one of the windows holding a length of fabric up to the light and scrutinising it. She was smartly dressed in neat black trousers and a pink and white patterned blouse. Her wavy blonde hair was immaculately styled and she was wearing her usual make-up.

Good, she must be feeling better, Sallie thought, as she rang the front doorbell. Louise smiled when she saw Sallie standing there after she opened the door.

'I spoke to Tracy this morning and she said she thought you might be up to having visitors so I decided to come round. I hope that's all right.'

'Of course it is. Please come in.'

Louise led the way into one of the two front reception rooms. There was a large square polished wood table under the front window with a sewing basket on it. The length of fabric was draped over the back of a chair.

Louise said: 'I was about to begin making some new curtains for the library, but my back has started playing up again. When we've had some tea, would you help me get my sewing machine out of the utility room?'

'Of course I will. I'm so pleased to see you looking better.'

'Well, I had to get back to some kind of normality eventually. I still get upset every now and then, but it doesn't do me any good. Whatever I say, whatever I do, it won't bring Don back, will it?'

'No, I'm afraid it won't. I'm so sorry, Louise, for your loss.'

'It still doesn't seem real. I knew he had a bad heart, of course, but he was always so full of life and energy. I suppose I expected him to live forever.' She gave a little laugh, but it turned into a sob.

'Oh, Louise! I'm so sorry.'

'I'll go and make some tea for us. You sit down and make yourself comfortable.'

Sallie settled back on one of the cream sofas and looked around the room appreciatively. There was a large vase of lilies standing in the hearth in front of the wood burner, which had probably not been used for weeks because of the hot weather. There were three, silver-framed photographs of Don and Louise displayed on a highly polished antique side table. She looked down admiringly at the thick, beige carpet, which was pristine.

Tracy was obviously a lot more thorough with her cleaning here than she had ever been at the library, Sallie thought.

Louise came back in with a tray of tea and set it down on another highly polished side table and poured Sallie a cup.

She poured one for herself and sat down on the settee opposite. Outside, the sky had turned darker and Sallie could hear rain hitting the multi-paned Georgian windows.

'Tracy has been very concerned about you. I could tell she was relieved that you have started to feel better,' Sallie said, after taking a sip of tea.

'Yes, Tracy has a good heart, I have to say, despite all her funny, little ways.'

'While I was talking to her this morning, Clive came round to the front of the library. He was behaving much more calmly today and was more like his old self. I mentioned this to Tracy and she says he has been okay all the while really and that he kept pretending to have outbursts in front of the volunteers because someone has been paying him to try to scare them off.'

Louise didn't seem surprised at all. She said. 'Well, the story is that his great-grandmother, or great, great-grandmother was murdered by her husband and then chopped up into small pieces. Her body parts were buried in the garden behind the library in an old tin trunk and the husband told everyone she had left him. When the man died, the house was sold and the new owners discovered the trunk while they were working on the garden.'

'Yes, I've heard the story many times before. But Clive apparently told the volunteers that the library was haunted by the ghost of the victim.'

‘I know. He must have been trying to frighten the knit and stitch ladies.’

‘But who would pay him to do that, and why?’

Louise just smiled. ‘I’ve absolutely no idea, Sallie.’

‘Tracy said Clive had denied being responsible for the practical jokes, so they must have been the work of someone else.’

‘Oh, you’re not still worrying about that, are you?’

Sallie took a deep breath. ‘Do you think Don knew who the practical joker was?’

Louise put her cup and saucer down on the small table in front of her. ‘It’s quite possible. Don usually knew what was going on in the village.’

‘Did he ever tell you who he thought was responsible?’

‘No, he didn’t. And anyway, why are you bothered about it now? What does any of it matter?’

‘To begin with we wanted to find out who was responsible so people wouldn’t blame us for playing tricks on the volunteers. But now it’s become a lot more serious than that because someone caused Don’s death in the library.’

‘But unmasking the practical joker won’t help me, will it? It won’t bring Don back and I will still have to get through the rest of my life on my own.’

‘I know, but it’s important you get to know the truth. How could you carry on living here, if you knew Don’s killer is almost certainly someone from the village?’

'Well, maybe I won't stay here much longer. Once the funeral is over and the will is settled there will be nothing to keep me here. I might go and live abroad.'

'Of course, you have the villa in Spain. You could go there whenever you want to.'

'No, I wasn't thinking of going there. That was Don's dream, not mine. Once it's finished I'm going to sell it.'

'Tracy was telling me this morning about your problem with the tiles.'

Louise stayed very still, her teacup poised a few inches from her mouth as she had been about to take a sip.

'What problem with the tiles?' Louise asked, putting her cup down carefully.

'She said you had a call from the villa company about the tiles you had chosen for the bathroom, but you told them you hadn't chosen any tiles yet.'

'It sounds like Tracy has been eavesdropping on my phone calls.'

'I don't think she intended to, but she said she couldn't help but hear what you said because you were shouting down the phone and at one point you asked them to describe the person they claimed was you.'

'Oh that! Yes, I remember the phone call now. They'd obviously got me mixed up with someone else.'

'Tracy said it was the day Don returned from Spain. I'm glad you didn't let it spoil your evening out together. I saw you both in the pub before you went to the restaurant and you looked fabulous and very happy to have him back.'

'But then the next day he was found dead.'

'Oh, Louise, I'm sorry. I shouldn't have mentioned your last evening together. It was very tactless of me.'

There was a brief silence and Sallie could hear the rain lashing against the window.

Louise picked up her tea cup again. 'So, Tracy was telling you all about the tiles at the villa, was she? What else did she tell you?'

'Nothing really. We were mainly talking about Clive being paid by someone to have his little tantrums to upset the volunteers. I'd like to know who was paying him and if it is the same person who was planting the joke items in the library.'

'I still don't understand why you're so interested in finding out.'

'I suppose it's because I hate unsolved mysteries. It must be because of my journalism training.'

'Oh yes, I'd forgotten you used to be a journalist,' Louise said vaguely.

Sallie took another sip of her tea while she thought about what to say next. 'There was a time when I even wondered whether it was Don playing tricks on the other volunteers,' she said, trying to sound casual. 'People have told me he had a quirky sense of humour. Also, after he went to Spain there weren't any more incidents at the library.'

Louise chuckled. 'You could say he had a quirky sense of humour. I might say he was a bit childish. He loved whoopee cushions and had a gadget you hold in the palm of your hand before you shake hands with someone so they get a sort of electric shock. He thought that type of thing was hilariously funny and was always buying stuff on the internet.'

'So, are you saying Don was the person responsible for playing the practical jokes at the library?'

'Well, of course it was Don! Who else would it be? But it was all harmless fun really. I didn't know about him paying Clive to kick off, but I certainly wouldn't put it past him. He wanted people to drop out so the library had to close. He thought the building would be easy to convert into another one of his convenience stores and that it was in an ideal location in the village.'

'But he might not have been able to get planning permission.'

'Oh, he knew how those sorts of things worked and he would have been able to find plenty of people to support his application by giving them the right kind of encouragement. He'd done it plenty of times before in other locations. He was a good businessman, you know.'

'But what was the point of doing all that if he was planning to go and live in Spain?'

'Money, of course. He would have got it all started up and then put a manager in to run it for him. Once everything was going smoothly he would go abroad and leave it to be run by his staff while he collected all the profits. He could still be in overall control whether he was living in Spain, or here.'

Sallie said: 'It's a shame you didn't get Don to admit what he was up to when people were pointing the finger at me and Jo.'

'Oh, I learnt a long while ago not to get involved in Don's business dealings. But I remember telling you both I knew it wasn't you two and not to worry about it. I told you all the sensible people would know it wasn't you two.'

'I never realised you were being so supportive because you knew who was really responsible. But what I still find puzzling is that the police are working on the theory that Don had a heart attack after he had been involved in a struggle with the practical joker in the library.'

'Are they? I didn't know that.'

'But I understood from Emma it was you who told her that was the theory the police were working on. Why didn't you tell them that Don was the practical joker himself so that they didn't waste their time?'

Louise was silent for a moment. 'It seems that a lot of gossiping has been going on behind my back and people have been getting hold of the wrong end of the stick.'

She got up from the settee. 'You won't want to walk home in this downpour and your tea must have gone cold by now, so why don't I open a bottle of wine for us instead? While I'm doing it you could perhaps get my sewing machine out for me. I'll show you where it's kept in the utility room.'

Sallie followed her across the hall to the utility room and lifted the sewing machine carefully out of the cupboard and carried it into the sitting room. She set it down on the wooden table next to Louise's sewing things. The rain was still coming down heavily and there was a distant rumble of thunder, which persuaded her that she would be much better off staying and having a glass of wine with Louise while she waited for the weather to improve.

Louise came back carrying two glasses of wine and put one in front of Sallie on the table nearest to her.

'Thanks, Louise,' Sallie said, raising the glass to take a sip. She coughed. The wine tasted foul, like she imagined nail varnish remover would taste, so she put it back down on the table. She wondered how she would be able to drink it. To just leave it would seem rude, but she never drank bad wine just for the sake of it.

'It's one of the wines stocked by Don's shops,' Louise said. 'It was his favourite so he would often bring home a few boxes for us.'

'So, where do you think you will go if you do decide to live abroad?'

'Oh, I haven't really thought about it properly yet, but maybe the south of France.'

'Are you imagining yourself living in an old French farmhouse?'

'No, I was thinking more of an apartment that is easy to maintain in a fashionable area where I would be able to have a good social life.'

'That sounds like a good plan.'

Louise took a sip of her wine and leant back against the cushions. 'So much has happened over the last few days it's difficult for me to remember exactly who said what to who and when they said it.

'I do seem to recall the police saying they thought Don had been involved in a struggle with someone in the library that had led to him having a heart attack and that maybe it was the practical joker, but they didn't go into any details. Whatever happened that morning, he's dead and that's that. Now, drink your wine and let's talk about something else.'

Sallie obediently took another sip of wine. The rain was still hammering down outside and she wouldn't be going anywhere for a while, so she decided to try to find out as much as she could.

'Did you know that Don nearly got engaged to Joyce Ferrier years ago?'

'That dried-up old spinster? Yes, I did know. Don told me her parents didn't think he was good enough for her and made her break it off with him. He said that was the turning point in his life, when he became determined to become rich and successful and he never looked back. He started a business and kept expanding until he made more money than her stuck-up parents could ever have dreamed of.'

'How did you meet Don?' Sallie asked interestedly.

'My father got to know him through doing business with him and was very impressed with his ability. I was living back at home at the time after giving up my job at the hospital. He introduced us to each other and I was immediately attracted to him. Daddy offered to put money into Don's business because he could see his potential and thought it would be a good investment. Don proposed to me a few weeks later and we got married quite quickly.'

'And were you happy ever after?'

'I suppose so, whatever happiness is. I've always had the money to do whatever I want to do and to buy whatever I decide I need. The only disappointment was that we never had any children. I would have liked at least one child. That would have been enough for me. I was an only child myself and was perfectly happy not to have a brother or sister. But we couldn't even manage one,' Louise said regretfully and then took a large gulp of her wine. 'Excuse me a minute, Sallie, but I have to nip to the little girls' room. I'll be back in a second.'

While Louise was out of the room, Sallie looked round to see if there was a way of getting rid of some of her wine. There was an aloe vera plant in a grey ceramic pot on top of a small chest of drawers by the window. She poured all but the last half inch of her wine into the top of the plant pot and sat down again where she had been sitting before.

When Louise came back into the room, she lifted Sallie's nearly empty glass from the table. 'Let me get you a top-up and I will try to explain what I've been through.'

She was back in the room in a matter of seconds and put a full glass of wine on the table in front of Sallie.

Sallie took a sip of the wine and put the glass down carefully on the table in front of her again. It tasted no better. It was a cheap Chardonnay that had gone off, she decided.

'When we eventually realised we weren't going to have any children we began to drift apart. He had his life and I had mine. I knew he occasionally had other women but that didn't bother me too much. To be honest, I was glad he lost interest in me in that way. We were reasonably civil to each other and still went out to do things together occasionally. If I ever thought there was a chance he was getting too serious with anyone I would drop a hint about Daddy's big investment in his business.'

'Was Deirdre one of them?' Sallie asked.

'Oh yes, dreary little Deirdre. She didn't last long when I found out about her.'

Sallie took another sip of the dreadful Chardonnay and leant back against the cushions as Louise carried on talking.

'Of course, after Mummy died, Daddy sadly died soon afterwards. Then there was never a threat that Daddy would ask for his money back, so Don was off the hook for a while. But then, Don had his heart scare and needed me to look after him. My nursing training came in very handy and I think he started to appreciate me more. That's when he came up with his plan of having a villa built in Spain and having other people look after his shops while we were enjoying the good life out there on the back of the profits.

'When the village library went over to the volunteers he was surprisingly keen to get involved and do the housebound deliveries with me. It was only later that I worked out that he wanted to buy the building so he could open one of his convenience stores in the village.

'Don made several trips to Spain on his own, supposedly to encourage the builders to get on with things and to sort out some of the problems that cropped up. I didn't realise what was really going on. I just thought he was keen for the builders to make progress with the villa. But during this last trip, while he was supposedly out there cracking the whip, I got that phone call.'

'The one about the green tiles?' Sallie asked.

Louise nodded. 'Yes it was only about the tiles but it gave away what Don was up to. I mean, who in their right minds would choose green tiles for the main bathroom? I would have chosen cream, or a soft pink myself. But, in any case, I knew I hadn't chosen any tiles yet and I didn't think Don would pick any without consulting me. But the silly little man at the villa company insisted I had chosen them and said he had been there when I made my choice and he remembered me well.

'But you knew you hadn't,' Sallie interjected.

'Of course I knew. In fact Don had given me the impression that things were being held up so much that we were a long way away from choosing tiles and colour schemes and that kind of thing.

'The problem was that the main bathroom was very spacious and the villa company couldn't get hold of enough of these green tiles to cover all the walls. The man wanted me to choose another type of tile that they could order in sufficient quantities to do the job. I kept insisting I hadn't chosen any tiles yet but he kept saying he'd been there when

I picked them. So I asked him if he could describe me. He was eager to do so. He said he remembered me well because I was tall, with long dark hair and that I was very attractive.'

'Oh no!' Sallie whispered.

'That's when the penny dropped and I became really angry. It was obvious Don had taken another woman with him to choose the tiles. Later that day when he got back home I tackled him about it.

'I was amazed that he stayed very calm and I could tell he was trying to be really honest with me. He said he had met her in a bar one evening. She was English but she lived and worked in Spain. He said he had fallen in love with her and that she was 'the one'. He explained that he wanted us to have an amicable divorce. I could continue to live here and he would make me a generous monthly allowance. Of course, I was completely shocked. In a matter of a few hours my whole life had been completely turned upside down. All I could manage to say was that I would think about it and then I went upstairs and carried on with getting ready to go out for dinner.

'And that's when I realised I was going to have to kill him.'

CHAPTER TWENTY-FOUR

Jo had abandoned painting plant pots and gone inside before the rain started. She was tidying and cleaning her kitchen when Tom rang the doorbell.

'Are you on your own?' he asked, looking round cautiously.

'Yes, apart from Mutz, that is. Sallie went a couple of hours ago.'

He wrapped his arms around her and pulled her towards him for a long kiss. Then he stroked her hair with one hand and caressed her back with the other, his face buried in her neck.

'She's gone to see Louise to ask her a few questions about Don,' Jo added.

Tom slowly let his arms drop and took a step back from her. 'Oh dear, I had high hopes for this afternoon,' he said. 'I wish you hadn't told me that.'

'She said she was going to be very tactful. She knows how vulnerable Louise is at the moment.'

Tom hesitated a moment. 'Look this is only for you to know, so don't tell anyone else about it, please. I was talking to the DI in charge of the investigation into Don's death this morning and he said Louise is their main suspect. They still don't know exactly how Don died but she has no alibi for the time of Don's death and she inherits all his money and businesses.'

Jo was appalled. 'I don't believe Louise would ever hurt anyone, let alone her own husband!'

'Well, you're wrong there. They've been doing a bit of digging into her past and apparently Louise left her job in nursing after she'd given an injection to a patient who then died. She was suspended while they held an inquiry. Nothing was ever proved against her, but she decided against going back to her job anyway.'

'But it still doesn't mean she would kill her own husband.'

'No, I agree. But she does stand to inherit a lot of money. The detectives are going to take their time and see if they can build a case against her. Sallie could ruin everything by going round there asking questions now. Grab a jacket because it's raining .We'd better drive there fast and make up some excuse about why Sallie needs to come back with us straight away. We mustn't do anything to let Louise know that she's a suspect.'

*

It was as though time stood still for a minute or two and there was silence in Louise's sitting room.

Sallie was confused. 'You're surely not saying you killed Don, are you?' She was beginning to feel hot and uncomfortable and was finding the smell of the lilies in the fireplace overpowering.

'Well, I had to do something. I wasn't going to stand by and watch him go off with another woman after I had devoted so much of my life to him and I certainly wasn't going to let another woman spend my father's money. He would have made me the laughing stock of the village by divorcing me for a younger woman.

'I kept calm and did what I had to do. I had already booked the table at the restaurant and he had agreed to go out for dinner with me. I let him think I was going to be reasonable about things. I put on a gorgeous new dress and plenty of bling. I knew I had to keep up appearances. While I was getting ready I could hear him banging about downstairs. It sounded like he was moving furniture in the utility room. He was obviously already looking for the things he wanted to take with him when he left. That made me even more determined. I planned exactly what I was going to do and so far it has worked out perfectly. Before we went out I told him I would agree to a divorce but that I didn't want anyone else to know about it yet. I suggested we went to the pub for a drink before dinner and he agreed. I wanted the whole village to see how devoted a couple we were and to remember it afterwards.

'At the restaurant I dropped one of my sedatives in his beer while he went to the little boys' room. In the taxi on the way home I could tell he was getting tired and I said it must have been because of his long journey. When we had been dropped off here and the taxi had driven off I suggested we went round to the library and collected the bags of books for the housebound deliveries so that we could have a lie-in the next day. He agreed to this and said he wasn't feeling very well but he thought a walk in the slightly cooler air might do him good. We let ourselves in the back door of the library and I took him straight into the kitchen so we never went anywhere covered by the CCTV. I suggested he sat down in one of the easy chairs while I collected the books. As I had predicted, he quickly fell asleep. I had noticed earlier, because he had been wearing a short-sleeved shirt, that he had two, nasty insect bites just below the inside of his elbow. I had even given him some cream to put on them. He had put on a long sleeved shirt to wear to go out for dinner so I rolled up the sleeves of his jacket and his shirt and used an empty syringe that I had ready in my handbag to inject him through the puncture mark in one of the bites and then I rubbed more of the cream into the bite afterwards and rolled his sleeves down again. He opened his eyes and looked straight into mine while I was doing it but within a minute or so he was dead.'

Sallie gasped. 'How could you kill him in that cold-blooded way just because he said he wanted a divorce?'

'He was going to humiliate me by divorcing me so he could be with another woman. He was planning to live in his Spanish villa with her and leave me here in this village to get by on a monthly allowance. I wasn't prepared to let him have all the money, so he had to die.'

Sallie was conscious her heart was beating fast and she didn't feel well. She tried to get to her feet.

'Sit down, Sallie, and finish your wine.'

'No, thank you, I don't want any more.'

'You might as well finish it. You've been knocking it back all afternoon and there's been one of my sedatives in each glass. If you're unconscious you won't feel a thing,' Louise said, suddenly producing a large syringe from her handbag, which was on the floor at the side of the settee.

Sallie thought desperately about how she could distract Louise. 'Please, just tell me one thing. The book he chose to put the finger in right at the start. Why did he choose that one?'

'What book was it?'

'Be Careful What You Wish For by Jeffrey Archer. Was he trying to send out some sort of message?'

'No. Of course he wasn't! It would have been the first book he picked up. He wasn't very literate, you know. I never remember him sitting down and reading a novel for enjoyment. Look, just finish your wine.'

Sallie knew she had drunk hardly any of the first glass. She got to her feet, grabbed one of the silver-framed photographs of Don and Louise and threw it straight at Louise's head and then ran for the door. She found her way into the kitchen and then ran to a door which she hoped would lead to the outside. She pulled it open but then felt Louise grab her from behind and slam the door shut again. She felt herself being pressed up against the door, hurting her nose. Louise then pulled her hair to make her turn her head. She pushed Sallie's glass of wine up to her lips.

'Now, drink your wine,' she yelled, her normally tranquil grey eyes glittering with anger. 'I'm going to chop you up into little pieces and scatter you all over the library. You won't want to be conscious for that.'

'You're mad!' Sallie screamed. Then she heard the doorbell ring and it gave her hope that help was coming.

'Just tell me one more thing,' she shouted, while Louise was momentarily distracted. 'How did you know that injecting him with an empty syringe would kill him?'

'Because I've done it before and the person died.'

Louise moved away to pull open one of the kitchen drawers. She produced a small black gun which she pointed at Sallie.

'Now, drink it all, unless you want me to shoot you somewhere that will be very painful.' She advanced towards Sallie, pointing the gun at her. Terrified, Sallie raised the glass to her lips with a trembling hand but when Louise got close enough she threw the drink in Louise's face. While Louise was temporarily blinded by the wine, Sallie opened the kitchen door, and ran through a small lobby to another door. She was able to turn the handle to open it and ran out into the rain.

*

Tom and Jo had run out to Tom's car and driven at high speed down the hill to Louise's house. They ran to the front door and rang the doorbell, but as they stood with the rain pouring down on them there was no sound from inside the house. They looked through the windows of the front reception rooms but could see no one.

'Perhaps they're in the kitchen at the back of the house,' Jo suggested.

They hurried down the path on the left side of the house until they came to a door.

It opened suddenly and Sallie came flying out. 'She's got a gun,' Sallie shrieked as soon as she saw them. Tom grabbed Sallie's hand and Jo's and ran back to his car with them. He gave his car keys to Jo. 'Take her home and I'll call for back-up,' he shouted at her.

Jo didn't move. 'Go!' he yelled.

'You're not going in there, are you?'

'Not till I've got back-up. Now please go and let me call it in.'

*

Sallie was still shaking with fear as she sat in the passenger seat of Tom's car on the short drive home.

'Louise told me she was going to kill me,' she said.

'Let's just get you home and you can tell me what happened to you while you were in there,' Jo said.

They got out of Tom's car and went down Sallie's path and stood outside her front door in the pouring rain.

'Oh my God, I've left my handbag at Louise's house. We can't get in,' Sallie wailed.

'It's okay. I'll nip home and get my spare key,' Jo said. 'Just wait here. You're safe now.'

Once Jo had returned with the key, they let themselves into Sallie's cosy sitting room where Des was sleeping peacefully on the settee.

Sallie was still shaking. 'She confessed to me. She admitted that she killed Don. What if she comes after me later and tries to kill me again?'

'I promise you she won't. You can tell me everything she said and I'll tell Tom to report it to the investigating officer. We'll stay the night with you. She won't be able to get anywhere near you with us staying here. But you're soaked to the skin. Why don't you go upstairs and have a hot shower while I make some tea.'

While Sallie was upstairs, Jo hung her wet jacket in the porch and took off her shoes and left them to dry out there.

Sallie came down in fresh jeans and a tee shirt. Her blonde hair was combed into its usual style but was still wet.

She collapsed on to the settee next to a sleepy Des and Jo gave her a cup of hot, strong tea. Jo sat in one of the armchairs facing the settee.

'She offered me a glass of wine but it tasted foul so I poured it into one of her plant pots when she was out of the room. She told me later she had put one of her sedatives in it. If I wasn't such a wine snob, I'd be dead by now.'

'But why did she think you were a threat to her? What happened?' Jo asked.

'I'd been asking questions about Don and eventually I got her to admit he was responsible for playing the tricks on the volunteers at the library. She also said Don was probably responsible for paying Clive to have his little tantrums and to put it about that the library was haunted.'

'But why did he do it?'

'He wanted the volunteers to drop out so the library would fail and he could buy the building and open another of his convenience stores in Upper Mickle.'

'So that's why he got so stroppy with George,' Jo said.

'I pointed out to Louise that she had told Emma the police were working on the theory that Don had suffered a heart attack after confronting the practical joker. I asked her why she hadn't told them it was Don playing the tricks so that they didn't waste their time.'

'The investigating officers didn't say that to her anyway, according to Tom,' Jo said. 'He says Louise is their main suspect. She probably made it up because that's what she wanted people to think and she hoped Emma would tell people so it would spread round the village and people would accept it as true.'

'Well, anyway, she said she wasn't bothered about finding Don's killer. She said she just wanted to get the funeral out of the way and wait for the will to be sorted out and then she was going to go and live abroad.'

'In Spain?' Jo asked.

'No, she said Spain wasn't good enough for her. She's planning to buy an apartment in the south of France.'

'But what made her kill him?' Jo asked.

'She said she'd always known he had affairs and she just let him get on with it. When she thought he was getting too involved in the past she would drop a hint about her father's investment in his business and he would put an end to it. But this time, when he got back from Spain, she said he was different. He said he wanted to be completely honest with her and he told her he'd met someone new. He said this time he'd fallen in love and that it was the real thing and he wanted a divorce.'

'The woman scorned,' Jo said thoughtfully.

'No, the more relevant quote is "the love of money" in this case,' Sallie said. 'She wasn't content to live in a beautiful house on a monthly allowance, she wanted the lot. To think I envied her for having plenty of money because it certainly didn't mean she had a happy marriage. Because of her father's investment in Don's business all those years ago she thought she was entitled to have all the money. That's why she gave me the glass of wine with the sedative in it because she knew she'd told me too much.'

'Could you taste the sedative?' Jo asked.

'No, I just thought it was a cheap Chardonnay that had gone off so I didn't drink much of it and poured it away into a plant pot when she was out the room. But once she got started she told me everything. She put one of her sedatives in his drink at the restaurant when he went to the toilet. Afterwards, she persuaded him to go to the library with her to pick up the bags of books for the housebound customers. She took him into the kitchen where there is no CCTV and sat him down. When he fell asleep she injected him with an empty syringe through the puncture mark on one of his insect bites.'

'The cunning bitch.'

'She gave me another glass of wine with a sedative in it and kept encouraging me to drink it but I still thought it tasted foul. I kept pretending to drink it so she would carry on with her story.

'When she suddenly produced a syringe from her handbag and threatened me, I threw one of her framed photographs at her and ran out of the room. She followed me and grabbed me as I was about to get out of the kitchen and pushed me up against the door. She pulled my head back by the hair and tried to pour the wine down my throat. When I heard the doorbell ring I hoped someone would wonder what was going on and come to investigate. I tried to distract her by asking how she knew that by injecting Don with an empty syringe she would definitely kill him and she said she knew it would work because she'd done it before and the person had died.

'Then she opened a drawer and got out the gun. I really thought that I was going to die,' Sallie said, beginning to cry again.

*

It was a couple of hours before Tom was dropped off outside Sallie's cottage by a police car. Jo went to the door to let him in and when he walked into the room Sallie could tell by his face that something bad had happened.

'I'm sorry I have to give you both some rather distressing news,' he said.

'Why, what's happened now?' Sallie asked, with a sinking feeling.

'I'm afraid that Louise is dead.'

'But she can't be. She was very much alive and well when I left her.'

'She was found dead in the house by armed officers when they gained entry.'

'She shot herself, didn't she? She didn't want to be arrested for murder. It's all my fault. I shouldn't have gone there interfering and making her confess.'

'No, Sallie, not a shot was fired either by her or any of my colleagues. But tell me, while you were there this afternoon, did you notice an electric sewing machine anywhere in the house?'

'Yes, I did. She asked me to get it out of the utility room for her because she said her back was hurting and she wanted to start making some new curtains for the library. I carried it into the room where we were sitting and put it on the table under the window.'

'Honestly, all the volunteers are far more interested in making soft furnishings for the library than having anything to do with the books. It's ridiculous,' Jo said angrily.

Tom ignored her. 'It seems that after you managed to get away from her this afternoon she calmly sat down at the machine to start sewing. But when she switched it on she had an electric shock that killed her. Obviously a proper investigation will have to be carried out but early indications are that someone had sabotaged the sewing machine and left it so that the next time she switched it on it would give her a fatal shock.'

'Well it wasn't me!'

'Of course, it wasn't,' Jo said. 'Thank God she didn't ask you to switch it on for her, or you would have been killed instead. She must have been completely insane to want to sit down and start sewing after the scene you had with her before you managed to get away.'

'I've never been any good at sewing. I don't think I would know how to switch on a sewing machine,' Sallie said.

'Another thing that's saved you, along with not drinking rubbish wine,' Jo said, smiling.

'When I was with her earlier, Louise mentioned to me that while she was getting ready to go out for dinner with Don last Sunday, she heard him moving furniture about in the utility room. She thought he was getting some of his stuff ready to take with him when he left her and she said it made her even more determined to kill him. But actually, what he might have been doing was tampering with the sewing machine so that the next time she switched it on it would kill her.'

'Perhaps he didn't believe she was going to give him an easy divorce and thought he would bump her off and have all the money for himself so he could live a new life out in Spain,' Jo suggested.

'Maybe, that's what happened,' Tom said. 'There will have to be a proper investigation and inquests will be held into both of the deaths, but the indications are that the officers won't be looking for anyone else in connection with the case. You will have to give a statement and tell them what you told me about the sewing machine, Sallie, but after that you will be able to put it all behind you.'

CHAPTER TWENTY-FIVE

Sallie woke up early the next morning and was relieved when she realised that she had slept for at least some of the night. She could remember having a confusing dream but it had been about working in the village library and hadn't involved Louise or Don. She lay in bed feeling weary and depressed. The horrible scene with Louise was in her mind and she could still hardly comprehend the fact that Louise was now dead. Life in this village was never going to be the same again and it all seemed very bleak.

Tom had gone back to Jo's house to sort Mutz out for the night while Jo had made up the bed in Sallie's spare room so they could stay in the cottage with her.

Sallie lay in her bed for a while listening to them moving about downstairs and talking to each other and then she went to the bathroom and had a shower. She didn't feel like getting dressed. After she had dried and styled her hair she put on a fresh pair of pyjamas and a towelling robe and thrust her feet into her slippers.

When she walked into the kitchen Jo, who was already dressed, was sitting at the table eating toast and drinking tea while Tom, wearing an old floral print dressing gown of Sallie's over his boxer shorts, was standing at the stove frying a pan of bacon and a pan of eggs.

'Sallie, how are you? Did you get any sleep?' Jo asked, standing. She poured Sallie a cup of tea and put some toast in front of her.

Tom gave Sallie a plate of bacon and eggs and sat down at the table opposite her. He managed to look serious despite the pink, flowery dressing gown.

He said: 'A full search of the house was made for the gun you said Louise threatened you with, but all they found was a novelty cigarette lighter that looked like a gun in one of the kitchen drawers.'

'That must have been it, then. It was probably another one of Don's silly gadgets. I'll never live it down, will I, claiming to have been threatened by a gun when it was just a joke cigarette lighter?'

'Not at all, Sallie. Any sensible person will be very sympathetic with you. It's a well-known fact that when people in shops and banks are held up by criminals with fake weapons, they feel just as scared as if they were real weapons because they don't know they're not going to die. That's why the police take those sorts of incidents seriously.

'But the officers also found Don's mobile phone in a drawer in the bedroom, hidden under some of Louise's underwear. She must have taken it from him, presumably after she killed him. The officers found texts that indicated he was planning to return to Spain as soon as possible after sorting things out here. Louise would not have wanted the police to know what Don's plans were.'

After they had finished their breakfast, Sallie and Jo sat and had another cup of tea together while Tom went upstairs to get showered and dressed.

Jo said: 'I'm going to have to go home when we've finished breakfast and see to Mutz. Then I'm planning to get dressed up in a pretty frock for the village show this afternoon. You will come to the village show later, won't you Sallie?'

'You've come a long way in a short time, Jo Pudsey, to want to wear a pretty dress rather than your usual jeans. But, I'm sorry, I don't really feel up to going out today. I'm still remembering how I felt when she pointed that gun at me. I'll be laughed at when people find out armed police were called out because I was threatened with a novelty cigarette lighter.'

'I'm sure people won't laugh at you. You heard what Tom just said. People will feel sorry for you. It will do you the world of good to get yourself dressed up and go out for a while. People will be glad to see you and you'll realise how many real friends you have here.'

'Real friends! That's a laugh. I thought Louise was a real friend and it turned out I didn't know her at all. I mean, what must Louise have been thinking when she turned a blind eye to Don's affairs and carried on pretending she had a perfect marriage? She was living in a fantasy world, but I believed everything she told me.'

'Well, it seems she was only with him because of the money. But then again, we'll never really know the truth about their relationship. You can't know what's going on in anyone else's marriage.'

'I always envied her because she never had to worry about money but I wouldn't have wanted to be with someone who was having constant affairs.'

'What made you think Louise might have killed him?'

'Well, I can't take the credit for a brilliant piece of deduction because I didn't realise for ages. But once you reminded me that Sandra had said he was wearing a suit when she found him dead in the chair at the library, it made me start to wonder. He always dressed casually when he was out and about in the village but he was wearing a suit when we saw him in the pub with Louise because he was about to take her out for a meal at a smart restaurant.

'It did make me wonder if he had been killed that night and left in the library in his suit. I thought it was highly unlikely he would have dressed like that again the next morning. Also, if Louise's story had been true and they went to bed together as soon as they got back from the restaurant, wouldn't she have known that he got up and got dressed and went out again? I was sure she knew more than she had told the police. But I must admit I never dreamt how things would turn out after I started asking her questions about it.'

*

After Jo and Tom had gone, Sallie snuggled down on the settee with Des and had another sleep. When she woke up she lay there for a while thinking about things. She was relieved she would never have to face Louise again.

Although it made her feel guilty to be glad someone was dead, it meant she wouldn't be looking over her shoulder every time she went down to the village or into the pub.

She saw it was nearly two o'clock and decided to get ready and go to the village show after all. She did her hair, put on some make-up and dressed in a smart skirt and top. Tom had promised to retrieve her handbag from Louise's house for her while the police were there securing the evidence, but for now she found another bag to use and put in some loose cash, a packet of tissues and Jo's spare key, which she would have to use until she got her own keys back.

Although there was a blue sky and the sun was shining as she walked down to the village green, she found the air was fresher and cooler than it had been before the heavy rain of the day before.

When she arrived at the green, the marquees and stalls were grouped together at one end as they had been in previous years and at the other end there was an open space in front of the copse of trees where children were playing.

The first person she saw was Eileen. She didn't feel like talking to her so she quickly went into the nearest marquee.

She saw Marco behind a table serving glasses of Prosecco and stood watching him. Then she heard her name called out by someone. She looked round and saw Geoffrey and Roger sitting at a table so she went across to them. Geoffrey fetched a chair from another table so she could sit with them.

'Oh, Sallie, we've heard all about what happened to you. It must have been terrible. We're so pleased to see you looking so well.'

'Let me get you a glass of Prosecco,' Roger said standing up.

'No, I'd better not have any. It's a bit early and once I start drinking I don't think I'll be able to stop.'

'I can understand that,' Geoffrey said. 'So, all the while it was Don Bainbridge doing those weird things at the library, was it? We always said it wasn't you and Jo, didn't we Rog?'

'Yes, we did.'

'I never liked his wife. She was a right stuck-up cow.'

'She always used to go to the big salon in Mickleton to have her hair done. She must have spent a fortune there, having to have her roots done so often,' Roger said.

Sallie didn't want to talk about Louise and stood up. 'Anyway, I think I'll go and look for Emma. I'll have a drink with you two later,' she said.

'All right, Sallie, love. See you later,' Geoffrey said.

The next tent she looked in was thronged with men and she could see Frank behind a table at one end doing brisk business selling beer. As Sallie came out again she walked straight into Sandra Thompson.

'Sallie! I'm so glad you've come. I was talking to Jo just now and she told me about what happened to you yesterday. It must have been terrible. I'm so grateful to you. I thought I was losing my mind, I've been so worried. But Jo's explained to me that Don was with his wife all evening and it was her that killed him, so it had nothing to do with me at all. I can't tell you how relieved I feel.'

'Good. I'm so pleased you're feeling better.'

'Oh yes, I feel as though a huge weight has been lifted. But it's all thanks to you. It was so brave of you to go and confront her like that.'

'Some people would say I was very foolish.'

'Well, I can't thank you enough for what you did. But the whole thing has taught me a lesson and I'm going to cut down on my drinking and look after myself better from now on.'

'Good, I'm glad to hear it. Have you seen Emma at all?'

'Yes, the last time I saw her she was on the Tombola stall with Rory. It's next to the tea tent.'

'Thanks, Sandra,' Sallie said and continued on her way. She suddenly realised she hadn't brought a notebook with her so she couldn't go round getting snippets from the stallholders for the local paper, but it didn't seem important any more. In any case, she told herself, she would find out from Emma how much money they had raised and email a paragraph to the newspaper about it on Monday.

She peered into the tea tent and saw Dolly behind the cake stall wearing a pretty pink ball gown with a matching fascinator. Dolly spotted her and came over to talk to her.

'Sallie, sweetheart, I'm so pleased to see you. I've heard all about what happened to you. She was about to stab you with a big carving knife, wasn't she? The horrid woman. You must have been terrified. Come and choose a nice sticky cake for yourself on the house.'

'I'm sorry, Dolly, I haven't got much appetite at the moment.'

'Oh, I understand, darling. You come back and see Dolly when you're feeling better.'

'Thank you,' Sallie said, moving on quickly.

Rory had been left on his own behind the Tombola stall. When he spotted her he came over and gave her a big hug.

'I've heard all about it from Jo. You must have been terrified. I'm pleased to see you looking so well today. I hope we can still be friends now it's all been resolved. I've been thinking - why don't we meet for a drink in the pub next week? I'm free every evening. Text me when you feel like going out.'

'The thing is, I don't have my phone at the moment. I left my bag in Louise's house when I escaped from her. Tom has offered to retrieve it while the police are there gathering evidence. Give me your number and I'll text you when I get it back.'

Rory wrote his mobile number on the back of a tombola ticket and Sallie put it carefully in her bag.

'Make sure you remember to text me,' he said firmly.

'Yes, I will, I promise.'

She left him when his next customer came to the stall and carried on walking round the village green.

The next person she ran into was Mrs Whittaker, who was looking very smart in a pale blue jacket with a diamante brooch on the lapel, which she was wearing over a blue and white summer dress despite the warmth of the afternoon.

'Hi, Sallie. How lovely to see you. I've heard all about your adventures yesterday. It's the talk of the village. You were very brave to confront a murderess.'

'More stupid than brave, I think,' Sallie said.

'Anyway, I've still not managed to get anyone to accept that I've returned my library books. I've decided to go in next week and pay for them. I just can't cope with the stress any longer.'

'No, Mrs Whittaker, you mustn't, it's not fair to you. I'll tell you what we'll do. I've decided I'm not going to worry about the volunteers any more. We'll meet at ten o'clock on Monday outside the library and go in together. I'll find the books on the shelves and stand over whoever's on duty until they discharge them retrospectively from your ticket so it doesn't show your account as owing anything. Then I will give the books to Malcolm Bray and make him eat them page by page.'

Mrs Whittaker tittered nervously. 'Well, that seems to be going a bit far.' Then she seemed to change her mind. 'But, on the other hand, I have been very worried about it. They need to be made to realise it was all their fault. All right, if you don't mind coming in with me, we'll do it.'

Sallie went past George's stall, where he was wearing a blue and white striped apron and a white chef's hat and doing brisk business selling hot dogs and burgers in buns. Then she encountered Joyce, who had Sebastian with her.

'Oh, Sallie! I'm glad I've seen you. Are you all right now? You must have had a terrible experience. Poor Donald! What a life he must have had married to a woman like that.'

'I think they were probably both as bad as each other,' Sallie said, thinking of the sewing machine she had carried into the sitting room for Louise that he had turned into a death trap.

'Maybe they were. I don't think people will miss them in the village.'

'You're probably right,' Sallie said.

She had to pass the loudspeaker system which was blaring out swing band music to get to the Bench of Sighs, right on the edge of the village green, so she could sit down and rest. She sat watching all the goings-on, feeling strangely detached from it all.

Deirdre was the next to spot her. 'How are you, Sallie? I didn't expect to see you here today. I was going to ring you next week to suggest meeting up. Jo's told me all about what happened to you yesterday. It must have been awful. I feel so sorry for Don to have been married to that woman. I didn't like to say too much the last time we met because I knew Louise was one of your friends, but Don had told me she had to leave her nursing job under a cloud after a patient died. She came back to live with her parents and they couldn't wait to offload her on to Don in return for investing money in his business. He tried to put up with her for all those years and now look what has happened to him.'

'To be honest, Deirdre, I'm fed up with talking about them. I came out to take my mind off things, not to keep going over it with different people.'

'Yes, of course. I'm sorry. I should have been more thoughtful. How about I give you a ring next week and we can arrange to go out for lunch? But, in the meantime, make sure you look after yourself.'

After she had gone, Sallie was glad to be left alone and sat back on the bench, enjoying watching the village show going on in front of her and pleased to be some distance from the loud music.

She closed her eyes and tried to count her blessings. She was lucky to still be alive. She loved her children. She and Jo were doing well with their shed library. She had a lovely home where she was comfortable. She had some good friends and Desdemona to keep her company. So what was the problem? What was preventing her from being happy? She just felt terribly bleak and as though everything was pointless.

She heard a discreet cough and opened her eyes. Marco was standing in front of her holding a silver tray with a glass of Prosecco on it. She suddenly realised how handsome he looked, his white shirt contrasting with his tanned skin, his immaculate dark, curly hair and his face with its high cheekbones and dark eyes.

'You didn't come to see Marco, so Marco has found you to give you a glass of Prosecco. I just wanted to say I am sorry you and your friend have been treated so badly by everyone and that you have had such a horrible experience.'

'Thank you Marco. That's very kind of you.'

'Come and see me at the restaurant next week and have a meal with my compliments. You can bring your friend, Jo.'

'That's very kind of you, but it's really not necessary…'

'No, I insist,' Marco said and gave her a little bow before returning to the Prosecco tent.

The next person to come over to the bench was Emma. She looked glowing with health in a pale blue sleeveless dress, her long blonde hair worn loose. 'Was that Marco I saw with you just then? He's always liked you, hasn't he? I think he's very handsome,' she said eagerly.

'Oh, I don't know, Emma. He's a nice bloke but I don't think we've got much in common.'

'Well, never mind about that now. You need to look after yourself and get plenty of rest. You must have been so frightened yesterday. Thank God Tom got there when he did.'

'I do thank God, Emma, I really do. I keep thinking, if things had turned out differently I wouldn't be here to see all this going on today. It's a terrible feeling.'

'It's bound to have knocked your confidence, but you'll bounce back, Sallie, I know you will.'

There was an awkward silence but then Emma said: 'If you don't mind talking about something else, I wanted to tell you that old Mrs Jenkins has received an overdue letter because of that book, Be Careful What You Wish For.'

'But it's on the shelves in the library. Jo's seen it. Have none of the volunteers had the wit to discharge it yet?'

Emma looked amused. 'Apparently not. But the thing is, she told Howard that she had asked Don to get her the next book in the series. She said she didn't normally read that kind of book but she really enjoyed it and wants to know what happens to the characters next. Do you know the title of the sequel?'

'Yes, it's Mightier than the Sword,' Sallie said at once.

'Well, I'll look in the library next week to see if it's in stock. I'm going to take books to her in future. I think doing the housebound deliveries might be more suitable for me than working behind the counter.' She smiled nervously at Sallie. 'You see, the thing is, I'm pregnant,' she said diffidently.

'Oh Emma! How marvellous! I'm thrilled for you. So that's why you've been a bit off colour recently. It all makes sense now. I'm so pleased for you and Howard, I really am.'

The two women hugged happily. Then Emma said: 'And I'm so pleased to see you are all right. You're bound to have been knocked back by this but I'm sure you have a lot to look forward to. Your new hairstyle looks fabulous, you have a lovely healthy colour because you've not been stuck in the library all summer and you've definitely lost weight. But you've emerged unscathed from your adventures, that's the main thing.'

'I know. I am glad to be alive, obviously, but the depressing thing is nothing's changed. I've proved Jo and I weren't responsible for the pranks at the library but that's about all. I don't have a job and I'm still all on my own.'

'But you never know what's round the next corner. That's the great thing about life, no one can predict the future.'

'Well, I can't imagine a knight in shining armour is suddenly going to appear and gather me into his arms.'

Emma smiled to herself as though something had amused her, but then stood up quickly. 'Look, I'm going to have to go. They're judging the cake competition at the moment and I'm supposed to be handing out the prizes. I'll come into the shed library and we'll have a proper catch-up next week.'

Left on her own again, Sallie sipped her Prosecco and watched what was going on in front of her. A breeze had got up and was rustling the leaves on the trees behind her and she was starting to feel cold but she still felt she did not want to leave the solitude of the bench.

She could hear the strains of the Blue Danube Waltz and saw couples had started to dance in the open area of the green in front of her.

She saw Eileen, playing the man's part, whirling Verity round, then came Rory and Alicia, not exactly in step with each other, but laughing happily as they went past. Roger was trying to steer Geoffrey round but they had both clearly spent too long in the Prosecco tent and were in danger of falling over. Tom and Jo held each other closely as they waltzed past, with Mutz, who was off his lead, walking along at the side looking rather forlorn. Then came Sandra Thompson, red in the face, clearly having been drinking, shrieking with laughter as she was whirled round in the arms of a large, fat, bald man wearing a high-vis jacket and a lanyard. God knows who he was, Sallie thought.

Suddenly she heard a twig snap behind her, the leaves rustled again and then there was a dull thud. She looked behind her anxiously. Emerging from the trees leading a white horse was a man in full armour wearing a helmet with a visor that covered his face. Sallie jumped up startled but then the man lifted the part that covered his face and smiled at her. Her heart pounded. She knew that smile.

'Jerry! What are you doing dressed like that?'

'I've been at the battle re-enactment. The editor wanted me to write a personal experience piece. I got fed up with being yelled at by Malcolm Bray, so I galloped off. I'd been talking to the Reverend Goodall at the tea break and he told me all about your ordeal yesterday. I wanted to make sure you were all right. I was hoping to find you here, or, if not, that one of your friends could tell me how you were.'

'But where have you been for the past week? I've been trying to contact you about the body in the library story.'

'Oh sorry, but I've been training for the battle re-enactment at the riding stables at Upper Morton. I used to ride but I'm very rusty and the only chance I had of staying in the saddle today was to have a refresher lesson every day last week. There's no signal up there so no one's been able to get me, apparently.'

'Oh well, it doesn't matter now,' Sallie said wearily sitting down on the bench again.

Jerry tied the horse's reins to a post next to the bench and sat down with her.

'When I heard about what happened to you in that woman's house yesterday I was horrified. I suddenly realised she might have killed you and that I would have never seen you again. That's why I decided to leave the battle. Although, Malcolm might come after me and have me shot for desertion.'

'I don't think you should have risked that.'

'Well, I think it was a risk worth taking because I've begun to realise how much I care about you. My trouble has always been that I get too wrapped up in my work and forget about what's really important. Can we start again and put last week behind us?'

'I suppose so. I'm unlikely to get a better offer this afternoon.'

'Well how about having a dance with me?'

He stood up and extended a hand to her gallantly.

'Are you sure you can dance wearing a suit of armour? And can you even do the waltz?' Sallie asked.

'I'm prepared to give it a go if you are. We'll just have to take it one step at a time.'

So Sallie's knight in shining armour led her on to the village green, where they joined in the dance and waltzed around on the grass with all the other oddly assorted couples from Upper Mickle, some of whom were much more in time to the music than others.

ABOUT THE AUTHOR

Val Culley was a journalist for more than 30 years, working in newspapers, television and PR.

She now writes about Italy as a freelance travel writer and combined her interest in Italy with her fascination for detective fiction with her first two crime novels, **Death in the High City** and **The Shooting in Sorrento.** They are both Butler and Bartorelli mysteries, one set in Bergamo in northern Italy, the other in Sorrento in southern Italy.

Her third novel, **The Body Parts in the Library** is set in a village in south Yorkshire and introduces the Library Ladies, Sallie Parker and Jo Pudsey.

Val spent some happy years working on a newspaper in Sheffield, where she met her husband, Jon Culley, a national newspaper sports writer. They now live in Leicestershire and have two grown-up children.

Visit valculley.com to find out more.

Printed in Great Britain
by Amazon

78461346R00189